Close to Home

PAMELA COOK

BOOKS

For John, the love of my life,
and
Kathie, my beautiful lifelong friend.

Thank you both for making my world
more wonderful.

Vinci Books

vinci-books.com

Published by Vinci Books Ltd in 2025

1

Copyright © Pamela Cook 2015

The author has asserted their moral right to be identified as the author of this work in accordance with the Copyright, Designs and Patents Act 1988. This work is a work of fiction. Names, characters, places and incidents are the product of the author's imagination or are used fictitiously. Any resemblance to actual persons, living or dead, places and incidents is entirely coincidental.

All rights reserved. No part of this publication may be copied, reproduced, distributed, stored in any retrieval system, or transmitted in any form or by any means, including photocopying, recording, or other electronic or mechanical methods, nor used as a source for any form of machine learning including AI datasets, without the prior written permission of the publisher.

The publisher and the author have made every effort to obtain permissions for any third party material used in this book and to comply with copyright law. Any queries in this respect should be brought to the attention of the publisher and any omissions will be corrected in future editions.

A CIP catalogue record for this book is available from the British Library.

Paperback ISBN: 9781036704308

Printed and bound in Great Britain by Clays Ltd, Elcograf S.p.A.

By Pamela Cook

The Homecoming Collection

All We Dream
Cross My Heart
The Crossroads
Close to Home

Chapter One

A sea of black wings beat against the sky, fanning the dying embers of the day. Charlie Anderson settled into the worn cane chair to watch the spectacle. Impossible as it was to make out the individual anatomy of the creatures, in her mind's eye she could see each small, furry body suspended between membranes of leathery skin. The bats flew silently, saving their chatter for darkness, when they would feast on the nectar of eucalyptus blossoms or the flesh of whatever exotic fruit they might find. She'd tried to count them once, but it had been a pointless exercise and she'd settled on 'hundreds' as a rough estimate. As twilight deepened into dusk and the last of the local colony of flying foxes disappeared, she wriggled forward and picked up her wine from the wooden crate she used as a makeshift table. Her Friday night treat, a glass of crisp, cool sauvignon blanc, signalling the end of her working week.

She gave a slight shiver and rubbed at the goosebumps dimpling her bare arms. There was a chill to the evening air, a sure sign autumn was well and truly here, but she was too comfortable to move inside. Taking another sip of wine, she leant back and gazed out at the curtain of greenery cocooning the house. Another rental place, like all the others she'd lived in, but this one was something special. The perfect place to unwind. Whether it was the warm timbers of the house itself or the calm dripping from the rainforest of trees that formed the backyard, Charlie wasn't sure, but there was a sense of peace here she'd never found anywhere else. A sense that both soothed and disturbed her in equal measure. This had been the closest she'd come to wanting to put down roots since she'd left university, and yet there was still something missing.

Or someone, a voice sighed into her ear, as she stared out at the deepening shadows, the house at rest behind her, silent and empty. She gulped at the wine. Work was what sustained her, defined her, the gauge by which she measured her success. The problem was she had too much time on her hands now with only routine vet consultations filling up her days, and that meant too much time to think. A plan for the weekend was what she needed to spark her up, maybe a hike up Mount Warning or a walk along the coastal track. Being outdoors, moving, getting out of her head, always helped.

Charlie's stomach growled. She hadn't eaten since breakfast – maybe it was time to see what she could rustle up from the leftovers crowding her fridge. The thought dragged her up and out of her chair just as a shrill ring fractured the quiet.

'Seriously?' she muttered, depositing her glass and picking up her phone. She raised an eyebrow when she noticed the caller ID. Why would her boss be calling at this time on a Friday night, all the way from Sydney? So much for relaxing. Swallowing back her annoyance, she answered in what she hoped was a breezy tone. 'Hi, Alex. How's things?'

'Good, good,' he replied, his voice smooth as honey on the other end of the line. 'Haven't caught you at a bad time, I hope?'

'No, just sitting out on my deck enjoying the ambience, usual Friday night thing.' She hesitated. 'You know, unwinding after a busy week.'

'So, no partying in town for you tonight?'

'You know that's not my scene, Alex.'

'Wouldn't hurt you to let your hair down occasionally.'

She had to smile at the irony of his advice. Alex was twelve years her senior and, while she appreciated his paternal interest in her welfare, she was quite capable of managing her own social life. 'Says the man who spends most of his time at the office.'

'You're not getting any younger, Charlie. That clock's going to start ticking soon and I wouldn't want you to be left on the shelf.'

Charlie rolled her eyes. 'I know about Chris's engagement, Alex, and his baby news. It doesn't bother me.'

'Hmm.'

Time to change the subject. 'Anyway, were you calling merely to see what I'm doing this weekend or is there another reason for this conversation?' While the two of them were friendly, he usually didn't ring her to make small talk.

'As a matter of fact, I'm calling about something quite serious.'

Charlie noticed the shift in tone from lighthearted to businesslike. She stood and stepped towards the edge of the deck, resting her free hand on the railing. 'Okay.'

'I got a call from the local Landcare manager down on

the south coast.' She heard him hesitate, weighing his words. 'He suspects they might have an outbreak of the virus down there.'

Charlie tightened her grip on the wooden balustrade. *Oh no, not hendra.*

'What's happened?'

'One horse dead,' replied Alex. 'Six days ago. Vet called it as colic.'

'But *you* don't think it's colic.'

'I don't, no. The vet who treated the horse . . .'

Charlie heard the words coming and felt her stomach coil.

'He's come down sick. Pretty bad, by the sounds of it. Fever, headache, sore throat. According to his doctor, it's a bout of the flu.'

She heard the scepticism in his voice and pressed the phone closer to her ear, looking out at the garden. 'We shouldn't jump to any panicky conclusions.'

Alex grunted. 'It's not just me. The vet nurse there rang it in and reported it as suspicious.'

'Right. How far south are we talking?'

'About three and a half hours out of Sydney.'

Her heart took another little jump.

'Horses all over the place,' Alex continued, 'so we need to check it out.'

Charlie kept her voice calm. 'It's unlikely the virus could have spread so far down the coast, though. Based on what we know, I mean, about how it's spread to date. Highly unlikely.'

'Yes, but you know how unpredictable this thing can be. We can't take any chances. And remember, a bat tested positive in South Australia a while back.'

'How's the uptake of the vaccine been in the area you're

talking about?' Charlie could feel her Friday night wellbeing draining away. The scientist in her could hear all the warning bells, and with each new piece of information from Alex, she felt another tiny tug of dread.

'Low uptake,' Alex replied. 'Low uptake, lots of horses, and one more worrying thing . . .'

'Don't tell me . . .' She knew what was coming now.

'There's a bat colony in the national park there – and the park adjoins the property in question.'

Bats.

Charlie looked out into the night. Not long ago this sky had been swarming with them. It was the bats that had brought her to Lismore, in a roundabout way. Or at least the virus that began with the bats, which saw her being called from property to property examining sick horses, spending hours, days and weeks dealing with distraught clients and reactions bordering on hysteria. Thankfully so much progress had been made in the eighteen months since she'd arrived, and so much data collected and analysed, that they now had a better handle on the disease. An outbreak on the south coast wasn't impossible, but it would be completely out of the blue.

The unease she was feeling was about more than the virus, though. Just over three hours south of the city? High numbers of horses? Charlie gazed steadily into the now-vacant sky, asking her next question out loud. 'So where exactly is this place?'

'Naringup. Thought you might know it. Didn't you grow up down there somewhere?'

She bit her bottom lip, but the gasp still escaped. 'Yeah, I did.'

Exactly there, she thought, picking up her glass and throwing back the last mouthful of wine.

'So how soon can you be packed and ready to leave?'

'You want *me* to go and investigate this?' She already knew the answer, but stalling seemed the only way of quelling the rising tide of nausea.

'Yes, Charlie, you. We need someone who knows this virus inside and out and you're the best we've got.'

'You mean I'm the only available person you've got.' There were other vets and scientists working for the Department of Primary Industries, her co-workers, who could do this job just as well as she could. She knew it and she knew Alex knew it. But most of the others had ties. Children and family commitments that meant they preferred to stay in one place, not travel the countryside like nomads.

'Charlie? Are you still there?'

'Yes.' Calm and professional, that was how she needed to deal with this.

'Like I said, I need the best. Won't hurt that you know the area and possibly some of the locals.'

'Look, Alex, I'm flattered, but I'm really busy up here. I don't think I can get away right now. Isn't there anyone else?'

'No, frankly, there's not. And this has nothing to do with flattery.' He was getting testy now, pulling rank. 'If this is what it looks like, we need to get on top of it fast. There's also the chance this could produce some important research, and it is your specialty area. You have the skills and the knowledge to handle it, Charlie. You're the one I want running the show.'

She tried, but failed, to suppress a sigh. Alex had so much faith in her, and she didn't want to let him down, but the thought of returning to the place where she'd spent her teenage years set not only her teeth but her entire body on edge. Taking a deep breath, she straightened up, as if standing the whole of her 177 centimetres would somehow give her the courage to agree to Alex's request. 'How long will I have to be down there?'

'Hard to tell. Might be a false alarm, or it could be a full-blown outbreak. If it is, we're going to need you there to manage things for the duration.' His tone softened. 'So, are you in?'

The duration. A month. Possibly more. She stared out into the almost dark, at the silhouette of a rambling bougainvillea bush growing completely out of control, its tendrils beginning to wrap themselves around the verandah post not far from where she was standing. She'd sworn to herself she'd never go back. The memories of the six years she'd spent in Naringup had been long since boxed away, but they began to creep out again now, tightening like a thorny vine around her heart.

This is your job.

It's important.

You can do this.

The voice that had given her the strength to stand on her own two feet all those years ago spoke to her again now, prompting her to finally answer Alex. 'Fine. I'll do it. When do you want me there?'

'Asap. I can book you on a flight down to Sydney tomorrow morning, meet you at the airport with a department car and you'll be there by late tomorrow afternoon.'

'No!' The night fell still around her. She sat back heavily into the chair, steadying herself before she continued. 'I mean, I'd rather have my own car. I've got all my equipment in the boot already, won't take me long to throw a bag of clothes together. I can leave tonight.'

Alex took his time absorbing her response. 'Charlie, are you crazy? You're – what – nine hours away from Sydney?

And it's another few hours on top of that. It's a hell of a drive, and it's late.'

'I'll be out of here within an hour. I know a place at Port Macquarie where I can stop over and then head off in the morning. I'll take a few breaks – it'll be fine.' She was trying hard to sound nonchalant and hoped it was working. There was no way she was getting on a plane. Even the thought of it made a thin film of perspiration break out across her temples. 'I really need my own car,' she repeated.

Alex sighed, clearly exasperated. 'Whatever you want, Charlie. I'll make a motel booking for you somewhere in the town and email you through all the information I've been given so far, including the address of the affected property and the contact details for the vet. I'll need you to keep me updated on a daily basis.'

And I need to get off the phone and get my head around this, she thought.

Now.

'Great – thanks, Alex. I'd better get packing.'

'Bye, Charlie. Drive safely.'

She lowered the phone and placed it on the table. Bundling her mane of blonde curls into a knot at the back of her head, she pinned it there beneath her hands, feeling the taut stretch of muscle in her armpits. She drew another deep draught of air into her lungs. It helped ease the panic that was beginning to take hold. Naringup. It wasn't the thought of returning to the place so much as the people. The ones who had let her down so badly – and the one she'd let down in turn.

You can do it.

Charlie listened to those words repeating themselves in her head – words she'd learnt from her mother, the same words that had helped her through the hard times when all she wanted to do was curl up in a ball and die. Now was not the time to give in to fear. She had a job to do, a job she loved, an important job that was helping to curb the spread of a deadly disease, deadly to both horses and humans. And if that meant facing a few demons from the past, then so be it.

She picked up her phone and the empty wineglass, thinking it was lucky she'd only had one. Hauling herself to her feet, she turned away from the dark indigo sky and the sounds of cicadas and frogs in the garden she now had to abandon. It was time to pack a bag and get ready for a long, unwelcome road trip south.

Chapter Two

Charlie's eyes watered as she stared at the ribbon of road unfurling in front of her. It had been almost eight hours behind the wheel after a restless sleep in the motel. And that wasn't counting the four and a half hours she'd done the previous night. Alex had been right when he said a flight would be more practical, but even this horrible driver fatigue wouldn't be enough to convince her to step through the doors of a plane. So, four cups of coffee, a barely edible burger and two headache pills later, she still hadn't arrived in Naringup. She checked the screen of her TomTom – thirteen minutes until she reached her destination.

'Hallelujah,' she muttered.

Operating from memory alone she wouldn't have had a clue. She'd only made this trip twice before – once when she was twelve, leaving Sydney, and once when she returned to the city at age eighteen. And nothing in between – no visits to friends left behind, no holidays, no shopping trips. A clean break. It was 'for the best' they'd said, and she'd had no choice but to fit in and toe the line. What else could she have done? She'd only been a child, at the mercy of adults who made all the decisions. Her old life was swapped for another, completely different world.

A churning began in her stomach and she wasn't sure if it was the takeaway food she'd eaten or her current thought pattern that was doing the damage. Either way she needed to get her mind focused on something else.

The scenery – always a good option. It was certainly a beautiful part of the world. Miles of tall, thin gums, grey bark peeling away to reveal the white flesh of trunks stretching skywards. Giant grass trees, their knobbly stumps sprouting headfuls of spiky green hair, brown spears standing to attention. And in between the stretches of state forest, acres of rolling farmlands dotted with cows and horses.

Horses. All over the place, just as Alex had said.

If his suspicions were right, and this developed into a serious outbreak, it could be as bad as – or worse than – what had already happened in Queensland and northern New South Wales. In the early days, before the sort of research she and her colleagues had undertaken, horse owners had no protection against the virus. But since the vaccine had been made available they had the choice to safeguard their animals – and themselves. So why did so many choose not to? Yes, the vaccine was relatively new and there was a cost involved, but wasn't saving lives the priority?

It is for me, Charlie thought, but obviously not for a lot of people. If the horses could speak I know what option they'd take.

She stifled a laugh. She'd always thought animals had more sense than humans. It was why she'd chosen to study veterinary science rather than medicine.

According to the Google search she'd done last night in the motel, Naringup was now full of tree changers, possibly ones who weren't into vaccinations of any kind – no matter the species. She'd added that observation to the notes in the file she'd made, skimming the reports Alex had emailed her and making a plan for when she arrived in the town.

There's probably been a lot of other changes too, she thought now, slowing down to take a tighter than expected bend. Then she saw the town up ahead, the faint glint of the river spanned by an arching steel bridge. She was almost there.

And that's when her stomach started to cartwheel rather than just spin.

Get a grip on yourself, Charlie.

Taking her own advice, she pushed back her shoulders, sat taller in the seat and started mentally reviewing what she knew of the case. Possible hendra – with the emphasis on *possible* – one dead horse, and a vet who could have a bad cold or who, looking at a worst-case scenario, could be dead within a matter of days. From what she'd been told and read on email, he was the best person to interview to try to glean more information. She hoped to god he was willing – and well enough. Hard evidence was the only way she would be able to determine what they were dealing with – tests would have to be done, people questioned, quarantine measures undertaken if it came to that – so she needed everyone involved to cooperate.

The vet, Walter Murray, lived on the same site as the surgery, so that was going to be her first stop. She knew from past experience that the disease could progress rapidly once it took hold, so it was crucial she speak to him sooner rather than later. The quicker she sorted this thing out, the faster she could get her job done and leave.

Again.

As soon as Charlie reached the edge of town she got her bearings. The vet surgery was at the southern end, a couple of blocks past the old bakery. She turned off the TomTom and cruised towards the main street. Her jaw dropped as she took in the sight, unconsciously lifting her foot from the accelerator. The slightly shabby street she remembered had been transformed into a vibrant village. She drove slowly, marvelling at the multitude of cafés, all with alfresco tables, a few up-market boutiques, a European-style delicatessen and gift shops dotted down its length. There was even a Spanish tapas restaurant called 'Flamenco'. Very chic. The old bakery, which she recalled as a worn building with pink paint peeling from its facade, had been revamped as an organic bread shop, the cream buns and lamingtons that once decorated its window replaced by loaves of sourdough and home-style muffins. The tired concrete footpath had been upgraded to terracotta paving, complete with rubbish bins that looked like abstract works of art and small, circular gardens bursting with lavender, musk-pink roses and sprays of white butterfly bush. Smartly dressed people sat sipping coffee or browsed in shop windows. For a Saturday afternoon in a country town, the place seemed surprisingly lively.

Charlie dragged her eyes back to the road, surprised to see a set of traffic lights changing from orange to red just up ahead. In the years she'd spent here, there'd barely been need for a stop sign, let alone a set of lights, but the onslaught of city escapees had obviously had a drastic impact. I wonder how the locals feel about the invasion, she thought with a wry grin. When she'd been forced to move here from the city, the almost mind-numbingly slow pace of the town had made her feel like she'd travelled back in time. She'd missed the hustle and bustle of Sydney streets, even at such a young age, craved the sense of variety that came with life in an inner-city suburb. Naringup definitely seemed to have had an injection of both in recent times.

She slowed to a stop not long after the intersection, outside a freshly painted cottage. Leaning over the dashboard, she read the sign on the fence: 'Walter Murray, Veterinary Surgeon, Opening Hours Monday–Friday 9 am–4 pm'. A second building sat at the far end of the driveway. Probably the vet's residence. She switched off the ignition, chewing on her bottom lip as she stared at the time – 2.10 pm. Should she really be disturbing the man on a Saturday afternoon, especially when he was sick? But the urgent need to get the facts and her worry that Walter Murray might deteriorate further stifled any doubt.

She locked the car and made her way to the back of the surgery. The house was a quaint colonial-style painted in various shades of cream, a replica of the main original building at the front of the block. Alex had told her that Walter had been the vet here for the last fifteen years, which meant he'd arrived about a year after she'd left. It was a good thing that she didn't actually know him – it would make it easier to keep the situation businesslike. She stepped up to the door and pressed the buzzer, triggering a raucous chorus of barking and the appearance of a black Scottish terrier behind the flyscreen.

'Hi there,' Charlie greeted the dog, who fell quiet and wagged his tail in reply. Footsteps sounded at the other end of the hallway before a stocky woman sporting a neat grey bob joined the Scotty at the door.

'Yes?'

'I'm Charlie Anderson. From the Department of Primary Industries.' She'd presumed Alex had told them she was coming, but the lack of response from the woman behind the screen door suggested otherwise. 'I was wondering if I could speak to Mr Murray?'

'My husband isn't well enough to see you right now, I'm sorry.' A steely tone belied the apology. 'You can come back tomorrow if he's feeling up to a visit.'

Tomorrow could be too late, Charlie thought. 'I was hoping I could chat to him straight away, before I head out to the affected property.' She smiled. 'I won't keep him long.'

'Walter already wrote a report and spoke to the Landcare people. He's done everything that was needed.'

'Absolutely, he has, Mrs Murray. I just thought he might be able to walk me through the case personally, so I know exactly what happened. It won't take long.'

The woman sighed, lifting her hand to the lock and flicking the key. 'Alright then. If it wasn't for that nosy vet nurse sticking her beak in, there wouldn't even be an issue. The last thing Walter needs is you people telling him how to do his job.'

'I wouldn't dream of it, Mrs Murray. I'm just here to do *my* job.'

Without another word the vet's wife turned and strode back down the hallway. Charlie followed, the black dog prancing at her heels. The whole place reeked of eucalyptus and she found herself lifting a hand to her nose in an effort to deal with the overpowering smell.

As they entered an open-plan living area at the back of the house, Mrs Murray turned the corner and spoke to a man lying back in a leather recliner, a red crocheted blanket draped across his lap. 'Wally, the DPI woman is here to see you.'

The man angled his head towards Charlie. His face was ashen, his eyes dull, as he reached down to flip the lever on the chair, bringing himself to an upright position. He held a blue handkerchief over his mouth as he gave a rattling cough.

Normally Charlie would have reached out to shake hands, but under the circumstances it probably wasn't a good idea. 'Hello, Mr Murray, I'm Charlie Anderson. I just wanted to go through the details of that horse case with you briefly.'

The vet cleared his throat. 'What do you want to know?'

She opened her notebook, slid the pen from its spine and, despite the lack of invitation, settled herself on the lounge across from Walter. His wife retreated to the kitchen at the far end of the room, but Charlie was aware of her eyes watching the pair of them and she was sure the woman would be listening to every word. 'According to your report, the symptoms the afflicted horse displayed were similar to colic – restlessness, refusal to eat, lying down.'

'That's right. I've treated plenty of cases of colic in my time. That's exactly what it looked like to me.' There was a distinct wheeze in the vet's voice, something heavy and clogging in his breath. The pen wobbled slightly in Charlie's hand as she scribbled her notes.

'So how rapidly did the horse deteriorate after you were called out?'

'Got the call just after seven in the morning – the owners found it in a state when they were doing the morning feeds. Since it looked like colic, there wasn't much I could do. Gave it a shot of phenylbutazone, told them to try to keep it mobile, offer it some grass.' He paused, took a few breaths and brought the handkerchief back to his mouth. 'They rang again around four, said it had got worse, so I went back out expecting to be euthanasing, but it had a convulsion and died just before I arrived.'

'And you performed an autopsy that afternoon?'

'At the owner's request. They were pretty upset, wanted to know exactly what had killed it. I didn't think there was much I could tell them, but I did the autopsy to keep them happy.'

'What did you find?'

'Fluid in the lungs, thickening of the ventricular walls. Told them it was heart failure . . .' he paused again, '. . . brought on by the stress of the colic.'

Charlie knew the next question was likely to stir things up. She softened her voice and turned slightly towards Walter. 'Can I ask what sort of protective clothing you were wearing?'

'Had a pair of gloves on but one of them split, so I ended up taking them off.'

'But no overalls or mask?'

'No, I already told you that.' He waved a hand in dismissal and bent over into another coughing fit. Charlie instinctively leant away. She could feel a set of eyes burning into her all the way from the kitchen.

'I'm sorry, but I just need to get the facts straight,' she said when the coughing bout subsided. She ploughed on. 'So, after the autopsy, the horse was buried and you returned home and showered?'

'That's right.'

'And was there anyone assisting you while you treated the horse or present during the autopsy?'

'The owner of the place was there. He helped shift the horse around and then dug a hole with his backhoe to bury it. Oh, and his wife – she was pretty distraught. Refused to leave its side.'

'And have either of them fallen ill?'

'How the bloody hell would I know? I treat animals, not people. I've seen my doctor and he's said it's the flu, nothing more.' Despite his pallor, the vet's cheeks flushed a deep crimson.

Charlie knew the interview was just about done. 'Are there other horses at the property with similar symptoms?'

'Not that I know of.' Walter rested an elbow on the arm of the chair and shifted forward, looking directly at Charlie for the first time. His eyes were watery and red-rimmed, his breathing laboured. 'Look, I know what you people are doing. You're trying to make a mountain out of a molehill. This could be equine flu or some sort of colic brought about by the feed, but it isn't hendra. We're miles away from all of that business. It's preposterous to even suggest such a thing.'

'Mr Murray, I know it seems improbable, but it's not beyond the realms of possibility. There's still a lot we don't know about the virus. This whole thing is one huge learning curve, and it's working with vets like yourself who deal with routine illnesses every day that's helped us make the progress we have.' She looked down at the list of points she'd made prior to the visit. 'Just one last question – what's the vaccination rate like around here?' Alex had already told her, but she hoped Walter could elaborate.

'Varied. Some of the show ponies have had it. A good number of others haven't. Costs are too high. They don't see the need for it down here. The anti-vaccine contingent don't believe in it.'

'And the property in question?'

'No. Not vaccinated. They breed and spell horses for the races.'

Charlie couldn't help but groan. Horses couldn't be exported once they were vaccinated, so the racing industry was resisting.

'Now if that's all, I'm feeling a little under the weather.' The vet slumped back and tilted his chair.

Charlie closed her book and stood. 'Of course, I'm sorry to have bothered you, Mr Murray. Thanks for taking the time to talk to me. I hope you're feeling better soon.'

The vet's eyes were already closed as his wife approached, ready to escort their visitor out. Charlie followed her lead, just as happy to be leaving as they were to get rid of her.

'Goodbye,' the woman said without even a hint of a smile as she opened the door.

'Oh, Mrs Murray, one more thing. I have the name of the property concerned, but I don't seem to have the address.'

'Far end of Comptons Creek Road. Fancy place. You can't miss it.'

Charlie jotted the directions in her book. 'And is there anything I should know about the owners – Mr and Mrs McDowell, is it?'

Now came a grim little smile. 'Only that you'll have your work cut out for you, dealing with Garth McDowell.'

'And his wife?'

'Emma. Don't know much about her, keeps to herself.'

'Thanks. I appreciate your help.'

Some help.

Charlie stepped outside and heard the doors – both of them – bang closed behind her. She stared down at the names she'd written on the page. Emma McDowell. Emma.

Her Emma? Surely not. It couldn't be. Of course there'd be more than one Emma in a town this size. And the address Walter's wife had given her was on the opposite side of town to where *that* Emma used to live. She snapped the notebook shut. There were more important issues at stake here. But replaying what she'd heard did nothing to ease her anxiety. A dead horse, a vet who used no protective gear, and the risk of other horses, and people, already being infected. Walter Murray, the horse's owner, the owner's wife – all in contact with what could be a highly contagious, dangerous virus. And a farm full of unvaccinated horses. Charlie's brow creased as she considered the situation. Whatever kind of resistance she was going to encounter at the property, it sounded like it was only going to get harder – in more ways than one. There was no point putting it off. She climbed back into the car, reprogrammed the TomTom and headed west out of town.

From memory, the area where the McDowells lived was quite well-to-do. So there wasn't much chance, Charlie thought, that the Emma who lived there would be her Emma. *Her* Emma? Who was she kidding? That relationship was long since gone, so it was ridiculous to dwell on any imagined personal connection. Moping over the past wouldn't get her anywhere – she needed to drag her mind back to the issue at hand. Once she got there she'd have to get as many facts as possible, from the owner's viewpoint, about the horse and the autopsy, and check whether any of the other horses had become sick. With a bit of luck the vet would turn out to be right – the department was erring on the side of too much caution and this whole thing was nothing more than a scare. That was a report she'd be delighted to send back to Alex.

Fat black cows lazed in the surrounding paddocks as she drove past what was once an old cheese factory, now converted into a coffee shop and guesthouse. Further along the road she passed a newly established vineyard with sloping hillsides of netted vines. From the pristinely manicured appearance of the land and the uses it had been put to, Charlie suspected this was the side of town the new arrivals had claimed. And why wouldn't they? Lush farmlands, only a fifteen-minute drive to the coast, close enough to Sydney to be accessible to weekenders and daytrippers. There were quite a few horse properties scattered along the road too — a fact that set off a fluttering in her stomach. If it was hendra they were dealing with, there was a chance it could spread through this entire area. Given the news of the low vaccination rate, it might have already, but there was only one way to find out.

She slowed down as the end of the road came into view and an elaborate pair of cast-iron gates appeared on her right. An image of a horse's head was fashioned into the metal above the name 'Willow Vale Park'. Charlie raised an eyebrow. Very fancy. The gates were shut, but there was a buzzer on the sandstone wall and she hopped out of the car to press it, taking in the size of the place. A red gravel drive led through a column of deciduous trees, currently changing colour from the iridescent green of summer to a buttery yellow. At the far end of the sweeping drive sat a smoke-grey house complete with a wraparound verandah and white French doors. Fruit trees bordered the closely trimmed lawn, which smelt freshly mown. Behind and alongside it all lay a state-of-the-art stable block, skirted by neatly fenced paddocks. An enormous shed, painted the same colour as the house, had a quad bike, a horse truck and a black four-wheel drive parked outside its doors. There was money in horse breeding, especially for the racing industry, if you got it right. Garth McDowell, it seemed, was on a winning streak.

Despite the presence of the car, Charlie's buzz remained unanswered. Maybe the McDowells were out with their horses. She pressed the buzzer again, holding it a little longer this time, and was startled when a deep voice boomed abruptly from behind the speaker.

'Yes.'

'Mr McDowell?'

'Yes. Who is it?'

'My name is Charlie Anderson. I'm from the DPI. I need to talk to you about the horse that died on your property last week.' Static crackled as Charlie waited once again for a reply, so long in fact that she thought she hadn't been heard. 'Mr Mc—'

'There's nothing to tell. The horse had colic, it died, end of story.'

Oh great, so this was how he wanted to play it. As much as Charlie would have liked to keep things casual, his attitude forced her to pull the official card.

She stepped closer to the wall, frowning. 'I'm afraid there could be more to it than that. We've had a report that there's the possibility of hendra here. It would be much easier having this conversation face to face, if I could just come in?'

'That's bullshit. And it's the weekend, in case you hadn't noticed. Like I said, there's nothing to discuss.'

Charlie sighed. What the hell was wrong with this guy? His family could be at risk and he wanted to argue? Deliberately hardening her tone, she gave it one last shot, glaring at the intercom as if he was actually standing in front of her. 'Look Mr McDowell, the vet who attended your horse is quite sick, and considering the circumstances around this case the department feels it needs to investigate. We have to do some tests and make sure that it isn't something more than colic. This isn't a request – once a possible case has been reported, we're obligated to check it out.'

There was a silence, in which she could almost hear his rage boiling. 'You listen to me. I don't want you or your people here on my property stirring up trouble. Am I making myself clear? And I don't give a rat's about obligation. This is my place and I get to say who comes here and when. Now piss off. And that's not a request either.'

Really? Did this idiot think she was here to while away a few spare hours because she had nothing better to do?

'Mr McDowell. Can you just let me in so we can have a sensible discussion about this?'

No response.

Charlie felt her frustration rising. She jammed her finger against the buzzer.

Nothing.

Damn! The vet's wife had been right. This guy was a piece of work. Well, if he was going to be difficult about it, she'd need to talk to Alex about forcing his hand. She got back into her car, yanking at the seatbelt, swearing when it caught. Making a deliberate effort to cool down, she pulled on the belt more gently, clicked it into place and started the engine. Alex had to know about this as soon as possible. One way or another, she'd get onto this property and do her job, and if Garth McDowell didn't like it, then it was just too bad.

Chapter Three

Alex answered after the first ring. 'Charlie. What have you got for me?'

'Not much, I'm afraid.' She tucked the phone between her shoulder and her ear as she picked up her bag and scanned the numbers on the doors of the motel.

'You spoke to the vet?'

'Yes, Mr Murray, but he didn't really give me any new information. He was pretty defensive. Doesn't like the idea of Big Brother looking over his shoulder.'

'Sounds like a bit of a redneck.'

'No, just old-school, I think, and completely in denial that the virus could spread this far south. But then I guess he's not the only one.'

'How was he? Physically, I mean.'

'Not too good. Fever, I'd say, and an horrendous cough. Adamant it's the flu, which it still could be, Alex.'

'Well, we live in hope, but you know the drill. How about the McDowells? What's the story there?'

Charlie hesitated. Here it was, number 12. She pushed

the key into the lock of the door. 'I spoke to the husband over an intercom at the gate. He refused to let me in.'

'You're kidding.' Charlie could hear the frustration in Alex's voice, could picture him taking off his glasses and pushing the pads of his fingers into his eyelids.

'I know, hard to believe, right?'

'Doesn't he know how serious this could be?'

'No, I don't think so. Or if he does, he doesn't want to let on. The place looks like it's worth a mint, by the way. Some pretty exxy horses involved. No doubt he's worried about his business.'

'Well, maybe he should be more worried about his health and his family. Presuming he has one.'

'Not everyone's got your priorities, Alex. He absolutely stonewalled me.'

'Right, well, I'll get all the authorisations we need – won't happen until tomorrow now. And I'll call the local police station and see if someone there can back you up. This joker needs to get the message that we're not playing games.'

'Sounds like a plan.'

'Is the motel okay?'

Charlie looked around the spartan room, wrinkling her nose at the smell – something between mothballs and dirty laundry. 'It'll do for the time being.'

'Great. Talk soon.'

'Bye, Alex.'

She walked to the window and pulled open the floral curtains. Grandvista Motel was nothing special – a bed, a bar fridge, a red-wine stain on the beige carpet – but it did live up to its name. The view was simply stunning. A wide expanse of farmland rolled out like a carpet fringed by bush, stretching all the way to a sweep of cloud-wisped sky.

Charlie was used to country scenery – after her stint in Sydney for uni, she'd spent most of her working life travelling from one rural area to the next. But nearly all of it had been in Queensland or at the northern end of New South Wales. It was only now she was back that she realised how much she had missed the south coast, the slower pace, the softer light, the untamed feel of the bush and beaches. This place had nurtured both her love of open spaces and her passion for animals. So it hadn't been all bad. And as long as she kept reminding herself that this particular visit was all about work, things would be fine.

Now that she'd called Alex, all she could do was sit back and wait. Paperwork had to be organised and the police possibly brought in, but that would have to be dealt with tomorrow. It was the tail end of the day and Charlie realised that apart from the cereal she'd choked down at some ridiculous hour this morning and the hideous burger she'd scoffed en route, she hadn't eaten. And when you were in desperate need of a decent meal in a country town on a Saturday night, there was only one sure bet: the pub.

Stepping into the bathroom she blinked as the fluorescent globe above the sink flickered to life, her eyes widening when she saw herself in the mirror. Was it just the light or were those grey circles beneath her eyes even worse than usual? And her hair – ugh. Unwinding it from the bun she habitually wore it in, she ran her fingers through the curls and decided they were better off restrained before bundling them straight back up. She sniffed her armpits – a shower was definitely called for, but now she'd started thinking about food she was totally ravenous, so she pulled a can of deodorant from her toiletry bag and gave a couple of squirts. That would have to do. It wasn't like she was here to impress anyone. In fact, the less interaction she had with the locals, the better. There was little chance of her getting out of this whole deal without running into anyone she knew, but it had been a while and she'd been in her teens when she left, so with a bit of luck no one would recognise her, at least not tonight.

A cool breeze stirred the leaves of the ornamental trees planted along the pavement as she headed into the town centre. They looked like some sort of miniature version of a maple tree, the unusual merlot-coloured foliage turning a dark shade of orange. Charlie pictured the street in a few weeks' time, a tapestry of gold and copper, local kids scuffing through the fallen leaves, watching them float into the air and drift back to the ground, collecting them and taking them home to press inside one of their favourite books, like she'd done as a child. She wondered what had happened to the leaves she and her mother had so lovingly gathered on their walks in the park not far from their beautiful old Federation house back in Sydney. Together, they'd arranged them just so between sheets of waxed paper and laid them down inside the pages. But for the life of her she couldn't remember what book it had been. Or where it had gone. What was it about the mind that meant the things you wanted to remember were lost to you, but the memories you so desperately wanted to forget seemed to be tattooed onto your brain?

The hum of a motor registered somewhere in Charlie's consciousness and she roused herself from her daze as the driver waved her across the street towards the pub. Like most of the other older buildings in town, it had been updated and was painted to match the streetscape in a deep shade of wheat, trimmed with crimson and bottle green. The smell of something warm and inviting wafted from the door as Charlie approached and she didn't hesitate to step inside.

The Centennial was a lot busier than she'd expected. Being a teenager when she'd lived here, she'd only peeked in the doorway as she was wandering past, and all she remembered was a few of the local men huddled around the bar while a commentator called the races from a too-loud television. Now that same bar had been converted into a stylish lounge area with comfy-looking armchairs arranged around coffee tables and abstract artworks hanging on mocha-coloured walls. The purr of conversation filled the room, backed by the soothing tones of mellow jazz. Hmm, very inviting. Might even grab a drink here later, she thought, but first things first. Food.

She followed the signs to the dining room, headed straight to the counter, ordered herself a medium-rare sirloin and found a small table in the corner. The bar was at the far end of the room, so she draped her jacket across the back of the chair and wandered over to order a glass of red. There was a long table just to the left filled with a bunch of guys who looked like they were in for a big night. The noise they were making and the assortment of empty beer glasses on the table told Charlie they'd made an early start. She smiled – it reminded her of her uni days in the city, playing sculling games at the bar down by the ovals, staggering back to the college at god knows what time and waking up with a head that refused to lift itself off the pillow.

'After you.' A friendly voice brought her back from her reverie and she turned to see a pair of clear blue eyes beaming at her.

'Sorry?' she said, shuffling back slightly.

The owner of the eyes nodded towards the burly barman standing opposite them. 'I thought you might like to order your drink.' He held an empty jug in each hand. One of the party boys.

'Oh, sorry, I was just daydreaming.'

'What would you like, love?' the barman asked.

'A glass of shiraz, please.' Charlie gave an awkward smile, conscious of the stranger beside her, who seemed to be waiting for her to continue speaking.

'Looks like you lot are in for a big night,' she said, gesturing towards the table.

'Looks that way,' he grinned. 'Bucks night.'

'Yours?' she asked, immediately kicking herself for getting into a conversation at all when she'd planned on lying low.

He laughed and shook his head. 'No. Mate of mine, the one at the head of the table who looks like he's about to keel over any minute.'

Charlie followed his eyes to the man in question, who had a half-full glass of beer precariously balanced on his head. 'I see what you mean. Hope the wedding's not tomorrow.'

The barman reappeared with her wine.

'Next weekend. Gives him a full week to recover.'

'Was that his fiancée's idea?'

'Sure was.' He passed the jugs across the counter. 'Two more, thanks, Andy.' He turned back to Charlie, who didn't quite understand why she was still standing at the bar. 'You just in town for the weekend?'

'Yeah,' she lied. Probably better not to give any details about the reason for her visit. Too many questions.

'That's a shame. Well, hope you enjoy it.' Picking up the amber-filled jugs, he headed back towards his mates.

'About time, Drummo!' Charlie heard one of them yell as she started towards her own table. She found herself swallowing another smile as she sat and sipped at the wine. After school she'd always gravitated towards men as friends rather than women. They were so much less complicated than her own sex, much less likely to have an agenda – apart from the obvious one – and often more fun to be around. Over the years she'd cultivated an easy sense of camaraderie with most of her male vet colleagues. She and Chris had worked together for years before their relationship morphed into something else when they'd both drunk far too much alcohol at a farewell dinner one night. After that it seemed logical to take the next step and let their friendship develop into a full-blown relationship, but Charlie realised too late that he was far more committed than she was ever going to be and that's when things went sour.

A waitress appeared, swapping a plate for the table number, leaving Charlie with a buffalo-sized steak and a mountain of salad. Tucking in, she watched the men at the far table. Boys will be boys, she thought, as the groom attempted to climb onto his chair, balancing a full glass of beer on his head, much to the delight of his audience, who clapped and cheered when it inevitably toppled and spilt down the front of his pants. She found herself laughing out loud just as the man from the bar – the one they'd called Drummo – looked over and caught her eye. Charlie's cheeks warmed and she focused her concentration back on her meal, careful not to look interested in the proceedings again. Once she'd eaten what she could and finished the shiraz, she slipped into her coat and headed back to the motel, glad to be out in the cool night air and away from the noise.

As she walked the few blocks in the dark a tide of melancholy swelled inside her. Maybe the antics of the guys in the pub had made her nostalgic for her lost youth, or maybe the mention of a wedding had stirred up some deep hidden regret over her break-up with Chris. It hadn't helped to learn he was getting married only a year after they'd split, or that he was soon to become a father. But then again, Charlie told herself, she'd been the one to end things. Maybe it was just being here in Naringup again, the place itself dredging up all the feelings she'd battled against in her teens.

How was it you could be in a bar – or a house – full of people and still feel so desperately alone?

Grey light leaked into the room as Charlie woke and pulled aside the curtains. Brooding clouds hung low in the dawn sky. A crow cawed somewhere in the distance. Everything was still. She let her head fall back to the pillow, and the room back into shadow. She thought again about her attempted visit to the McDowells. Garth and Emma. Emma. The name conjured an image of a teenage girl, petite, with dark brown hair falling straight down her back like a chocolate waterfall, olive skin that accentuated her green eyes and an expression Charlie had never quite been able to define. As she pictured her again now, the word came to her: lost. Emma had always looked so lost. And really, was it any wonder, considering her family? Our family, Charlie thought bitterly. But that was a can of worms she didn't want to – couldn't – open if she was going to get through this case.

Tossing back the covers, she clambered out of bed and found her phone. One text, from Alex: Will have the paperwork couriered down to you later today. Have spoken to the police sergeant. Should be ready to go first thing tomorrow morning.

Charlie cursed and plugged the phone into the charger. Great! A wasted day, stuck in a town she didn't want to be in with nothing to do but bide her time. No point sulking about it, though. She stripped off her PJs and hopped into the shower. Clean and a whole lot more awake, she dressed in a pair of jeans and a grey cotton shirt and inspected herself once again in the bathroom mirror. Better than last night – at least the hair's washed and I don't smell like I just stepped out of a sauna, she thought. She combed her fingers roughly through her curls, brushed some mascara across her lashes and decided a buffet breakfast would be the best way to kick off what was bound to be a long, boring day.

Replaying yesterday's exchange with McDowell in her head over a starter bowl of cereal, Charlie found herself getting more and more wound up. She needed a distraction, but while she didn't want to mosey about town, the idea of spending the day in the plain, serviceable motel room hardly appealed. Her nerves could do with a little soothing, she thought, so maybe a drive out to the coast was the best bet. It wasn't far, and a walk along the beach might be the perfect way to relax.

The road dipped as it crossed a bridge and a smile hovered on Charlie's lips as she read the sign: *Gumbie Gumbie Creek*. The nonsense name had always made her laugh. At least to herself. She and her relatives hadn't visited the beach much as a 'family' – the odd visit in summer if the day was truly scorching – but as she got older and was allowed to venture out more on her own, she'd taken to catching the bus to and from Curlew Point and spending hours wandering the shoreline, fossicking around in rock pools, watching the rise and fall of the sea. In the city, where the beaches had been crowded and swimming restricted to the patrolled areas between the flags, the whole exercise had seemed pointless to her, even as a child. It was only here on the wild stretch of shore strung like a hammock between two cliff-ends that Charlie had found a true passion for the wildness and ferocity of the ocean. It had become both her escape and her consolation, a place of refuge and of hope.

A sense of anticipation grew in her now as the road carried her closer and closer. Farmhouses on acreages flashed past, and fragments of bush, much of which seemed to have been recently cleared. An entire valley was being converted from forest into perfectly groomed blocks of land. Some already sported two-storey cement-rendered mansions complete with symmetrically paved driveways, kerbs and guttering. All neatly packaged together as 'Boronia Grove'. It would be a miracle if there was a boronia left, she thought sadly. People had to live somewhere, of course, yet the sight of steel and concrete where there used to be nothing but trees made her body sag. Nothing stayed the same, at least not for very long. Sometimes that was a good thing, of course – you could endure the bad times if you thought that something better might be around the corner. Her mother had been an eternal optimist, the glass-half-full type. 'Never give up, Charlie,' she'd tell her. 'Always keep trying, there's no such word as *can't*.' That seemingly simple phrase had kept her going more times than she cared to remember, had become a kind of personal mantra, in fact, and still was after all these years.

She opened her window as far as it would go, letting the rush of air bring her back to the present, and flicked on the car stereo. The tension seeped from her shoulders as the soulful sounds of her favourite Café Classics CD floated from the speakers. Turning up the volume, she leant into the headrest, resisting the temptation to close her eyes as sunlight flickered between tree branches and danced across her face. She could taste the salt on her tongue. It made her eager now to get to the beach and sift the sand between her toes. A few more bends, a right-hand turn and there it was in front of her.

She cruised into the deserted car park and sat for a moment, taking in the view. When she stepped out of the car a gust of wind whipped strands of hair across her face and she instantly regretted her decision to wear it loose. Oh well, she thought with a resigned smile, too late. She slipped out of her Converse, rolled up the legs of her jeans and padded down the wooden steps onto the almost deserted stretch of beach. Her skin tingled. If animals were her first love, the ocean came a close second.

It reminded her she was alive.

Today the sea was a solid sheet of navy beneath a slate grey sky. Charlie dipped her toes in as a wave bubbled to shore. The chill of it made her shiver. Her feet sank deeper when a second wave washed across them, swirling around her ankles. She took a step back and ambled along the beach, bending to pick up the occasional shell, her mind returning to that one day, years ago, when she'd come here and almost hadn't left . . .

Her eighteenth birthday. Six years since her parents' deaths, six years since she'd been sent to Naringup to live with her aunt and uncle, and after all that time the cloud of loss and pain still hovered. People told her it would get better but they were wrong. 'Time heals all wounds,' they said, trying to give comfort. 'You have to go on living.' Not that what she'd been doing could really be called living. Existing maybe, going through the motions, but it could hardly be called living. Six years of pretending that she was doing okay, that she'd pulled through, when all the while darker thoughts lurked in the undertow.

She had waded out into the water, an awareness coming from deep inside her that it was time to let go. Let go of the misery, let *them* go, her beloved lost parents.

But as the waves sucked and pulled, more enticing thoughts surfaced. Thoughts that had kept her company for six long years, thoughts that had held her hand in the middle of the night and wrapped her tightly in their arms. The same thoughts that had led her to this isolated beach and promised her oblivion.

Grief-stricken and lonely, her face awash with tears, she had waded into the sea, wanting, craving, that oblivion . . .

And yet here she was. All this time later. Here, still.

A sob caught at the back of Charlie's throat as she remembered. She'd been so young and vulnerable.

Thinking now about what she had almost done was painfully confronting. What if coming back to Naringup again opened up all those old wounds, the ones she'd spent years trying to heal with hard work and study? What if—

You can't live your life playing the 'what if' game, Charlie.

Her mum again. The truth, again.

But was it better not to take the risk?

Her phone rang and she pulled it from her back pocket. Alex. Perfect timing. She could tell him he needed to find somebody else. Somebody who had no emotional ties to Naringup, who wouldn't be preoccupied with their own personal history. It wasn't like she'd made much progress anyway.

'Hi, Alex.'

'Charlie. How's it going down there?'

'Oh, you know . . . Sunday in a country town.'

'Well, you may as well enjoy it – might not last long.'

'Why? Have you had more news?'

'No, but chances are we'll have some soon, now the paperwork is signed and on its way. Should be at the motel in a couple of hours.'

'Right. Actually, Alex, I wanted to talk to you about—'

'What was that? Hang on a bit until I find somewhere quieter.' There was talking in the background, the sounds of laughter and a child's high-pitched squeal. 'That's better. At my nephew's christening party. It's like a battleground out there. Now I can hear myself think. Fire away.'

What was the best way of putting this? She stalled. She could hardly say, 'I'm too much of a coward to be back here, so get someone else to do the job.'

'Charlie? Are you still there?'

'Yeah, I'm here.' She made sure her voice was steady

when she continued. 'Look, I'm not sure I'm the best person for this job, Alex.'

A loud sigh of annoyance echoed down the line. 'Not this again. I thought we sorted things out the other night. Has something changed now you're there?'

'No, no.' It was true – essentially nothing had changed. It was just that her fears about coming back were starting to be realised, and it hadn't even been twenty-four hours.

'Good. Well, I don't really see that there's anything to discuss, then, is there? You've handled worse cases than this before. You've got the power of the department on your side, and me, of course.' He gave an apologetic laugh. 'I've got faith in you, Charlie. Don't let a defensive bully get to you – this is more important than whether he's happy with policy or not. With a bit of luck, the tests will come back negative and you'll be out of there in a couple of days.' He paused, changing tone. 'What's it like being back in your old stomping ground, anyway?'

Alex had been so good to her over the years. He'd given her opportunities some of her colleagues would have killed for, encouraged her to submit research papers, made sure she got the placement in Lismore. How could she disappoint him now?

'Great. It's great.' She examined the series of circles she'd drawn in the wet sand with her big toe. Circles – the same pattern her thoughts seemed to be following.

'Give me a call tomorrow and let me know how it goes.'

'Will do.'

Pushing the phone back into her pocket, Charlie stared out at the water once more. She hated herself for being such a wimp, for not confessing the truth to Alex – ironically, because she didn't want to look like a coward in the first place. She'd always thought of herself as a survivor.

And after all, wasn't she? When she'd first arrived in Naringup, against her will, she'd been a gangly young girl, just twelve years old, left stunned by her parents' accident, nobody really understanding enough to see the pain she was in and rescue her from it. In the end she'd saved herself, and that's the way things had been ever since.

Charlie Anderson against the world.

She could do this, she could. She'd been through a lot worse.

A flash of colour grabbed her attention from the far end of the beach. A para-surfer sliced effortlessly through the water, flying over a wave before becoming airborne, the sails of the parachute bobbing like a brilliant orange bird over the metallic surface of the sea. *Exhilaration.* That was the word that came to mind as she watched. *Thrill* was the second. Closely followed by that strange, small word that promised so much.

Joy.

It had been quite a long while since she'd experienced true joy. Alex had been right when he'd suggested her life could do with a good injection of fun. But it certainly wasn't going to happen while she was in Naringup, that much was clear.

She turned and headed back along the beach, tucking wisps of hair behind her ears, shivering a little now that she was walking into the breeze. A laugh escaped as she thought about why she'd come here today in the first place – to relax.

So much for that idea.

Chapter Four

Being out early on a Monday morning meant there was plenty of parking, so Charlie pulled up outside what looked to be the only place open for breakfast, Country Harvest. According to the sign, it was vegetarian, which was a good thing considering the greasy bacon and sausages she'd choked down after her cereal yesterday morning at the motel. Something meatless was much more appealing. She swept aside the curtain of amber beads hanging in the doorframe and entered a virtual garden – the mint-coloured walls were decorated with brightly painted images of eggplants, cauliflowers, watermelons and lemons. Underneath a sign saying *Local Produce* sat jars of muesli, nuts and honey, and cartons of eggs labelled free range with a thick black texta. A basket of the most delicious-looking berry muffins she'd ever laid eyes on waited on the counter. She ordered immediately and took a window seat where she could sit back and watch the world go by.

Not much appeared to be happening. It was a weekday, so daytrippers were scarce, but a few of the shopkeepers had started opening their doors and rattling their shutters. The boutique across the road looked like it might be worth a visit. Jeans and overalls were fine for work, but it had been a while since she'd treated herself and a little retail therapy never went astray. Stolen Moments, the bookstore a little further along, looked interesting too. She would definitely have to find time to browse through its shelves. Buying books was Charlie's favourite guilty pleasure. She loved the smell of the untouched pages, the promise of the story as she held it in her hands. Crime fiction was her latest genre of choice – something she could really get her teeth into, a page-turner. If she wrapped things up here quickly, she thought, she might be able to take her time driving back up the coast, and a new book would be excellent company at pit stops. But there was no point getting ahead of herself. Right now it was good just to sit and gather her thoughts before the hard yakka of the day began.

The door beads jangled behind her.

'Hi, Mel, can I order the usual?'

Charlie knew that voice. Swivelling slightly in her seat and taking a surreptitious peek, she recognised its owner in an instant. The guy from the pub. Drummo, as his mates had called him, stood at the counter and pulled his wallet from his back pocket. She couldn't help noticing how nicely his arse filled out his khaki work pants.

'Sure thing,' the girl said. 'Take a seat. Won't be long.'

Turning quickly back towards the window, Charlie propped an elbow on the table and rested her palm against her cheek. She wasn't in the mood for small talk. And she wasn't good at it. But it was no use. He'd seen her.

'Making a long weekend of it, I see.' There was a playful tinge of sarcasm in his tone and she wondered, quickly, if he'd noticed her attempt to hide.

She attempted a breezy wave. 'Oh, yeah, still here.'

He shoved his hands in his pockets and smiled. The navy blue wind-jacket he was wearing brought out the colour of his eyes. 'Came to the right place for breakfast – the pancakes are killers.'

'Glad I ordered them then.'

'Mind if I take a seat while I wait for my smoothie?' Before Charlie could come up with an answer, he'd pulled out the chair opposite her and sat himself down. Generally she'd feel affronted at such an intrusion, but there was something so beguiling about the guy she didn't really mind. 'My name's Joel, by the way,' he added.

'Charlie.'

'Charlie? Short for Charlotte?'

'Not exactly. My father wanted to call me Charlotte and my mother wanted to call me Annie. They couldn't decide, so they went for a combination of the two.' She was used to people's curiosity about her name and the story that explained it came as easily as ever.

'I like it.'

'Thanks.' There was a moment's silence that neither of them seemed to know how to fill. Charlie searched for something to break it. 'I hope your head wasn't too sore after the bucks party the other night.'

Joel gave a laugh that came out more like a snort. 'I've been better, but I wasn't half as bad as the groom. Think he's probably still in bed this morning.' He reached for the small metal jug stuffed with packets of sugar and spun it around on the table. 'So how long are you in town?'

'Not sure yet.' It wasn't a lie, but she didn't want to reveal the truth either. She knew from past experience that the words *hendra virus* had a way of starting the alarm bells ringing, and there was no need to be doing that at this point.

'Good time of year for a holiday. You been here before?'

The waitress arrived with her order just in the nick of time – buttermilk pancakes with blueberry sauce.

'Your smoothie's ready,' the girl said to Joel.

'Thanks, Mel,' he smiled before turning back to Charlie.

'Guess I'd better get going. Sorry you're not hanging around a little longer. Could've given you the guided tour.' The offer sounded genuine and Charlie found herself focusing very hard on the plate in front of her, trying to ignore the way his self-effacing charm made her insides turn to mush. 'Nice seeing you. Enjoy your breakfast.'

'You too,' Charlie said. 'I mean, nice seeing you too.' She stumbled over her words. What in the hell was it about this guy that had her acting like a smitten schoolgirl?

When she glanced out the window just in time to see the man in question turn and wink at her, the answer to that particular mystery was glaringly obvious. The guy was both hot and cheeky. A deadly combination. A pity really, because fraternising with the locals wasn't exactly a part of her plan, although she had to admit that, in some other universe, she wouldn't be sorry to see Joel again. She picked up her knife and fork and ploughed into her breakfast, thankful that she'd been blessed with a good metabolism.

Joel was right, the pancakes were delicious, but as much as she hated to leave food – especially food this heavenly – there was no way she was going to be able to polish off the whole lot. Pushing the plate away, Charlie arched her back in an effort to make sure her stomach wouldn't burst and took a sip of the coffee she'd ordered. The intense flavour of the espresso coated her tongue. She savoured it and checked the time on her phone – only 8.20. No need to rush. Having to get the police involved was a complication she could have lived without, but there was still plenty of time to get to the station and out to Willow Vale Park before the courier arrived for the samples. Taking another sip, she scanned the café, which, she realised, was now almost completely full. The two women seated at the table beside her were deep in conversation, and even if she tried it would have been impossible not to overhear every word.

'Apparently he took a turn for the worse and was taken to hospital yesterday afternoon.'

'Really?'

'Hmm. His temperature's through the roof and he's having seizures and all sorts.'

'Do they know what it is?'

'No. They're still doing tests, but Val's beside herself. He doesn't even know who she is.'

'Poor thing. Isn't he due to retire soon?'

'Yes, he's been waiting to find someone to replace him. He's been the vet here for the last fifteen years – won't be easy . . .'

A distant siren started wailing in Charlie's brain. They were talking about Walter Murray, and it didn't sound good. At all. Before she could pick up any more gossip the women changed topics and were onto discussing the benefits of vitamin supplements. She drained her coffee, grabbed her bag, nodded a thanks to the waitress and made for the door. Back in the car she let the engine idle for a minute as she considered the situation. There was no doubt the hospital would be doing blood tests, but if they weren't testing specifically for HeV it could easily be missed. The virus couldn't be transmitted from person to person, but if that's what was causing the vet's illness they needed to find out sooner rather than later. If he had been infected, anyone else who had been present the day the horse died could have contracted the disease as well.

First stop this morning was going to have to be the hospital.

Charlie marched along the corridor, already squeamish at the smell that sat somewhere between bleach and disinfectant. A memory materialised: the broken arm she'd suffered falling off Emma's horse all those years ago, the awful pain, waiting for attention in this very hospital. She wriggled her elbow. It had been the last time her aunt had let her ride. She'd said if Charlie couldn't manage to stay on, then she shouldn't be up there at all. After that Charlie had taken to caring for the horses rather than riding them, feeding them and grooming them, talking to them in the stables when there was no one else around, finding some comfort in the warm softness of their coats beneath her fingertips and their gentle breath in her ear as she poured out all her secrets. All the things she couldn't say to anyone else because there was no one to tell. Emma might have listened, of course, if Charlie had mustered the courage to confide in her. But Emma had had enough problems of her own to handle.

No one was waiting, so Charlie stepped up to the reception desk and pulled her DPI identification card from her wallet. The receptionist, who looked like she was just out of school, was on the phone.

'I know, that's what I told her,' the girl said, doodling a

hexagonal pattern on a sheet of paper. 'But she thinks she knows everything, so what can I do?'

Charlie tapped the ID card against her thigh. Really, she didn't have all day. She stared at the curtain of hair hiding the girl's face. Something must have registered, because the receptionist – Elysha, according to her name tag – lifted her head and stared straight back.

'Well, looks like I have to go,' she said to whoever was on the other end of the line, making little effort to hide her resentment. 'I'll talk to you later.' She hung up and, without any attempt at a smile, finally turned her attention to Charlie. 'Yes?'

If there was a customer service questionnaire, Charlie thought fleetingly, Elysha would be scoring very low on the friendliness scale.

'Hi. My name is Charlie Anderson. I'm from the Department of Primary Industries,' she said. 'I'd like to speak to the doctor in charge of Mr Walter Murray, the town veterinarian, please.'

The girl squinted at the ID card and then back up at Charlie, frowning. 'May I ask what it's in regard to?'

Charlie didn't want to say too much until her suspicions had been properly confirmed. 'It's a confidential matter,' she said pointedly.

The girl twisted her mouth into a sideways pout. 'You'll need to make an appointment or leave your number and I can get the doctor to call you.'

Charlie could see there was no way Elysha was going to cooperate unless she had more information. She exhaled heavily. 'It's in relation to a very serious public health issue. It's crucial I see the doctor concerned immediately.'

'Oh, I see.' Elysha's eyebrows arched. Great – news would be spreading like wildfire as soon as the girl got the chance to pick up the phone again. 'Well, the doctor you'd be needing to speak to is Dr Brunton. I'll see if he's on duty.' As the girl tapped away at the computer keyboard, Charlie couldn't help but notice her neatly sculpted turquoise nails. She shot a look down at her own bare, stumpy nails and dropped her hands to her sides. One more thing she'd been meaning to do but never seemed to manage.

'Ah, yes, he is here. Clocked on an hour ago. I'll just phone and see if he's available. You can wait over there.' The girl pointed towards the lounge in the waiting area.

'Thanks,' Charlie said bluntly. She took a seat and picked up a magazine, thumbing idly through the pages while she waited. Celebrity gossip, fashion, a story about a man who had received a lung transplant from his dead brother, more celebrity gossip. None of it was enough to distract her from her thoughts about Walter Murray. How bad was he really? Perhaps the women in the café had been wrong, and hearsay and rumours had blown the story out of proportion. Charlie glanced over at the receptionist, who was once again on the phone, talking in a low whisper. It wasn't hard to work out what she was talking about.

The gravelly voice of Jimmy Barnes filled the waiting area and Charlie silently sang along with the lyrics – she knew them off by heart. Both her parents had been huge fans of Cold Chisel, and although she'd only been a kid at the peak of the band's popularity, their CDs had been the backing tracks to her childhood. She still had two of them in her glove box, now she came to think of it, the cases cracked and the discs scratched with time and use. This particular song had always been a favourite – the image of the flame trees lining the streets and the girl falling in love by the pianola. How appropriate, she thought ruefully, as she remembered the story of the singer returning to his old home town.

'Miss Anderson.' She looked up to see a tall, balding man peering down at her. 'I'm Anthony Brunton. I understand you wish to speak to me about Mr Murray.'

Charlie sprang to her feet, holding out her hand in introduction. 'Nice to meet you, doctor. I know you must be busy, but I'm afraid this is rather urgent.'

'We can talk in my office,' he said flatly.

Evidently cordiality wasn't high on the agenda around here.

Charlie followed him along the hall and into a sparsely furnished office. He positioned himself behind his desk, clasped his hands together and waited for Charlie to take the chair opposite him.

'So, would you like to tell me what this is all about?'

'Certainly,' she said, adopting the formality of the doctor's tone. She relayed the history of the case, including her meeting with the vet and his wife the previous day and her visit to the McDowell property. 'I was actually on my way out there again now when I happened to overhear a conversation in the café – that's how I found out Mr Murray had been brought in and was in a serious condition.'

'You can't believe everything you hear in a coffee shop, Miss Anderson.' He made no effort to disguise his disapproval.

'I wasn't eavesdropping, if that's what you're implying, doctor. The conversation was quite loud.' Why was she even trying to justify herself? 'But regardless of how I found out, I thought you should know there could be more to this than meets the eye. I'd like to ask you to take blood samples to test specifically for hendra virus.'

The doctor leant forward on his elbows. 'Miss Anderson, I'm a doctor, not a vet, but from what I've read about the spread of this virus to date there's been no recorded cases south of Macksville. Isn't that right?'

'Kempsey, actually, but—'

'Please, let me continue.' The man's condescending attitude was bringing Charlie's blood to a fast boil, but there was no point getting him offside. She nodded as a signal for him to continue, not that he needed prompting. 'From what you've just told me, though, it would appear . . .' he hesitated, choosing his words carefully, 'there are some grounds for concern. Mr Murray's condition has deteriorated from serious to critical. He's on a respirator. He already has a weak heart, and his ability to fight whatever is causing his illness is severely compromised.'

He paused again and felt in his pocket, bringing out a notebook and pen. 'If there is any chance at all that this is what you say it is, Mr Murray's prognosis is not good. And I agree with you. If hendra's the problem and there's a risk of anybody else being infected, then testing is essential.'

Charlie could have stood and cheered. Finally, somebody was cooperating.

'Thank you, doctor.' She wasn't really sure what she was thanking him for – they were both just doing their jobs – but he had that authoritarian way about him that demanded respect. Even if she found herself giving it grudgingly. She passed him her business card. 'These are my contact details. If you could let me know the results as soon as you have them, I'd appreciate it.'

Brunton nodded and stood, indicating the end of their 'consultation'. Charlie thanked him again for his time and made a quick exit, feeling like she'd just been dismissed from the headmaster's office. Pulling her phone out, she checked her messages. There was one from Alex saying he'd been in touch with the local police, that they were expecting her visit and she should ask for Sergeant Pearce. Time was running out to get out to Willow Vale Park. Hurrying along the hallway and out to the car park, she ignored the knot in her stomach that pulled a little tighter as she thought about returning to the property and the greeting she was sure to receive there. Would involving the police make it better or worse?

There was only one way to find out.

The police station was just down the road, so it was only a few minutes before Charlie was out of the car and standing at the counter. A constable so young he still had traces of acne sat at a desk, busy at his computer, not noticing her entrance until she cleared her throat.

'Oh, sorry, hi there. What can I do for you?'

Friendly. Nice change.

'My name is Charlie Anderson, and I'm from the DPI. I think Sergeant Pearce is expecting me.'

He rolled his chair backwards, calling through the doorway into the next room. 'Sarge, someone here to see you.'

When a woman appeared, Charlie was taken by surprise, but not because she'd expected a man. She uttered a silent groan as she saw recognition register in the woman's eyes.

'Charlie Anderson! I was wondering if it was you when I heard the name. Fancy seeing you back in town after all this time.'

'Hi, Jacqueline. It's been a while, hasn't it?' Up until

now Charlie hadn't run into anyone she'd known back then, but it had been bound to happen sooner or later. 'So you're a policewoman?' Stupid, stupid question.

'No such thing these days, we're all *officers*.' Jacqueline made air quotes and laughed. Her straight auburn hair was pulled back in a ponytail, just as Charlie remembered her wearing it at school. In fact she seemed to have hardly changed. Freckles still darkened her otherwise pale complexion and she still had that same wide, bright smile. Jacqueline had been in the year above her and Charlie had never known her well, but the girl had always been friendly towards her, as friendly as Charlie ever allowed anyone to be, at least.

'And you're a bigwig at the DPI these days. I hear you're having a bit of trouble with one of our locals.' Jacqueline swung open the door and came out into the foyer. Even leaning against the counter she was still slightly taller than Charlie.

'Certainly not a bigwig, more of a foot soldier, to be honest. But yes, I am having a problem. Did my boss fill you in?'

'He sure did. Doesn't surprise me. Just between you and me, McDowell's a bloody tool. I have no idea what Emma ever saw in him. Thinks his money puts him above the law.'

Charlie was a bit taken aback by the woman's frankness, and her comment about McDowell's wife. Hardly tactful. 'Not in this case, I'm afraid.'

'No. Well, maybe he just needs a little more encouragement. Let's get out there and give it to him, shall we?' There was a gleam in Jacqueline's eye, but Charlie couldn't find it in her to share the enthusiasm.

'What happens if he won't let us in? Like yesterday?'

'You have the right documents, don't you?'

Charlie held up the papers the courier had delivered to the motel. 'Right here.'

'No problem then.' A smug look crept across the sergeant's face. 'Oh, and I think once he knows I'm out there backing you up, he'll cooperate. Let's just say we've had . . . ah . . . *previous dealings.*'

Charlie opened her mouth to ask what she meant, but thought better of it. McDowell's personal issues weren't her concern, and if they involved something illegal she was probably better off not knowing. 'I hope you're right. I really need to get these tests done as soon as possible.'

'Not a problem. My car's out back. You can follow me.'

'Great. Thanks, Jacqueline.'

'Everybody calls me Jac.'

Charlie nodded and headed to her car. Everything about this woman said *don't mess with me,* which eased some of her own nervousness. With a bit of luck, they'd be onto the property and doing tests within the hour.

She pulled out behind the police car, trying to ignore her thudding heart. While she had no qualms about serving the papers, she was pretty sure Garth McDowell wasn't going to just roll over and comply. Then there was that niggling issue of his wife. Had she imagined it, or had Jacqueline said the name Emma like Charlie knew who she was talking about? The question spiralled inside her head as she turned onto Comptons Creek Road.

Spots of rain pattered against the windscreen. Peering through the water-streaked glass, she waited until it was good and soaked before flicking on the wipers. They swished backwards and forwards in a steady beat. All that Charlie could hear was the name being repeated, over and over again with each swipe – *Em-ma, Em-ma, Em-ma* – as she followed Jacqueline's car all the way to the end of the road.

Chapter Five

Wet gravel crunched beneath the tyres as Charlie pulled up outside the gate. She let herself be hypnotised by the sound of the rain for a moment, until a tap on her window broke the spell.

'Shall we?' the sergeant asked. Was she actually enjoying this? They approached the buzzer together, but a noise over the intercom had Charlie pulling her hand back in haste.

'It's open.' A man's voice.

The gates parted automatically, sliding along a track and disappearing behind the columns of sandstone framing the entrance.

'Well, waddaya know?' Jac tossed her head, tiny drops of rain flying from the hood of her spray jacket.

'Looks like I've wasted your time,' Charlie said. 'Sorry.'

'Not at all. He's only letting us in. Doesn't mean he'll continue to cooperate. I'll hang around while you do the tests. Just in case.'

'Thanks, Jac, I appreciate it.'

'My pleasure. After you.' Jac gestured towards the house and Charlie took the signal to hop back in the car.

At least this time she actually had some backup, Charlie thought. And maybe she'd caught McDowell at a bad time yesterday – now he'd had a chance to think about it, he might be more obliging. She drove slowly up towards the house, mentally going through the procedure she was about to undertake. There were rules to be followed and she wanted to make sure, as always, that she dotted all the i's and crossed all the t's.

First things first: keep a record of everything. She switched off the engine and reached for her notebook and document folder on the back seat of the car, turning quickly when she heard the door of the house open. A broad-shouldered man in a plaid shirt with sleeves rolled up to his elbows stood at the top of the steps. He had a buzz cut, a barely there goatee and a scowl on his face that suggested his attitude hadn't changed at all.

Don't judge a book by its cover, Charlie.

Right. Be pleasant. Start afresh.

'Hello, Mr McDowell.' She made her way up the steps towards the man, who remained motionless on the verandah. 'Charlie Anderson.' Holding out her hand towards him, she let it drop when it was clear he wasn't going to reciprocate. McDowell towered over her. His hands hung in loose fists at his sides.

'I hope you're going to be more agreeable than you were yesterday, Mr McDowell,' said Jac in firm but faintly jovial tones, moving up to join Charlie.

McDowell took two slow steps down. 'I want to see the authorisation,' he said, directing his comment to Charlie, totally ignoring the police officer.

She pulled the papers from her folder. She'd made sure to highlight the words *mandatory testing* and *required procedures*. Passing them across, she looked over at Jac, who gave a slight nod, before returning her attention to McDowell.

Inside the house there was movement and Charlie heard voices, but nothing she could distinctly make out. The paperwork was all in order, but the time the man was taking told her he was reading every word. She clutched the folder tightly, staring at the jagged scar on McDowell's left temple while she waited him out. After a good few minutes, he fixed his dark eyes back on her.

'You need to test all of the horses then.' It was a statement rather than a question, one that hopefully meant he wasn't going to stand in her way.

'Yes, but we'll start with the ones who were in closest contact with the horse that died. And I'd like to find out more about the circumstances surrounding its death. The more information we—'

The door opened and the rest of Charlie's sentence lodged in her throat as she took in the woman who appeared. Her long dark hair was now shoulder length and streaked with blonde, but the eyes were unmistakeable. Almost identical to Charlie's own. The woman moved to the top step and stood beside her husband, her arm touching his as if to form a united front. Charlie had forgotten how petite her cousin was. She suddenly remembered, though, how Emma hadn't even come up to her chin when they'd clung together that last day. Thinking about it left Charlie's mouth so dry she didn't think she'd be able to speak.

The patterned timber door had been left ajar and a child's voice called from inside the house, 'Mummy, who is it?'

The woman ignored the question and stared straight at Charlie.

There was a hardness in Emma's face that Charlie didn't recognise. The stony look made her want to turn around, climb in the car and drive away, but her feet were suddenly stuck on the hard tiles beneath them, and her brain seemed incapable of sending through a signal strong enough to make them move. The job was the important thing, Charlie told herself quickly. The job.

'Charlie.' Emma's tone was only momentarily civil before it turned hostile. 'What are you doing here?'

The question galvanised Charlie into action. She slipped her ID card from her pocket and thrust it forward.

'Hello, Emma.' Her voice sounded high and strained but she pressed on. 'I'm investigating a possible outbreak of hendra virus.'

Emma rolled her eyes. 'Hendra? You've got to be kidding. Where did that information come from?'

'The source doesn't matter,' Charlie said, trying to keep her voice even. 'Once a suspected case has been reported, we have to carry out certain procedures.'

'Do you now?' Emma folded her arms.

It didn't seem like Mrs McDowell was going to be the voice of reason in this scenario. Or that she was even remotely pleased to see her long-lost cousin.

Mind on the task, Charlie.

'Well, look, it's in your best interests. If this is hendra, your family could be at risk.'

Was Charlie imagining it, or had the look of defiance stamped across Emma's features softened just a little at the word *family*?

'And why would you care?' Despite the challenge in her words, there was definitely a quaver in Emma's voice.

This was exactly the reaction Charlie had feared. Emma was not the same sweet girl she had once thought of as a sister. 'It's not a matter of what I care about, although I certainly wouldn't want to see anyone suffer if the case is confirmed.' *Especially not you.* 'I'm here to do my job, pure and simple.'

'And then you can up and leave again, right?'

Conscious of the sudden trembling in her knees, Charlie closed her eyes for just a second in an effort to regain some sense of control.

You can do this.

Jac stepped in to fill the void. 'I know you two have a history, but I can tell you now that Ms Anderson has the law on her side, and if you make this difficult I can and will be taking action.'

McDowell bristled at her words, throwing back his head and jutting out his jaw. The look he gave the two women was pure contempt and Charlie had to brace herself to meet his eyes and not look away. But even that was better than dealing with her cousin.

Jac's implied threat seemed to have an impact on Emma, who looked first at her husband and then back at Charlie. 'What do you need to know?'

How have you been all these years? thought Charlie wildly, automatically. Why didn't you answer my letters?

Then another, sterner inner voice: *Focus.*

'I need you to walk me through what happened last week and show me where the horse was when it died.'

Emma pointed towards the back of the house. 'It was out in the stable block.'

'Are there horses in there now?' Charlie asked.

'Of course there are. This is a fully functioning thoroughbred breeding facility,' McDowell snapped.

'Right,' said Charlie, opening her notebook. 'Were there any other horses in the stable with the afflicted horse prior to his death?' She could get through this if she could just manage to stick to the facts.

'When we moved Amigo into the stable, there was my daughter's pony, Star – they were good mates. They fret without each other. Or they did.' Emma's voice had lost its aggressive edge now she was talking about the horses, making her sound more like the teenager Charlie remembered. 'And Jewel, my mare. The others were all grazing.'

Charlie looked out across the farm. Fruit trees were scattered at intervals throughout the paddocks closest to the house: apples, peaches, an enormous fig tree and a few others. Some were netted, some not. A magnificent-looking horse, coal black with a white blaze, wandered over to the dam not far from the house, dipped its head and drank, pawing with its front leg, splashing water everywhere.

Scribbling a few more notes in her book, Charlie continued, 'Mr Murray has told me he diagnosed the horse with colic. Did you notice anything other than the usual signs?'

Emma shook her head decisively. 'Not until the end. He had some sort of fit and there was . . . blood coming out of his nose. Foaming at the mouth too. It was terrible to see him suffer like that. With the colic, I mean.' Emma was doing all the talking now, but McDowell had his eyes trained on Charlie the whole time. The scrutiny was unnerving and she was extremely glad to have Jac's calm presence beside her.

'So who was with him when he died?'

'Both of us. And . . .'

McDowell cut his wife short. 'That's it. Just us. And the vet.'

'Were any of you wearing protective clothing? Face masks?'

He frowned, his face dark. 'Of course we weren't. It was bloody colic, Wally said, so why would we?'

'Have any of the other horses come down with similar symptoms?'

'No.' McDowell was back in the driver's seat, his thick arms crossed, Emma standing mute at his side. 'Honestly, I mean think about it, *Ms* Anderson.' She caught the derision in the *Ms*. 'Don't you think we would have called a vet if they were sick?'

Charlie assumed the question was rhetorical and fired back another of her own. 'And none of your horses have been vaccinated against hendra?'

'No, they haven't. The horses we breed are for racing. Other countries won't import them if they're vaccinated, as I'm sure you're aware, being the *expert* from the department. And Wally told us there was nothing to worry about down here.'

His tone was becoming more and more heated. Charlie really didn't want to fuel the fire, but she had to make sure he knew the facts. She took a deep, calming breath.

'Well, I'm afraid the information you were given was a little misleading, Mr McDowell. There's still a lot we don't know about the virus, but one thing we do know is that it's spread by flying foxes. I believe there's a colony in the national park not far from here. Have you seen any on your property recently?'

Emma looked at her husband, who was staring out into the paddock where a second horse had now wandered in to stand beside the taller black. 'We get a few coming to feed on the figs,' he said finally. 'Used to have them all covered, but some of the nets broke and I haven't had a chance to fix 'em.' He shifted his eyes back to Charlie. 'Still doesn't mean you're right.'

'Mr McDowell, this isn't a matter of being right.' The guy was really pushing her buttons. 'You probably aren't aware, but your vet was admitted to hospital yesterday and the doctor is currently testing him for hendra. Now that the horse has been buried, it's hard to say if that's what killed him, but we will need to test the other horses, starting with the two that were in closest contact. Today. If the tests come back positive, your property will have to be quarantined until all the horses are cleared.'

This time his look was full of venomous disbelief. 'Quarantined? Like hell! We've got horses coming and going from here all the time. There's no way you're putting this place under lock and key. Out of the question.'

'You won't have a say in the matter.' Jac shifted closer until she was standing directly in front of McDowell. Charlie could have sworn that she saw him flinch slightly.

She jumped in to the silence that followed. 'How many horses do you have here, Mr McDowell?'

'Eighteen. Not that it's any of your business.'

Charlie scribbled a note in her book. 'All of them will have to be tested if the pony or the mare test positive for the virus,' she said evenly. 'The tests will be repeated over the next couple of weeks and the horses closely monitored. No animals will be entering or exiting the property. Now, if you can show me out to the stable, I need to get on with things so the samples can be transported to the lab in Sydney. The courier is due here in the next couple of hours.'

McDowell looked like he was on the verge of speaking again. Speaking, or punching her. Emma placed a restraining hand on his arm. Charlie saw the way she squeezed her thumb into the flesh just above her husband's elbow. 'People can die of it too, can't they?' Emma said.

'Yes,' said Charlie. 'I don't want to alarm you, but if Mr Murray tests positive for the virus, you'll both need to be tested too. In the meantime, it's probably a good idea to keep away from the horses. If either of you are in close proximity to them, you'll need to wear full protection: overalls and gloves, and face masks.'

Charlie turned and went back to the car, where she fished around in the boot and opened the crate of protective gear. Climbing into the disposable overalls and pulling on a pair of black rubber boots, she slipped goggles and a mask over her head. Everything else she needed was inside the bag she lifted from the boot – the syringes, antiseptic, swabs, saline and cold packs she'd stored in the motel fridge overnight. The courier would have a chilled crate to transport the samples, but they needed to be kept cold until he arrived. If she didn't get her backside into gear, though, there was a good chance he'd be here before the tests were even done.

Two children had appeared by Emma's side, both dressed in school uniforms – a girl, maybe eight or nine, and a boy who looked a few years younger. They stared at Charlie like she was something from outer space.

'Mummy, why is there a police here? And why is that lady wearing those funny clothes?' the boy asked, squinting up at his mother. Again, no answer from Emma, who seemed to be fixated on a stain marking the toe of her leather boot.

'That's a bit much, isn't it?' McDowell snarled at Charlie.

'Department regulations,' she shot back. 'Now, if you could direct me to the horses, I'll get on with the testing.'

'Tori, Matt. Go inside,' Emma said.

'But, Mum,' the girl said, 'we're late for school.'

'Don't argue with your mother. Get inside,' McDowell bellowed, pointing towards the house. 'Now!'

Both children jumped to attention when their father spoke and did as they were told. He wheeled around and followed them, slamming the door shut behind him. Emma dropped her head and walked down the steps past Jac and Charlie without a word.

It was clear who wore the pants in the McDowell household.

Rain had started falling again, but with both her hands full there was nothing Charlie could do but blink it away and pick up the pace. The musty scent of hay and sawdust drifted from the stables. Inside, two horses were corralled side by side in their pens, a bay pony who whinnied as the group approached and a striking dappled grey with one of the sweetest faces Charlie had ever laid eyes on. She stopped just inside the door and pulled her face shield down over her eyes before wriggling her hands into a pair of close-fitting disposable gloves.

'Probably best if you wait here,' she said to Emma, who crossed her arms and slouched against the doorframe. Jac stood on the opposite side of the entrance. The place was beautifully fitted out with timber panelling, exposed arched beams and a row of windows just below ceiling height allowing natural light to filter through the entire complex. More luxurious than most of the houses I've lived in, thought Charlie.

She opened the gate into the first stall and held a hand

out towards the pony, rubbing his cheek when he stretched his neck forward and sniffed.

'Hey there, what's your name?' She assumed that Emma knew the question was really directed at her, but when there was no reply she gave her cousin a questioning look.

'Star,' was the grudging response.

Charlie stroked her hand over the small white blaze on the pony's forehead. 'I can see where that comes from,' she smiled.

Horses were the most sensitive creatures on earth and being around them usually made her feel peaceful, but today was a little different. Emma's open hostility towards her was unsettling, and testing for something like hendra, a disease which could prove fatal to all of these horses, was always disturbing. She had to make herself concentrate and forget that Emma was watching her every move. After giving Star one more scratch behind the ear, she opened her bag and took out what she needed. It was important not to screw this up. If any of the samples became contaminated, the whole process would have to be carried out again. And she was pretty sure that neither she nor the McDowells wanted to prolong her stay.

Working efficiently, Charlie collected nasal, oral and rectal swabs, depositing each in a sterile container before starting on the bloods, uncapping a syringe and feeling for the correct vein in the pony's neck. She swiped it with disinfectant before gently inserting the needle.

Star didn't even squirm. 'Good boy,' murmured Charlie, drawing back the plunger so that the vial filled with deep crimson liquid. She sealed it and placed it inside a container of saline, which she then packed inside the cooler bag. Just as she prepared to repeat the process, Emma spoke up.

'Why are you doing it again? Isn't once enough?' Her

cousin's expression was hard to read and Charlie wasn't sure if it was curiosity or sarcasm lacing her questions.

'The lab likes to have multiple samples, just in case.'

'In case of what?'

'In case the first, or even the second, is tainted in any way.' The greater number of samples she could provide, the more conclusive the tests.

'Or in case you stuff up.' The animosity was clear now.

Ignore it and get on with what you have to do.

Charlie kept her eyes on the pony. 'That wasn't so bad, was it?' Star nickered, hopefully in agreement, as she gave him a final pat and moved on to the grey mare in the next stall. She reached a gentle hand to the horse's face but was greeted by a definite pinning back of its ears.

'Careful, that one can be nasty.' Emma tossed the words at her and Charlie could almost taste the spite.

At times Charlie had wondered what it would be like to see Emma again but this was nothing like the daydreams she'd had about a family reunion with her cousin. She'd imagined if it ever happened it would be awkward but warm, certainly not distant and decidedly frosty. If anything, this was more like their very first meeting. Only back then it had been Charlie, numb with grief, who had made no effort at all to be friendly. It was only later she'd realised that a small piece of her wanted comfort, needed some sort of security. And Emma had needed it just as much as Charlie. But now they were grown women with too many years and too much heartache between them.

Ignoring Emma's comment, she talked softly to the horse, waiting for it to relax, and before long the mare lowered her head, even nudging at Charlie's hand to see if she had any food.

'You're all bravado, aren't you?' Charlie said soothingly,

and although she was speaking to the horse, she hoped her cousin was considering her meaning.

She went through the same procedure she had with the pony, Emma watching her without another word. As the final sample bag was zipped and stored, the sound of a car engine disturbed the brittle silence. The courier. Perfect timing. Charlie tugged the goggles over her head, snapped off her gloves and pulled the protective shield from her mouth.

'The test results usually take a couple of days,' she said to Emma, still wintry-faced at the stable door. 'I'll call you as soon as I hear anything. You're not officially quarantined at this stage but until the results come back, please don't move any horses on or off the property, and keep the pony and mare away from the others.'

'You're wasting your time, you know. And ours.'

Charlie felt the heat rise to her cheeks. She'd spent far too many years learning to control her emotions and maintain the mask to let it slip now. Part of her wanted to grab this older, tougher version of Emma and shake her, remind her of the laughs they used to have together and the tears they'd shared, but this wasn't the time.

'Emma,' she said, waiting until her cousin looked her in the eye. 'This is serious. If these test results are positive, I'm afraid your horses are going to have to be euthanased. Believe me, that's the last thing I want. But if I were you I'd be a little more worried about the risk to your own health – and your *children's*.' Okay, maybe that was digging the knife in a bit too far, but the McDowells needed to face reality.

The blood drained from Emma's face. 'Oh, god.' She raised her hand to her mouth. 'Tori.'

'Your daughter?'

Emma gave a slight nod of her head. 'I let her come out

to say goodbye to Amigo. She was holding his face, cuddling him after he died. She was really upset.' There was a frantic look in her eyes. Her voice faltered, then trailed away. 'We thought it was colic.'

'I thought you said it was just you and your husband with the horse when it was euthanased?'

Tears brimmed in Emma's eyes. As Charlie watched the black trail one made down her cheek, she was back on those cold cement steps, her younger cousin's fingers gripping her arm as she begged, *Please don't leave me, Charlie. Please don't go. Stay. For me. Please.*

She swallowed hard, forcing away the memory. This was a completely different Emma, and a whole new set of circumstances.

'Look, let's not get ahead of ourselves,' she said gently. 'We need to wait until all the test results are back before we can work out how to proceed. The sooner we get these to the lab, the better.'

Emma tried to nod, swiping the back of her hand across her face. Charlie took a step forward, but the younger woman spun away and marched off towards the house.

Jac let out a sigh. 'So,' she said wryly, 'I gather you didn't leave on the best of terms?'

'No.' The single syllable was the only word Charlie could summon. She picked up the storage crate, letting Jac take her bag. The rain had stopped but the sky remained dull and heavy. Apart from the high-pitched chirping of some lorikeets in the branches of the gum trees flanking the house and the far-off screeching of a black cockatoo, there wasn't a sound. The courier took the samples and was gone in a matter of minutes. Stripping off her suit and gloves, Charlie shoved them into a garbage bag, which she sealed and deposited in the back of the car along with the rest of her equipment. She could sense Emma standing alone on the verandah watching, but couldn't bring herself to look at her.

'I hope Ms Anderson won't be having any more trouble out here,' she heard Jac say through the fog that seemed to have addled her brain.

'We'll do what we have to do and nothing more.' The timid, shaky voice had gone. In its place was cold, hard steel.

'That's all we ask,' Jac replied and turned to Charlie. 'Let me know if you have any problems,' she said as she opened the door of the police car.

'I will,' muttered Charlie. 'Thanks.'

She climbed into her car, not bothering with any further farewells. What was the point? Once she'd started down the driveway, she looked in the rear-view mirror to see that Emma was still there, arms wrapped tightly around her middle as if she was trying to hold herself together. Just like she'd been sixteen years ago, when Charlie had turned around one last time to wave goodbye.

Charlie clamped her fingers to the steering wheel. Somehow she'd managed to keep her composure while she was at Willow Vale Park, but the minute she closed the car door she lost it. She cringed, thinking about how Jac had come to her rescue when meeting Emma again had left her speechless, but the embarrassment swiftly morphed into anger as she thought about McDowell's attitude. Her foot flattened against the accelerator, the bend ahead appearing way too fast so that when she hit the brakes, the car started to fishtail. Just in the nick of time the road straightened and she regained control. Her heart was in her throat. She pulled over into a clearing and killed the engine. She shut her eyes, blood pounding at her temples.

What the hell is the matter with you, Charlie?

She'd always been able to keep her head on the job, even when she'd dealt with overwrought clients, convinced they or their animals were going to die. Cool, calm and collected – yes, it was a cliché, but it was a way of operating on which she prided herself. This whole situation with Emma had her completely rattled, though. Okay, so she might have been able to keep a lid on her emotions while she was there, but that lid had blown off the minute she'd left. Really, it just wasn't good enough. It was way too risky.

Of all the people to have to be dealing with at a time like this, why did it have to be Emma? And why had she treated Charlie with such obvious contempt?

The idea of calling Alex again and demanding to be taken off the case crossed her mind briefly, but she dismissed it almost immediately. She could do this, she knew she could, and she wasn't going to let Emma or her pig of a husband screw things up.

There was no point sitting here by the side of the road. The space she'd pulled into was a parking bay, and glancing up, she caught sight of an information board and map showing a network of tracks. Fresh air, stretching her legs, losing herself in the middle of nowhere – that was more than tempting. Her eyes fell on the folder on the passenger seat – there was paperwork to complete and emails to send, but it would all still be there when she got back. Walking was the best way to clear her head and that was exactly what she was going to do right now.

The track sloped gently, winding between tall, thin gums. Scattered through the scrub were spindly bushes of grevillea, their stems sprouting spidery white blooms, stark against the dull browns of the undergrowth. Charlie's footsteps were swallowed by the damp earth as she moved quietly through the bush, listening to the lizards scurrying through leaf litter and an occasional wren hopping between the branches, flashing a sudden red breast before flitting away. She wandered off on side trails, taking her time, losing herself quite deliberately. The rain had held off, and although the temperature was only around seventeen degrees, the walking kept her warm. Gradually the solitude and peace of the bush eased her tension, loosening the knots between her shoulderblades, and she found herself drifting along the path, taking one turn and then the next as it wound downhill, towards the sound of running water.

At the bottom, what she thought would be a creek turned out to be a series of small waterfalls spilling onto moss-covered rocks, all meeting in a wide pool rimmed by lacy tree ferns. It was an oasis of calm. Cool. Quiet. Inviting. A fallen tree by the side of the pond was the perfect resting place. Charlie hoisted herself onto the long-dead trunk and ran her fingertips over the lichen patterning its surface.

The way her feet hovered a few centimetres above the ground made her feel like a child again, climbing that enormous fig in the park just near home, back in the city. She would shimmy along the branches, her bare feet finding crevices and bumps to anchor her toes and push herself higher until she was nearly at the top, surrounded by velvety leaves, stretching her fingers up until she could almost touch the sky. At least that's what it felt like then. Back when everything had been so simple. So easy. It was usually her father who took her to the park on weekends. She'd climb trees and spin cartwheels across the grass while he sat on the bench reading the paper, his head disappearing between the gigantic pages. They'd stay for hours if the weather was fine, both of them happy to be there doing their own thing, knowing the other was close by. Sometimes she'd call to him from the treetop, dare him to find her. Sometimes he'd try to climb up too, but he could never get as high as she did; she was always the winner. When it was time to go, she'd scoot back down and he'd catch her in his arms as she jumped from one of the lower branches. He'd play-wrestle her to the ground and tickle her mercilessly until she almost choked on her giggles, begging him to stop.

'Please, Daddy, no more, I can't stand it.'

'Alright, my little monkey.' He'd stop then and lie beside her on the grass, the two of them watching the clouds shift and change shape as the wind moved across the sky. Grass prickled the backs of her knees as she lay there beside her father, listening to the in-and-out of his breath, seeing the sure, steady rise and fall of his chest from the corner of her eye, knowing she was safe and secure and loved.

All the years of training herself to forget couldn't stop the ache that began at the base of Charlie's throat. What was the point of reliving the past when all it did was remind you of what you had lost? That was why she'd thrown herself so vehemently into her studies and later into her job: so she didn't have time to deal with any stray memories.

It was being back in Naringup that was doing it to her now. Once she was done here, the reminders would be gone and she could return to her normal life. Her uncomplicated, emotionally stable life.

Charlie picked up her water bottle from the log beside her and took a good long swig. It was time to be getting back, time to give Alex a call and get started on the report. Hopefully this was going to be nothing more than a scare, yet, even as she made her way back up the track to her car, deep down her instincts were telling her something completely different.

Chapter Six

It was late afternoon when Charlie arrived back at the car and checked her phone, more out of habit than necessity. No messages or missed calls, but looking at the number of bars displayed on the screen there was minimal reception here anyway. Driving back towards town, she mentally divided the remainder of the day into paperwork, a shower, a room service meal and possibly a movie before closing her eyes for a decent night's sleep.

Images of other eyes flashed through her mind on the way back to the motel: the long white lashes of the dappled mare, the wide black pools of Emma's pupils when she'd told her about the vet, and then, out of nowhere, the clear blue spark of another set of eyes smiling at her through the café window. Charlie gave her head a shake to rid herself of these visions, especially the last. Her relationships with men over the years had been one of two things: short-lived time fillers, which she usually ended out of boredom, or longer term live-ins that ended when they started talking about the future, which was when Charlie made a beeline for the door.

With Chris, things had been different for a while, but really they were more like brother and sister, friends rather than lovers. She wasn't a nun, though – she did admire a nice backside and good set of biceps. Both of which Joel certainly possessed. Maybe if she ended up staying in town longer than expected and maybe if their paths crossed again . . .

Get a grip, Charlie, she told herself sternly. You didn't come here to fool around.

But a girl can still daydream.

Her phone chimed as she pulled into the motel car park, signalling an end to that particular fantasy. Two missed calls from a number she didn't recognise. If they'd rung twice it must be important, so she hit the reply button and waited while it dialled.

It rang only once before a deep, no-nonsense voice answered. 'Anthony Brunton.'

The doctor.

'It's Charlie Anderson here.'

'Ah, Miss Anderson, thanks for calling back. I have some bad news.'

Charlie sat completely still, grasping the handbrake. The engine idled as she found her voice.

'What is it?'

'I'm afraid Mr Murray passed away a little earlier this afternoon. His condition continued to deteriorate and his body just couldn't cope with it. He suffered a cardiac arrest.'

'Oh, I'm sorry to hear that.' And she genuinely was. Walter Murray had been due to retire, presumably about to kick up his heels. Enjoy his twilight years. Now he was another statistic, possibly even a victim of a virus they still knew far too little about. Charlie thought momentarily of his wife, her strained face behind the screen door, the fear and stress in her expression. She paused, the weight of the question she was about to ask heavy on her tongue. 'So there's a good chance his death may have been caused by hendra?'

'Too soon to say. The results won't be back until at least the end of the week. We'll also need to do an autopsy.'

The doctor was right – it was too early to jump to conclusions – but given the circumstances, things were not looking good. 'Could you let me know as soon as you hear anything?'

'Of course.'

Charlie pressed the end button and dropped the phone into her lap. While she didn't want to indulge in any worst-case-scenario thinking, there was no avoiding the grim reality. Seven people had contracted the disease nationally so far, four of them fatally. It was looking like Walter Murray could be the fifth victim. And even more people could be at risk: Emma, her husband and even their daughter, Tori. Charlie's hopes for a quick resolution to this case were fading rapidly, along with any sense of escape she might have felt on her afternoon jaunt in the bush. She picked up the phone to fill Alex in on the latest development, knowing she was in for a long, sleepless night, nervous about what the next few days could bring.

The gates were open the next morning when Charlie made an early visit to Willow Vale Park, a fact she took advantage of by heading straight up the driveway. Both the cars she'd seen parked there yesterday were missing. Maybe no one was home. She'd toyed with the idea of calling first but wanted to tell Emma about the vet's death in person – assuming she hadn't already heard on the town grapevine.

Charlie parked and made her way up the steps to the verandah. Cartoon voices blared from a television somewhere inside the house. She rapped her knuckle against the door and waited.

Footsteps thumped along the hallway and Charlie fidgeted as she realised who might actually be here minding the children. Dealing with Emma was difficult enough. She hadn't yet contemplated facing her aunt.

When the door opened and a stranger appeared, she exhaled with relief. 'Hello, I was wondering if Emma or Garth might be here?' she asked.

'No. I'm their neighbour. Matt's sick and I'm keeping an eye on him. Emma does school canteen every second Tuesday.' The woman tucked a strand of jet black hair behind her ear. 'Can I help you with anything?'

If Emma was in town there was a good chance she'd hear about Walter's death before Charlie could break the news herself. She hesitated. 'I need to speak to them. Would you mind passing on a message for me?'

The woman nodded. 'Sure.'

'Could you please ask Emma to ring Charlie urgently.' She pulled a business card from her wallet just in case the one she'd given them yesterday had been mislaid. Or tossed.

'You work for the DPI?' The woman lifted a hand to the back of her neck, kneading it with her fingers as she studied the card. 'Does this have anything to do with the horse that died here last week?'

Charlie wasn't sure how much she should reveal. She didn't want to risk unnecessary rumours flying around, but if hendra was confirmed, adjoining properties would have to be notified. 'Are you an immediate neighbour?'

'Yeah. We live next door.'

'Do you have horses or livestock yourself?'

The woman's eyes narrowed. 'Yes, we have three horses. My daughters ride. We have a few cows too.'

Charlie made an effort to keep her tone neutral. 'Look, Ms ... ?'

'Mrs Turner. Larissa Turner.'

'Mrs Turner, I can't really say what this is about, but it's really important Emma calls me as soon as she gets home.'

Larissa visibly paled and looked blankly at the card in her hand without speaking. There was really nothing more Charlie could say, so she said goodbye and then turned and made her way back to the car. In the paddock adjacent to the house a group of grey and white geese were settled by the dam, beady black eyes peering at Charlie over the bridges of their orange beaks. A couple of horses nibbled lazily at the grass nearby and Charlie stopped in her tracks, clutching the handle of the car door. One of the horses she recognised – it was the bay pony she'd tested yesterday. She'd told Emma to keep Star separated, along with the grey mare, until the results came back. For heaven's sake, did these people think this whole thing was a joke? Anger curled deep in the pit of her belly. She had a good mind to storm into the paddock and take the pony back to the stable, but she could just imagine the McDowells' response to her interference. Stirring up further trouble with them was the last thing she needed. If they could find any grounds at all to keep her off the place, they probably would, and as much as Charlie would rather be anywhere else than here, once she started a job it was a matter of professional pride that she see it through. This case was no different from any other.

Glancing through the windscreen as she started the car,

she noticed Emma's neighbour was still on the verandah. Leaning against the pole at the top of the stairs, phone to her ear, she was already deep in conversation. Her lips were moving quickly and there was an animated expression on her face. Despite Charlie's refusal to reveal anything Larissa Turner clearly wasn't averse to speculation. It was hardly surprising, but any hope of keeping this under wraps for as long as possible was rapidly evaporating. From here on in it was all about damage control.

A tiny garden lizard had somehow made its way inside the motel room. Charlie watched it slip across the windowsill as Alex rattled off a list of instructions, outlining what needed to happen next. Even though she knew the procedure backwards, it was crucial everything was handled properly.

'We need to keep on top of this as much as we can, Charlie,' he cautioned. 'The last thing we need is a media circus. So far nothing's been reported outside of this office. I'd like to keep it that way if possible.'

'No one will be hearing it from me, but this is a country town, Alex.'

'Yes, I know. I'm not sure how long Walter Murray's autopsy will take, but we should have the horse test results some time tomorrow. You know the procedure if they're positive.'

She certainly did. The whole scenario was way too familiar – testing, quarantining, euthanasing. It was the path her research had led her down, but sometimes it seemed a very long way from her original career plan.

'Unfortunately, yes, I do,' she answered, her voice cheerless.

'I'll let you know as soon as I hear anything. Is the motel okay?'

Charlie looked around the room, at the dim lighting and closet-sized bathroom. 'I might ask around, see if there's somewhere a bit cosier, if it turns out I'm here for a longer stay,' she said.

'Oh yeah, I forgot you had connections down there. Maybe you can stay with some of your old pals.'

And pigs might fly, she thought. 'So you'll contact me the minute the results are through?'

'Charlie, I just said I would, didn't I?'

'Yes, Alex, you did.'

They were both a little testy, nervous about the outcome. She poked her tongue out and said goodbye in the sweetest voice she could muster. Of course she had other reasons to be jittery, but Alex didn't know the whole story – her whole story. Telling him would mean going through the saga of her youth, dredging up memories she really didn't want to relive. Especially not right now. This case had the potential to expand on what they knew about the virus, and writing a research paper about it would hold her in good stead for more prestigious positions. And wasn't that what she ultimately wanted? It's what her parents had drummed into her from an early age – *Be the best, Charlie, don't settle for less, make your mark.* If she could just stay focused there was a chance she could contribute some really meaningful data to what was known about the virus so far.

At eighteen, she'd made plans to leave this town, make her own way in the world. After walking out of the water that day at the beach, she'd decided to rely on nobody but herself. She'd thrown herself into her studies, surprising her teachers and classmates with dazzling marks. Really, she was only using the brains she'd previously kept well hidden.

Working like an automaton, she blitzed exam after exam, leaving the other students reeling in her wake. The day they'd finished that last HSC exam, the second she put down that pen, Charlie felt the chains loosen. Confident she'd nailed it, she knew her results – hopefully high enough for a scholarship – would be her ticket out of there. And they had been.

Now was not the time to sabotage her career.

She fell onto the bed, pulled off her boots and socks, and ran her eyes over the tomb-like space of the room. There were plenty of places better than this to stay in town, and she didn't have much else to do until the test results were back. Slipping into her sandals, she pulled a clean white T-shirt over her head. She'd walk to the café where she'd had breakfast yesterday, grab a coffee and ask about potential accommodation while she was at it. Just as she was about to step outside, a loud knock sounded against the door. Expecting the motel owner or possibly a cleaner, Charlie opened it and was stunned to see who was standing on the other side.

'Emma.'

Her cousin's eyes were moist and puffy, her fingers crumpled around a tissue.

'Is it true?' Emma blurted. 'Did Wally Murray die from hendra? I asked down at the hospital but they wouldn't tell me.'

'It's too early to say. The autopsy will take a while.'

'But if Amigo had it, does that mean Wally had it too?' There was dread in Emma's question, a dread that Charlie would have liked to quell. There was a fine line between being up-front and saying too much too soon, and she had to find a way to tiptoe along it.

She cleared her throat. 'We can't be sure about anything until the results come back.'

'Don't screw with me, Charlie.' Emma's volume had gone way up. 'If there's a chance any of us could have picked up this thing, I need to know.'

Charlie knew she shouldn't say any more. She should stick to the facts, follow Alex's instructions to keep this as low-key as possible. But as she paused, she thought about the pony she'd seen grazing in the paddock a couple of hours ago, about the McDowells' stubborn refusal to follow her directions. Maybe a good hard dose of reality would bring them to their senses.

'Well, considering the time line of events and the information I've gathered so far, there's a strong chance Mr Murray – and your horse – did die from hendra.'

Emma moved like a sleepwalker into the motel room and sat down slowly on the single chair at the table where Charlie had been working. She stared blankly at the reports open on its surface, at the notes on the screen of the laptop. Charlie moved across to her and closed the lid of the computer. Once upon a time she would have hugged her cousin, reassured her. Now there was a rock-solid wall between them and all she could do was wait for Emma to compose herself.

It took a minute or two. Emma didn't look at Charlie when she spoke but down at the floor. 'Garth told me not to tell anyone . . .' – her voice was low, cracking – 'but he . . . we . . . moved some of our horses.'

'You what? After I'd specifically told you not to?'

'He doesn't believe this is what you say it is.' Emma turned to look up at Charlie, chin forward, hands gripping her knees. 'You have to understand, we have a lot of money tied up in these horses. The ones he moved are the most valuable we have, a couple of mares and our best stallion. He didn't want them stuck out at Willow Vale Park and not be able to get them out if you did shut us down.'

Or risk them being infected if this is hendra, Charlie thought. Maybe he wasn't so stupid after all.

Anger crept its way up Charlie's spine. What was Emma doing, married to someone like this? Was her husband really so arrogant that he would ignore expert advice and endanger other people's lives? As Emma dragged herself back to her feet, Charlie made a concerted effort to keep her voice under control. 'Where did you move them to?'

'A friend's place. On the other side of town.'

'And does this friend know they could be carrying a contagious disease?'

Emma shook her head. 'Garth said it would all blow over in a couple of days, and since we weren't officially quarantined, we could do whatever we wanted.'

She could hear the childish spite in Emma's voice as she mimicked her husband and had to fight to keep her response professional. 'Tell me, are there other horses on this property they've been moved to?'

'No,' Emma barely whispered.

Charlie rubbed a finger across her lips. She would have liked to slap a quarantine order on the place straight away, but the usual procedure was to wait for the official test results. The delay had given the McDowells more time to get their heads around the situation, and this was the upshot. Now all she could do was try to rectify the situation.

'You're going to have to take me to the property so I can talk to your friend. It's too risky moving the horses back again, but they may have to be confined where they are and tested.'

'No,' Emma almost choked. 'I can't.'

'What do you mean, you can't?'

Emma's cheeks grew even more wan. 'Look,' she confessed urgently. 'I just can't. Garth thinks I've come into town to grab a few groceries. I have to get straight back.'

Charlie's original assessment that Garth McDowell was a control freak was looking like an understatement, and this was getting more frustrating by the second.

'Why did you even come here and tell me this, if you weren't prepared to do something about it?'

'I don't know,' Emma yelled, staring directly at Charlie. 'I flipped out when I heard about the vet. I needed to know what happened to him. Look, I can tell you where the horses are, but Garth can't find out that I've been here.'

'I'm pretty sure that once your friends hear about it they're going to be calling him to find out what the hell he was thinking.'

'No. They won't.' Emma dropped her eyes to the ground again. 'They're not at a friend's place. They're at Mum's.'

Charlie lifted a hand to the doorframe, taking in this new information. While she'd secretly hoped to meet up with Emma again on this visit, her aunt and uncle were the two people she most desperately wanted to avoid. When she'd left all those years ago, the guilt and worry she'd felt about leaving Emma behind in such a dysfunctional family were equalled only by the burning need to get away from Jim and Hazel Roberts. Now it seemed the universe had conspired to bring them together again in a way she could never have foreseen.

'Did you hear me?' Emma's voice cut through the haze.

'Yes. I heard you. The horses are at your parents' place.' Charlie repeated the phrase robotically.

'It's only Mum there now.'

'Right.' Logic told her she should ask why, but she had more than enough information to process. She knew what she had to do, but she didn't want to look at her cousin's ashen face for one second longer. She turned, moving her body out of the open doorway, signalling the conversation was over. 'Thank you for letting me know,' she said flatly.

Emma began to hurry out, then stopped. 'You won't tell Garth I said anything?'

Charlie realised it then, saw clearly what was in her cousin's eyes when she spoke about the man, about the possibility of him finding out she had broken his trust. Fear. Emma McDowell was deathly afraid of her husband. She'd married a bully – possibly worse. Wouldn't growing up with one for a father have been enough of a lesson? Hadn't she learnt to read the signs? It took every ounce of restraint Charlie had not to lock the door, sit Emma down and find out what the hell was going on.

'There's no need for me to report your visit here to your husband. But I will need to go and check on the horses that you've moved, to test them and warn your mother that she could be at risk. There's no point testing more horses until we know for sure it is hendra we're dealing with. Please let her know that I'll be out there as soon as possible.'

Charlie closed the door behind Emma and collapsed against it, letting it support her weight as she closed her eyes. Now that she was alone she allowed herself to crumble at the thought of returning to the house where she'd spent six long, miserable years.

It took the rest of the afternoon to write up the reports. The whole process needed to be thoroughly documented, for both public health and research purposes. She kept her eye on the clock, but when it hit 6 pm she knew it was too late for anything to be coming through from the lab. May as well clock off and do something about her grumbling stomach.

She pulled out a pre-packaged dinner from the fridge, peeled back the foil and stuck it in the microwave. *Dinner 4 One*. She tossed the lid in the bin, slamming it shut. This certainly wasn't the first frozen meal she'd eaten, and it probably wouldn't be the last. A bell dinged two minutes later and she settled in at the small corner table, poking around at the beef stroganoff with her plastic fork, stabbing at a mushroom swimming in some sort of creamy sauce, wishing it at least smelt appetising. *Bland* was the word that came to mind. A solitary, adequate but bland microwave meal for one.

The room was deathly quiet, only the occasional sound of a car humming past on the highway. Some background noise might help improve the atmosphere. She picked up the remote, flicking from channel to channel, deciding an old episode of *Seinfeld* was about as good as it was going to get. Scripted comedy and canned laughter – appropriate side dishes, considering the meal she was making her way through. But it wasn't enough to keep her mind off the day's events. Four days she'd been here and there was still nothing concrete. She needed those test results so she could move forward with a plan. Now they were dealing with two potential hazard sites. What the hell had Emma and that idiot husband of hers been thinking? McDowell knew he could do whatever he damn well liked with his horses without an official quarantine order, and until the virus was confirmed that couldn't be issued. Now all she could do was hope that he didn't attempt to move them again, possibly out of the district. The man was a loose cannon, liable to do anything.

Swiping a piece of broccoli through the pool of sauce, she considered her to-do list. First thing tomorrow, no way round it, she was going to have to visit Hazel's. Her stomach lurched and it wasn't anything to do with the food. She wouldn't think about it now, though. The cheap wooden chair caught on the carpet as she pushed it back. Grabbing it just in time before it toppled over, she shoved it against the table with more force than was strictly necessary. She binned the plastic container and took in the empty room. Her paperwork was up to date, but her mind was too skittish to focus on words on the pages of a book. More mindless television was probably the best alternative.

Crawling into her pyjamas, she settled back on the bed, surfing the channels until Tom Hanks and Meg Ryan appeared on the screen and she put down the remote: *Sleepless in Seattle*. She'd seen the feel good rom-com at least four times before and it was one of her favourites – not that she'd admit it to anyone. Even after multiple viewings, she still found herself urging Meg Ryan up and out of that chair as she stared across the New York City skyline to the Empire State Building, wondering about her destiny. Charlie would never use the word *romantic* to describe herself, but it was one of those movies she just couldn't resist. Settled beneath the doona, humming along to 'As Time Goes By', the faintest hint of a smile skimmed her lips and she found her eyes were watering ever so slightly.

Up early the next morning, Charlie decided on a quick motel breakfast but definitely not the fried variety. Juggling a bowl of cereal and a glass of orange juice, she slid into a chair by the window. The thick grey blanket of cloud had cleared overnight to reveal a sheer sweep of pale blue, but the bent angles of the grevillea bushes in the garden suggested a fairly strong wind. At least it wasn't raining. Someone had left a copy of the local paper on the table. Charlie's spoonful of cornflakes hovered midair as she read the front-page headline: *Hendra Scare as Local Vet Dies.*

She dropped her spoon back into the bowl. Ignoring the splash of milk on the tablecloth, she picked up the newspaper and continued reading, her hunger for anything other than the information in front of her suddenly vanishing.

Naringup vet Walter Murray is believed to have died after contracting the mysterious hendra virus. Mr Murray had been suffering flu-like symptoms for a week but was rushed to hospital on Sunday when his condition deteriorated. He fell into a coma and died late Monday afternoon. While the doctor attending Mr Murray refused to confirm reports of hendra, sources report that test results proved he had contracted the deadly virus. Representatives from the Department of Primary Industries are in the area investigating a possible outbreak of the disease, which until now has been contained on the far north coast of New South Wales and Queensland.

Oh, no.

Charlie threw the paper down on the table and took a snapshot of the headline with her phone, sending it to Alex along with a message: Just what we need. They'd both been crazy to think there was any chance of keeping it hidden from the public. News travelled fast in small country towns, but who would have leaked this sort of information? Not the McDowells, surely, and the doctor would definitely have kept it all confidential. There were others in the hospital, though, who might not be so discreet, she reflected. The snooty receptionist for one.

Well, whoever it was, she concluded with a sigh, judging by the headline the bush telegraph was alive and well. Charlie had handled press and media releases, but never before things were confirmed. She needed to know the whole story so she could stop any panic before it started. There was no reply yet from Alex, but she shot off another text: Any news from the lab?

Slumping back into her chair, she folded the paper and chewed her way through what was now a very soggy bowl of cereal. When the phone rang she pounced, but it was a number she didn't recognise.

'Charlie Anderson,' she said, hurriedly swallowing the last of her cornflakes.

'Hi, Charlie, it's Jac Pearce. Have you seen this morning's paper?'

'Yes, I have. Could've done without that.'

'Tell me about it. The phone here at the station has been running hot for the last hour. Horse owners demanding to know where Wally picked up the virus, what they should do to isolate their places, how far the thing has spread, if anybody else has contracted it. One nutter even asked if she should keep her kids away from school.'

'Doesn't surprise me,' said Charlie. 'People often jump to the worst conclusions when they don't know the facts. And it's not like anyone around here has had to worry about it before.'

'True enough.' There was a long pause before Jac continued. 'I know McDowell is a complete moron, Charlie, but I'd rather we don't mention that it's out at his place. At least for now. It would be good to try to calm the whole thing down if we can.'

'I agree, but it's hard when the paper is spreading the news like this. We're not even certain Walter Murray had the virus.'

'Do you have those test results from McDowell's place back yet?'

'Expecting them any minute. Once they're in we can officially quarantine the place if we need to.' Charlie hesitated, knowing there was no way she could avoid telling Jac about the latest development. She ploughed on as the image of her distraught cousin flashed into her mind. 'There is one problem, though. Emma came to see me.'

'And?'

'Guess who moved a few of his horses yesterday?'

'You're kidding.'

'Unfortunately not. He took the lack of an official notice as a signal to ignore my request. Emma was adamant that he doesn't find out she told me.'

Jac sighed heavily before speaking again. 'She would be. So what does that mean for you?'

'Well, it means I have to pay a visit to the property where he's put them, which just happens to be Emma's mother's place. And I have to make sure the horses aren't moved again. And then when we do the rest of the testing, we'll have to do those horses too.'

'Do you want me to come out there with you? Just in case?'

Charlie wasn't sure if Jac meant just in case Hazel refused to cooperate, or just in case Garth McDowell showed up and caused trouble. Either way, it would be good to have the moral support, given who she was dealing with. The fact that Jac was wearing a police uniform would lend weight to Charlie's own authority, as well as making the visit purely about work. Not that she had any intention of making it anything else. 'That'd be great.'

'If you're ready to go, I can come and pick you up now.'

'Thanks, Jac. I'm staying at the Grandvista Motel.' Charlie peeked over her shoulder and lowered her voice. 'Oh, by the way, you wouldn't happen to know of any other accommodation, would you? Preferably with a little more ambience than this place?'

'Really? You're not a fan of seventies-style decor?' Charlie could hear the tease in Jac's voice. 'As a matter of fact, I would. How about I fill you in on our way out to the Roberts' place?'

'Great, see you soon.'

Charlie hung up and hurried to her room. She was just about to step inside when a voice behind her made her jump.

'Excuse me, ma'am. Are you Charlie Anderson?'

Really? Who called anyone *ma'am*? She turned to see a man in black-rimmed glasses wearing jeans and a bomber jacket, dark hair slicked back from his face. He had an iPad tucked under his arm.

'Yes?'

'I believe you work for the Department of Primary Industries? I wondered if I could ask you a few questions about the hendra outbreak.'

'And you are?' Charlie asked, even though she had a fair idea who he was, or at least what he wanted.

'Simon Morelli from the *Naringup Times*.' He gave her a tight smile that didn't even begin to reach his eyes.

'Well, I don't know where you got your information, Mr Morelli, but at this stage there is actually no confirmed outbreak of hendra.'

'But you do work for the DPI? And you are here investigating?' He'd slipped the device out from under his arm and was already thumbing the screen.

As much as Charlie wanted to snatch the thing and fling it at the wall, there was no point getting the locals offside, especially the press. Better to be as calm and noncommittal as possible. 'I have no comment to make on the situation at present.' She turned the door key and stepped into her room.

Morelli moved towards her as if he was about to follow her inside. 'If people are at risk, don't you think they have the right to know the truth?' The guy obviously came from the scaremonger school of journalism.

'As I said, I have no comment at the moment.'

She closed the door and reached for her phone. Alex still hadn't replied to her message. It wasn't like him, but he was probably in a meeting. Jac would be here any minute. Thinking back over her conversation with the police officer, Charlie moved efficiently around the room getting ready. It had sounded like Jac knew more than she was letting on about the McDowells. And she'd been so quick to offer to escort Charlie to Hazel's place. Charlie couldn't help wondering why.

Now that word was out about the virus, she would have to do some troubleshooting, but first off came the thing she was really dreading – the visit she had to pay to her aunt. Even the idea of it made her want to hide in the bathroom and refuse to budge.

'You can do this,' she told her reflection, as she ran a comb through her hair.

A car horn beeped. Collecting her phone, her bag and her courage, Charlie headed out to face the day and whatever new disasters it had in store.

Chapter Seven

'Thanks for picking me up.'

Jac drummed her fingers against the steering wheel, waiting for the road to clear before turning north onto the highway. 'Not a problem. No point taking two cars.'

'Have you had any more phone calls?' Charlie asked.

'Phone calls, visitors, emails. You name it, we're copping it.' She crinkled her nose. 'Pardon the pun. It didn't help that the paper hyped the whole thing up, especially when they don't even have their facts straight.'

'Well, that's pretty typical. People are always afraid of what they don't understand.'

Jac nodded. 'Human nature, I guess.'

'I had a reporter at my door just before you arrived trying to prise information out of me.'

'Shit. Who was it?'

'Simon someone . . . Moretti?'

'Morelli.' Jac laughed. 'Looks a bit like Clark Kent.'

'Yeah, that's the one. He got a bit snarky when I said I

had no comment, pulled the "public has a right to know" line.'

'When there's something they *need* to know, they will.'

'Exactly.'

Charlie gazed out the window at the broad stretch of the escarpment, its sharp lines dark and angry in the distance. The slab of sky beyond never seemed to end. It was all so familiar and yet so unsettling.

'I was wondering . . .' Jac's voice was a welcome interruption. 'News travels pretty fast around here. Rather than everyone going off the deep end with inaccurate information, would it make sense to have some sort of public meeting, an educational forum type thing, where you and anyone else who might be relevant – a medico maybe – could give people the facts and answer any questions they might have?'

'Yeah, we could do that. When were you thinking?'

'The sooner the better, if it's alright with you. I might be able to arrange something for tomorrow night. I know you don't have the test results back from the lab yet, but even if they come back negative at least we can put everyone's minds at rest. And if they're positive, people are going to need to know what precautions to take.'

'I couldn't agree with you more.' Charlie knew from experience that lack of information only spread mistrust and suspicion. 'The Local Land Services rep for the area will probably come along. I contacted him yesterday to be on the alert, depending on what we get back.'

'And I can get the doctor who treated Wally Murray to speak. I'm sure he'd agree.'

'You really think that's a good idea? Pretty brusque sort of guy, if you ask me.'

'Not a great bedside manner, I'll give you that. But he's

not so bad underneath, and he's well respected around here. Anyone else we should include?'

Charlie thought for a bit. 'I've heard there's a bat colony in the national park. People are bound to ask questions about how this thing spreads. Is there a local Parks and Wildlife officer who might be willing to join in?'

'There sure is, and he just so happens to be my brother-in-law. I know he wouldn't mind being there. And you're right. I've already had people on the phone wanting to know what we're going to do about the "bloody bats". Leave it with me and I'll see what we can pull together.'

'Great.'

Jac turned off onto a tarred side road that soon gave way to dirt – a road Charlie knew too well. The conversation had distracted her for a while, so she'd almost forgotten where they were actually going. But now they were on Spring Hill Road, the landscape was disconcertingly recognisable. The old Webster place still had that rusty iron roof and a yard full of decrepit cars, discarded pipes, toilet cisterns and a jumble of plumbing equipment. It looked like the Williams place further along had been renovated, its faded weatherboards now painted a fashionable shade of pewter, with a matching awning over the front porch and a shiny green hedge dividing it from the neighbours. There were a couple of newer places, almost identical to each other, project-style homes perched on small acreages complete with pristine gardens and expertly paved drives. Charlie mentally ticked each place off on the map imprinted on her mind. As they passed a field full of slick black cows and another of scruffy goats, she knew it was only a matter of minutes until they arrived at the Roberts' farm. So far she'd resisted asking about her relatives, but the closer they got, the more pressing the need to prepare herself became.

'Emma mentioned that Hazel is on her own out here now. Do you know what happened to Jim?' She tried to keep her tone as light as possible.

'Died a few years ago. Cirrhosis of the liver. Big drinker, from what I heard.' Jac threw her a sideways glance. 'But I guess you knew that already.'

Charlie looked out the passenger window and swallowed back the memories of her uncle's drinking: the screaming matches between him and her aunt that had sent both her and Emma scuttling to their room; the slamming of doors that had more than the windowpanes shuddering; the brooding silence, while everyone in the family hid away for hours in case the storm hadn't yet passed. *Family*. What a joke that word had become, or at least what a farce he had made of it. Why hadn't Hazel left? Even after the terrible night when Nathan, older than Emma by seven years, left the house for good after that savage brawl with his father. Even then she had stayed. Her own son had walked out and never come back. Although, come to think of it, maybe he had. After all, Charlie herself hadn't planned on ever returning – and here she was driving again down this same old road. She turned her attention to the bush flickering by – tree trunks scarred and blackened, bunches of fresh green shoots stark against the deadened branches. Life sprouting from death.

'How long ago was the fire?' she asked Jac, relieved at the chance to change the subject.

'Couple of years back now. Bad one too. A few houses along this stretch were damaged pretty badly, some burnt to the ground.'

'The Roberts' place?' she asked, immediately ashamed

at the hope her voice betrayed. She didn't want to be vindictive, had trained herself not to be bitter, but when it came to her relatives, she didn't seem to have full control of her emotions.

If Jac noticed it, she didn't give any clue. 'Hazel saved the place almost single-handedly. She ignored the evacuation warnings and decided to stay and fight. Not sure what I think of that myself, whether it's plain stupid or amazingly brave. Don't think I could do it.'

She was always dauntless, Charlie thought, at least in some ways.

'Here we are.' Jac steered the car onto a rough dirt access road, bouncing along over a series of potholes that had never been filled. Charlie could feel herself being dragged back in time, back to that first bumpy trip, when everything inside of her was numb but the outside parts of her seemed to act of their own accord, her feet braced against the rubber matting in the back of the car, her elbow bumping against the window, her head lurching from side to side as if it might detach itself from her neck. Her body had registered the movement in all these physical ways, she remembered, but her mind – and her heart – had been too broken to register a thing. It was only when they'd pulled up outside the house and Aunty Hazel had opened the door that her brain had switched jarringly into gear, making her legs unfold and carry her out of the car, up those steps into that grim, unfamiliar house.

'Charlie, are you okay?' There was a hand on her arm and she turned towards the voice. 'You're as white as a sheet.'

Jac. It was Jac speaking, leaning towards her, snapping her back to the present. Charlie lifted a damp hand to her face, pressed it against the tightness of her jaw. 'Yeah, I'm okay. A little nauseous, that's all. Car sick.'

'I hope it wasn't my driving.'

'No, not at all.' Charlie unclasped her seatbelt to get out, busying herself to avoid Jac's concerned gaze. This was not the time to start falling apart. She had to pull herself together.

'Look, I'm happy to do most of the talking here if that's okay with you,' Jac was saying. 'We need to scare the shit out of these people so they don't go pulling any more stunts – not that I think Hazel is behind it, it's definitely Garth McDowell – but if we can make sure she knows the consequences, then she might alert us if her dickhead son-in-law tries to go behind our backs again.'

'That'd be great,' Charlie offered feebly. All things considered, it was probably best for Jac to take charge. Part of her would even be happy to stay in the car, just as she'd wanted to all those years ago, but now wasn't the time for cowardice. She followed Jac, standing slightly behind and to her left as the police officer banged on the metal frame of the flyscreen door.

A body materialised behind the wire. The figure was in shadow so that Charlie couldn't see exactly who it was. When the door finally opened, though, the look on the woman's face told her that despite the years, Hazel Roberts instantly recognised her niece. As the two women stood there taking each other in, Charlie noticed the lines that had carved themselves across her aunt's forehead, the deep wrinkles framing her eyes. In her head she'd pictured Hazel exactly as she'd last seen her – and the shock of seeing her so much older snatched away any words Charlie might have been able to utter.

'Good morning, Mrs Roberts,' Jac greeted the woman.

'We're here to discuss the horses your son-in-law brought round yesterday.'

The door swung outwards, forcing the two visitors to take a step back. 'Emma said you'd be coming out here,' Hazel said, gazing directly at her niece.

Charlie looked at Jac, willing her to speak.

'Is that correct, Mrs Roberts? About the horses being moved?'

Hazel pursed her lips and nodded.

'Well, to tell you the truth, I'm a little confused,' Jac continued. 'Mr McDowell was well aware those horses shouldn't be shifted, that his property was, to all intents and purposes, in lockdown.'

Hazel folded her arms. 'He hadn't received any formal quarantine notice at that stage. Still hasn't, as far as I know.' The tremor in her voice was making a mockery of her attempted bravado.

'That may be the case, Mrs Roberts, but he had – and has – a moral obligation not to move any of his animals off that land until it has been one hundred per cent cleared. And now that some of those animals are here, you have the same obligation.'

'Nothing to do with me.' Hazel kept her hand on the door as if she was waiting to snap it shut at any moment.

Charlie's phone beeped in her pocket. She pulled it out and read the message from Alex: Lab results back. Positive for hendra. Call me.

Positive. It was all Charlie needed to spur her back into work mode. 'He's not going to be taking them anywhere,' she said shortly. 'The test results have come back. There is definitely hendra on that property, which means it is *officially* quarantined as of now.' Hazel's mouth opened, but nothing came out. 'You'll need to make sure the horses that were brought here are kept well away from any other livestock you have, and you'll need to take precautions around them: overalls, gloves and mask. They'll have to undergo testing and a quarantine order will be placed on your property as well.' She turned to Jac. 'We need to go.'

'Make sure you follow our instructions, Mrs Roberts,' the police officer added as they moved towards the car.

'Wait!' Hazel's voice came from behind them. 'If you put me under quarantine, he's going to find out that you know the horses are here. And he'll work out who told you. Isn't there some other way?' Hazel sounded like a frightened child. She was as afraid of McDowell as her daughter, Charlie realised.

Quarantine was mandatory for infected properties. The regulations were there to keep both people and livestock safe. But if she followed them to the letter, would she be putting Emma – and possibly her children – in danger? Would there be any harm in bending the rules just this once? She could feel Jac's eyes on her as she ran through the options in her mind. When it came down to it there was only one.

'I don't have a choice,' she said at last.

Hazel seemed to physically shrink, clinging to the doorhandle as her chin dropped. There was a jarring silence as the three of them waited for someone to speak.

Finally Jac stepped in. 'If it comes to that, we'll say we had an anonymous tip-off. If Garth comes back at any time and tries to move them, call me straight away and I'll be onto it.'

'It's crucial you follow the instructions regarding the handling of the horses,' Charlie added. 'I'll bring a set of protective clothing with me next time. After the initial tests I'll need to come back and do regular follow-up tests.' The thought of returning even once more filled Charlie with dismay, but she simply didn't have an alternative.

Hazel nodded. 'Funny that you're the one to be here doing all this.' Her tone was more amiable than it had been when they arrived and Charlie turned briefly towards her, not sure what she'd meant by that comment. 'Might be fate bringing you back here after all these years.'

Fate. Was she serious? People talked about fate like it was a good thing, but the hand Charlie had been dealt when she was little more than a child had made her pretty cynical about the idea of some guiding hand steering the course of a life. If there was one, it certainly hadn't done her any favours.

'It's not *fate*,' she said stiffly. 'It's my job.' She made her way down the steps to the car without once looking back.

Sliding into the seat beside Jac, she squeezed her knees together as tightly as she could and closed her eyes. They were a good way down the road before Jac's voice floated through the fog and stirred Charlie back to reality.

'That was pretty tough for you, huh?'

'Yeah.'

'I don't know what happened with you and the Roberts, but I'm guessing it wasn't exactly nirvana living there.'

Charlie gave a strangled laugh. 'The opposite, in fact.'

Jac nodded. 'Thought as much.'

Charlie wasn't normally one to share, but the emotions simmering inside her after seeing Hazel again suddenly boiled over. 'Jim Roberts was a controlling, nasty man. Abusive.'

Jac twisted her head towards Charlie, concern flashing across her face.

'Not to me. Or Emma. At least, not physically. But he was to Hazel. The fights they had were . . .' Charlie shuddered as she thought about it all over again. 'They were frightening. Plates smashing, doors slamming. He threw a pair of scissors at her once. Missed her eye by a couple of centimetres.' She flinched. 'And she just put up with it. We all had to put up with it. He never touched Emma or me, but we were always scared. Petrified. It made the two of us closer.'

Not that you'd know it now.

'And Hazel? She was the one you were related to, right?'

'Yeah. She's my mother's sister. When my parents . . . when they passed away, they didn't leave a will. Hazel was my closest relative and she agreed to take me in. They hadn't seen each other in years, so it was like living with strangers.'

'Charlie, that's terrible. I never knew that when we were at school.'

'I wasn't the most talkative person back then.' Charlie gave a dry laugh.

'You think?'

Charlie watched the farms slide by outside the window. She swallowed hard. 'I was pretty shell-shocked when I arrived. My whole life had been turned upside down.'

'I can't even imagine what that must have been like.' Jac brushed a hand against Charlie's shoulder. 'And you haven't kept in touch with the family at all?'

Charlie remembered the letters she'd sent her cousin, the replies she'd never received. 'No. I didn't leave on the best of terms. Emma hated me for going.' She sighed. 'As for Hazel, let's just say she did something I couldn't forgive.'

'Families are complicated beasts, that's for sure.'

Jac turned the car back onto the main road and Charlie used the pause in conversation to reply to Alex's text. Now the results were in, there was a stack of things to be done:

organising the quarantine, additional testing and the inevitable damage control. 'The sooner we organise that public meeting, the better,' she said to Jac.

'I was just thinking the same thing. I'll start on it as soon as I get back to the station. Is there anything else you need me to do?'

Charlie thought for a minute. The presence of the virus meant she was now going to be in town for longer than she'd expected – certainly for longer than she'd hoped. If she could find somewhere better to stay, she could check out of the motel before things got too crazy. 'That accommodation you mentioned, is it a room in someone's house?'

'Actually it's the granny flat at the back of my place. Tenant vacated a few weeks ago and I haven't had a chance to organise anyone else. Pretty basic, but it does have a small kitchen, a bedroom and a living area.'

'Sounds perfect. Anything would be an improvement on the Grandvista.'

'I can believe that. I'll drop you back there now, if you like, then I'll swing by again and pick you up later.'

Charlie felt a rush of relief. 'Are you sure?'

'Absolutely. You can follow me to my place, dump your stuff and get settled. You have a busy few days coming up. That'll be one less thing you have to worry about.' Jac smiled. 'And I'll make sure to keep my two-and-a-half-year-old terror out of your way.'

'You have kids?'

'One, a little girl, Hannah.'

Charlie's eyes widened. 'Must be hard, being a cop and a mother. How do you manage?'

'Day care, family, and my husband's a huge help too. I couldn't do it on my own, that's for sure. You married?'

'Me?' Charlie laughed. 'God, no. Work's always been the priority for me.'

Which wasn't entirely a lie, she told herself. She had often used her job as an excuse to avoid commitment, even if the real reason was more to do with her fear of letting anyone get too close.

'Marriage and kids aren't for all of us, I guess. As much as Hannah's turned my world upside down, I wouldn't be without her. But then, I love working too. I'm lucky I can do both.'

Charlie listened while Jac told her more about her daughter, and how she'd met her husband, a landscaper, the day after he'd arrived in town eight years earlier.

'It was a whirlwind romance,' Jac said dreamily. 'He swept me off my feet. We were married six months after we met and we haven't looked back since.'

Jac's face lit up when she talked about her family and, not for the first time, Charlie wondered what it would be like to have that feeling of security and love, to have somewhere – and someone – that felt like home. Along with that thought came a distant ache, deep down inside. She shuffled back in her seat in an effort to push it away. Jac was right, that kind of fairytale wasn't for everyone.

The motel came into view and they said their farewells, agreeing to meet again an hour later. Charlie had just enough time to pack up her gear, phone her boss and prepare herself for another visit to the McDowells. This one was going to involve a discussion about euthanasing at least one of their horses. The day hadn't started well and she knew with a heavy heart that it wasn't going to get any better.

Before Jac had returned to the motel, Charlie had called Alex, arranged for the Land Services officer to meet her at the McDowells' place in a couple of hours, packed up her things and checked out. For the time being they'd decided to keep personnel to a minimum, but Charlie assured Alex that if things got too much she'd let him know. Apart from the quarantining and the testing, there wasn't a whole lot to be done other than manage community reactions. And she already had help with that.

'We're just on the other side of town,' Jac called through the car window. 'Follow me.'

Charlie signalled back with a wave as they drove away from the motel. The idea of staying at Jac's place was curiously comfortable. She was one of the few women Charlie had ever met who she warmed to right away — there was something simultaneously strong and soft about her that made her instantly likeable. And her no-nonsense streak had already come in very handy. Charlie switched on the radio, wound the window down and cruised past the cheerful buildings of the town, feeling her heart lift a little.

Despite everything, there were probably worse places to be stuck.

Jac's house was on the southern outskirts — a pretty weatherboard cottage, painted a pale lavender. A hedge dripping with white camellias bordered the driveway and an arched portico smothered in pale pink roses framed the gate. It could've been straight out of the pages of *Country Style* magazine. Charlie parked her car behind Jac's on the street out front as a white ute reversed out of the driveway.

Jac blew a kiss to the driver, who waved in reply.

'That's my hubby,' Jac called. 'Must have called in to pick something up. I'll introduce you two later.'

You don't need to bother, Charlie thought as she gazed

at the man behind the wheel, we've already met. It was him. The guy from the pub. And the café. The one who had winked at her as he'd walked past, who she'd thought she wouldn't mind running into again. And now she had, because he was married to the police sergeant.

Joel. Joel Drummond.

What the hell was this guy playing at? She hauled her bag from the car, trying to tamp down the irritation, keeping her focus firmly on the ground so Jac couldn't see her reaction.

'You shouldn't have any problem with McDowell,' Jac was saying as she led the way around to the back of the house, dodging a scooter and veering around a swing set. 'I've told him he'll be prosecuted if he causes any more trouble.'

'Did you go out there?'

'Yep. Thought it wouldn't hurt to let him know I'm onto him.'

'Did you say anything about visiting his mother-in-law, or him moving the horses?'

'Nope. No point dobbing his wife in if it's not necessary.'

Charlie sensed there was more going on here than Jac was willing to tell her, but really, the less she knew about the whole family situation, the better. As long as Emma was okay, she didn't need to be involved.

Jac stopped and gave Charlie a knowing look. 'Let's just say that it's in Emma McDowell's best interests that her husband doesn't know she came and saw you. And here we are.' She made a flourishing motion with her hand. 'Home sweet home.'

The small building mirrored the look of the main cottage, with a porch fronting the mauve-painted weatherboards. Stone pots of brightly blooming daisies flanked the doorway, and a wrought-iron table and chairs completed the perfect picture.

'This is gorgeous!' Charlie felt the load of her day lighten as she followed Jac inside.

'It's not exactly the Taj Mahal but it's comfy, and better than the motel.'

'You're not wrong.' Charlie laughed. 'Thank you so much. Let me know about the rent.'

'Oh, we can sort all that out later.'

Charlie checked her watch. 'Look, I can't thank you enough, but I'd better get going. I'm supposed to meet the Land Services guy out at the property around now.'

'If you have any problems, give me a call. I'll be at the station dealing with the masses.' They walked together out to the street and parted ways.

Turning the key in the ignition, Charlie took a minute to settle herself before driving off. The conversation with Jac had diverted her attention for a while, but now her mind drifted back to thoughts of her new landlord. God, if her first impressions of Joel Drummond were right, staying here could be way too awkward. But how was she going to explain that to Jac? *Sorry, but your husband was flirting with me, so I need to find another place to stay.* The words sounded ridiculous even without being said out loud. Maybe she'd read the signals wrong and Joel hadn't been flirting. Maybe he was just friendly. Some guys were like that – a smile for everyone. Her eyes flicked to the clock on the dashboard – the day was ticking away. She really didn't have time to worry about this right now.

The work situation had to take precedence and it certainly wasn't going to be a breeze. Apart from the animosity the McDowells clearly felt towards her, she was going to have to euthanase a horse today, one that she knew was dearly loved. And to make it worse, it was Emma's daughter's pony that had tested positive and would have to be put down. Charlie thought about the soft dark eyes that had held hers as she'd taken the blood samples, the way the horse had stood there so willingly while she'd poked and prodded. Her throat constricted as she thought about the next needle the pony was going to feel. She blinked deliberately, trying to remove the image she knew would all too soon become a reality. It was a horrible, horrible thing to have to do, but she had no choice. The only consolation was that she was helping to stop the spread of the damn disease. Not that an eight-year-old child was going to understand.

Enough.

It was time to get on with what she needed to do.

Chapter Eight

Back at the front gate of Willow Vale Park, Charlie parked beside a van with the Local Land Services initials and logo painted on the side. A man leaning against the side of it straightened up and waved.

'Charlie Anderson?' he asked. He was short and stocky, his dark hair greying at the temples beneath the frames of his silver-rimmed glasses. Charlie nodded. 'Ross Chalmers.' He extended a hand to her through the car window and gave a good, firm shake. 'Thought I'd wait for you and we'd go in together, considering what your boss has told me about the bloke we're dealing with.'

'Good idea. The local police sergeant has already been out this morning and read him the riot act, so hopefully things will run smoothly.' As smoothly as this sort of situation can go, she thought.

'Right behind you,' he said.

Charlie pressed the buzzer and the gates opened without her having to say a word. She drove slowly towards the house, the reason for her visit a heavy weight in the pit of her stomach. It anchored her to the seat, making her wait a few seconds before she opened the door and stepped out of the car, carrying a laminated procedure sheet and a photocopied version of it to hand to the McDowells. She needed to make sure she followed it to the letter, not just for her own benefit but so there wouldn't be any questions later about whether or not she'd followed protocol.

As she suited up, she was relieved to see Ross doing the same. It was his job to make sure the property was secure rather than to deal with the horses, but it looked like he was happy to take all the usual precautions anyway.

The front door opened and Emma and Garth appeared, both of them standing silent, watching. Charlie was relieved to see that the kids weren't with them – presumably they were at school. Nodding at Ross when they were both ready, she turned to the McDowells.

There was no point pussyfooting around. Charlie launched straight in. 'As you've been told by Sergeant Pearce, the tests for hendra that I did on Monday have come back positive for one of your horses.'

'Which one?' Emma asked, her voice scratchy.

'The pony.'

Even from a distance Charlie heard the hitch of Emma's breath as her hand flew to her mouth. Her husband stood stock still beside her, his expression completely blank.

'I'm sorry, but once a horse tests positive it's mandatory to euthanase.' Charlie knew she was repeating herself, but it was important they understood that this was out of her hands; that Emma understood there was nothing she could do to change things.

'What about the other one, the mare?' Garth asked,

ignoring his wife standing beside him, whose shoulders were shuddering despite the tight grip she had on her forearms.

'She'll have to be monitored daily for the next three weeks and retested once a week. And of course she'll need to be kept in quarantine, along with the rest of your horses.'

From the corner of her eye, she saw Ross wave a sheaf of papers. 'I have all the legal documents here,' he said. 'Quarantine order, infected property order—'

Garth cut him off before he could finish. 'And who are you?'

'Ross Chalmers. From the Local Land Services. I'm here to make sure that all the required procedures are followed. Now, we're happy to run through everything with you, so you know how this is going to work.' Even though Ross looked pretty mild mannered, there was something formidable about him that made even Charlie stand up and pay attention. He must have had the same effect on Garth, who shut up and listened as Ross explained that his first task would be erecting the quarantine signs. There was still the issue of the horses on Hazel's property to deal with, but Charlie didn't want to get Garth offside any further by bringing that up now. What she was about to do was hard enough.

'Any questions?' Ross finally asked the McDowells, who had descended the steps and were standing right in front of them. Charlie kept trying to catch Emma's eye, to give her a signal she was on her side in all of this, but Emma steadfastly refused to look at her.

'Do I get compensated for the loss of any of my horses or any of the business I'm going to lose as a result of this?' McDowell asked.

Charlie couldn't believe her ears. 'I'm sorry?'

'You come barging onto my property, telling me what I

can and can't do with my own livestock, prevent me from bringing any others onto the place for at least a month, not to mention souring my name with my clients. I didn't ask for any of this shit and I want to be compensated for the money I'm going to lose.'

'Listen, mate.' Ross took a step forward. Even though McDowell towered over him, the officer's stance and the warning that flared in his eyes told Charlie that if it came to fisticuffs, he'd be a force to be reckoned with. 'Nobody asked for any of this *shit*, as you call it. But it's got to be dealt with. And no, you will not be compensated. We're here to do a job, and if you stand in our way you'll find yourself with even more to fork out, in the way of a huge fine. Or you'll be arrested. Now, since you don't have any other questions, Ms Anderson and I will be getting on with it.'

Charlie watched a vein in the middle of McDowell's forehead pulse. His hands were balled, and his chest heaved. This man had an appalling temper, there was no doubt about it, one he was barely managing to keep under control. No wonder Emma didn't want him to know she'd gone behind his back.

'I have a question,' Emma asked, breaking the tension.

All three of them looked at her.

'Can I be with Star?' Her voice cracked and she took a few seconds to get it even again. 'While you . . . when he gets the needle? I don't want him to die alone. And I want it done before Tori finishes school.'

This fragile, caring version of Emma was the one that Charlie remembered. So different to the aloof, defensive woman she'd been dealing with so far. It was a relief to know there was still some of the old Emma hidden beneath the frosty exterior. As much as Charlie was a stickler for procedure, surely it wouldn't hurt to bend the rules this time around.

'There should be as few people exposed to the horse as possible,' she said. 'But if you suit up and take all the necessary precautions, I think it would be okay.'

She hoped for some sort of sign that Emma knew why she was giving her this concession, but there was nothing.

'The carcass is going to have to be buried immediately, I take it?' Ross asked Charlie. Really, the man could show a little sensitivity, she thought, use a better word than *carcass*, but she nodded her agreement.

'We're going to need a trench dug then, somewhere away from the house and the other horses. Do you have the equipment here to do that?' The question was directed at McDowell, who merely gave a grunt in reply. 'I'll take that as a yes,' Ross continued. 'I'm going to go and erect the quarantine signs and put the tape up at the gate. How many horses need to be tested?'

Charlie looked at McDowell, curious to see if the figure he gave today was the same as he'd given her on Monday. Two horses had already been tested so that left sixteen to be done. Was he going to acknowledge the horses he'd moved? He stared off into the distance, but she could see the battle raging behind his storm-grey eyes. Would he admit it or wouldn't he? 'Mr McDowell?' she urged.

'Thirteen,' he spat.

'You told me a few days ago there were eighteen horses here, including the two in the stable.' Maybe if she pushed hard enough he would admit to the move, make her life a little easier. And Emma's.

He refused to look at Charlie or Ross, but his voice became even more belligerent. 'You must have heard wrong.'

Charlie could feel Emma's eyes on her, willing her not to give up her secret. 'Hmm, maybe I did. But just in case I didn't make myself clear, the quarantine is now official, so any attempt to move horses from this point on means you will be prosecuted.'

'And wherever you've already moved the other three horses will be put under quarantine as well,' Ross added casually, his thumbs hooked through the belt tabs on his jeans.

Shit.

Charlie bit her bottom lip. When they'd spoken over the phone, she'd brought Ross up to speed on the horses being moved but hadn't told him that the information was confidential. Somehow she'd hoped to get that out of McDowell surreptitiously. But this had turned into a battle of egos and Ross was obviously determined to win.

Emma's shoulders slumped, her hair hanging forward to cover her face, but Charlie knew what her expression would be. If McDowell registered anything, he didn't comment, simply snorted in response, shifting his eyes from Charlie to Ross and back again, refusing to be intimidated.

The best bet now was to keep things on track. 'Look, we've wasted enough time,' Charlie said, moving back to the car. She took out another set of protective clothing for Emma and handed it to her. As her cousin pulled on the disposable overalls and a pair of long black gumboots, Charlie picked up her bag. 'I'm going to need some halters to put on the horses as I'm testing them. We can do it out in the paddock if someone's there to hold them while I take the samples. Let's do that first, before . . .' She looked at Emma, who was now fully suited up.

Emma gave a slight nod, not even bothering to hide the look of defeat in her eyes. 'I can get some headstalls from the tack room on the way out to the paddock,' she said quietly.

Charlie watched as Emma walked towards the stable block. I wish I could do something to make this better for you, she thought. But the girl she remembered was long gone and there was nothing Charlie could do to reach her. She made her way out to the paddock as Ross started down the driveway, leaving Garth McDowell alone, bristling with anger.

Rather than bring all the horses into the stable, which was now considered a hot zone, Charlie went ahead with her decision to take the blood samples out in the paddocks. Once he'd finished with the quarantine notices, Ross came and helped, carrying her equipment and assisting with the collection and collation of the vials. Again she'd opted for double samples – it took longer, but she knew only too well that things could go wrong, either during the delivery or in the lab, and it was better than having to do the whole thing over. Emma haltered and held each of the horses, patting them and calming them but otherwise not talking, for which Charlie was thankful. Apart from the awkwardness between the two of them, she needed all her concentration to ensure she didn't make any mistakes. They were both very conscious of what was coming next and neither wanted to get there too quickly. The noise of the backhoe thrumming nearby was reminder enough.

Ross fell into the silence along with them, asking only the odd question about what Charlie was doing. By the time they got to the last of the thirteen horses, a good few hours had passed. The day was unseasonably hot for late autumn and Charlie had worked up quite a sweat under the nylon suit. She wiped the back of her hand across her forehead as she turned to Emma.

'The courier will be here soon to pick these up,' she said, motioning towards the cooler bag where she'd stored all the vials in saline.

Emma nodded.

'What time does your daughter get home from school?'

'Three-thirty. The bus drops her off just outside the gate.'

Charlie looked at her watch. It was 1.15. 'It would be better to get this done as soon as possible, so we can bury the horse before she gets here.'

Emma raised her head, and even through the plastic of the protective goggles she wore, Charlie could see the tears.

'Do you have children?'

The question took Charlie by surprise, but then it shouldn't have. It wasn't as if the two of them had caught up on the events of the last sixteen years over a friendly coffee. They knew so little about each other's lives. This was the closest they had come to reconnecting. 'No, I don't,' she replied softly.

'Then you don't know what it's like to break their hearts.'

All Charlie could do was shake her head in reply. 'No, you're right, I don't. And I am sorry, I truly am. But the sooner we do this, the better.'

Emma didn't say anything, just turned and headed back towards the stable, arms hanging limply by her side. Charlie and Ross followed at a distance, carrying the bags and equipment.

Ross waited until Emma was a good few metres ahead before he spoke. 'What do you want me to do for this bit?'

'Just be around. I'm not sure how she's going to react when it comes to the crunch and I doubt her husband's going to be much help.'

He raised an eyebrow. 'I know what you mean. Real gentleman, isn't he?'

Charlie didn't bother answering. When they arrived at the stable door, Emma was already in the pen with Star, running her hands across the pony's forehead, her face nestled against his cheek. Even though the pony showed no symptoms of the virus, the tests were conclusive. The vet part of Charlie wanted to scream at the woman to get away from the infected horse, but the more vulnerable side was deeply moved by the sorrow in her cousin's eyes. Thank god she was suited up. Charlie coughed in an effort to remove the lump that had lodged itself firmly at the bottom of her throat. She truly hated this part of her job. She'd become a vet because of her passion for animals, because she wanted to do something that mattered, not because she wanted to create pain and misery. Nevertheless, it had to be done.

After depositing the cooler bags securely inside the large styrofoam crates and storing them in the shade of the stable, Charlie collected her bag and approached Emma.

'We need to walk him out to the trench,' she said gently. 'Would you like me to take him?'

Emma gave an immediate shake of her head, and with gloved hands, slipped a purple halter over the pony's head. As Charlie got closer, she saw Star's name spelt across it in diamantes. Inside the mask, tears streamed down Emma's face as she clipped on the lead rope and led the pony out of the stall.

Charlie had had to euthanase a few horses in her work to date, but none of them had been cute ponies owned by a child. She pushed that thought out of her mind as she followed Emma in the direction of the trench McDowell had now finished digging. As Ross followed along behind, Charlie had a vision of what the scene must look like from a distance: a bizarre sort of funeral procession made up of a bunch of strangely incongruent people.

The noise of the backhoe had ceased, leaving the afternoon eerily quiet. When they reached the trench, Emma stopped by the pony's side, her hand resting on Star's withers. The horse stretched his head down and sniffed at the freshly dug soil. Charlie wished there was some small patch of green still left, some final morsel for the pony to nibble. And yet there was no use delaying the inevitable – best to get this over and done with. She pulled the needle and vial of sedative from her bag. It sounded like such a kind word, *sedative*, something soothing, and in fact the injection was no more than a strong dose, one the pony wouldn't wake up from. But try as she might, Charlie couldn't muster the feeling of kindness that the word conjured.

Get on with it, get it over with.

'It won't hurt and it won't take long,' she said. If Emma heard her, there was no acknowledgement. McDowell remained seated on the backhoe. He hadn't spoken a word as they'd approached.

Charlie rubbed behind the pony's ears. 'Good boy,' she whispered, 'good boy.' As she pressed the plunger on the syringe, Emma let out a sob and laid her head against the horse's neck. Charlie continued to stroke the pony's face, watching closely as his eyes began to flutter. Within minutes, Star's front knees buckled, and almost in slow motion he crumpled to the ground and lay on his side in the dirt, his head resting on the rim of the trench. Emma fell beside him, and even though she was wearing protective clothing, Charlie had to resist the urge to drag her away.

She let it go and waited, watching the rise and fall of the pony's belly until it finally came to a halt. Only then did she pull her stethoscope from her bag and listen for a heartbeat.

'He's gone.'

Charlie watched a wagtail flit down to the ground, the white of its breast bobbing left and right as it hopped across the freshly turned soil, stopping now and then to peck at a grub or worm. It seemed an age before anybody spoke – the only sound Emma's muffled weeping.

Garth McDowell finally broke the silence. 'We need to get him buried.' He said it gruffly, without a trace of empathy or concern for his distraught wife, who stood and backed away, her eyes still trained on the now lifeless pony, then turned on her heel and ran.

Charlie nodded at McDowell, gathered her things and stepped back with Ross as the backhoe roared to life, pushing the body into the trench and covering it with soil. Ross headed off, but it was part of Charlie's job to make sure the body was properly disposed of, so she waited until the trench had been filled completely before turning back towards the house.

Even though it was still midafternoon and the worst part of the day was over, Charlie knew that she had hours more work ahead of her. There were reports to write up, long phone calls with Alex and things to organise with the lab. She still needed to test the horses out at Hazel's place, too, but the lab would be overloaded as it was, so that would have to wait a day or two.

Back at the house, Ross was already in his car. Emma was sitting on the top step of the verandah, her goggles discarded beside her and her suit unbuttoned halfway down.

'What do I do with all this stuff?' she asked, her voice dull with grief.

Charlie pulled a heavy-duty garbage bag from the car. 'I'll get rid of it.'

'Do we have to use a new suit every time we go near the horses?'

'Only if one of them starts to show symptoms.' Charlie handed the protection guidelines to Emma. 'Washing and disinfecting are important, especially until we get all the results back. And it's best if just one of you does the feeds and wears all the gear. If you have any questions, you can call me, and there are a couple of websites listed on the sheet I gave you that you can refer to.'

'But you need to come back, right?' There was an expectant tone in Emma's voice that Charlie took as a sign things might improve between them after all.

She nodded. 'Since there's been a positive case on the property, I'll be here every day for the next three weeks. And, Emma, I really am sorry about the pony.'

'I don't know what I'm going to tell Tori.'

'Do you want me to stay and explain things to her?' Charlie didn't have much experience with kids, but maybe having someone official there would help.

Emma looked across to the shed, where Garth was parking the backhoe. 'I don't think that's a good idea,' she said.

'Okay.' Charlie went to leave and then remembered something. 'There's going to be an information session tomorrow night at the community centre. A lot of people are concerned about what's happened . . . so we thought it would be a good idea to answer their questions and address some of their concerns. Will you be able to make it?'

Emma gave her a blank look.

'Well, hopefully I'll see you there.' Charlie followed Ross's lead and headed back to her car. At the door she turned back to Emma.

'The tests,' she said, 'for all of you. You really should get them as soon as you can.'

'Garth refuses to do anything until we know for sure.'

'Emma, the horse tested positive and Walter Murray is dead. Isn't that enough?'

'We'll see, when his autopsy results are back.'

'I think you'd be better not to wait.'

'Why, so we can find out sooner if we're going to die?'

The bitterness lacing the question left Charlie mute. Keep it professional, she told herself, and without another word she got in the car and drove away, unable to shake the nagging feeling that the presence of the virus wasn't the only problem at Willow Vale Park.

Chapter Nine

Crisp autumn air nipped at Charlie's cheeks as she walked up the driveway towards the back gate. It had been a long, exhausting day and it was already dark, and she was so thankful she was spending the night in Jac's little guest cottage instead of within the four walls of that dour motel room. Inside the house the murmur of voices mingled with the high-pitched squeals of a child and the rhythmic hum of music. She smiled wistfully at the simplicity of the sounds, wondering if she should knock and say hello. Too bone-tired, she decided against it, and anyway, she didn't want to intrude. And then she remembered. Jac was married to Joel. No, she definitely wasn't up to chatting with the man she'd had less-than-chaste thoughts about . . . which may have been reciprocated. Not now he was her new landlord.

She crept past the back door, making her way towards the granny flat in the darkness. Suddenly her leg connected with something blocking the path and she tripped, letting out an involuntary yelp as she sprawled face first on the ground. In an instant a light flicked on, illuminating the yard, and Jac came to her rescue.

'Charlie, I'm so sorry. I should have made sure the path was clear. Are you alright?'

'Yeah, I'm fine.' Charlie pushed herself up off the ground, brushing away the clumps of dirt and grass stuck to the knees of her jeans. 'Sorry if I disturbed you.'

'Don't be silly, I should have left a light on. We were having dinner and I didn't even notice how dark it was. Have you eaten?'

'No, not yet. The whole day's been crazy.'

'I can imagine. I've saved you something. Come in and eat.'

'No, really, thanks, it's fine.'

Jac laughed. 'What, you're going to whip up a storm from that well-stocked pantry of yours?'

Charlie hesitated. Jac did have a point — she'd had no time at all to grab supplies from the supermarket yet.

'I don't want to butt in on your family time.'

Jac waved an impatient hand. 'Oh, come on.'

Charlie could see there was no use arguing. 'Well, thanks, I'd love to, but I need to shower first. I won't be long.'

'Okay. Just come up when you're ready. And I'll move this, so you don't break any bones on your way back.' Jac picked up the tricycle that had been responsible for Charlie's fall and carried it to the back porch.

The decision to move her stuff here this morning had been a good one, Charlie decided. The flat was warm and welcoming. If Jac had decorated it — and Charlie assumed she had — she certainly had a flair. Even though the space was relatively small, the off-white walls and cleverly placed furnishings made it feel a lot bigger. There were shutters on the windows and a bright coil rug covering the shiny timbers of the floor. The perfect place to relax after a nightmare of a day.

Charlie peeled off her clothes and dumped them in a pile by the bathroom door. They needed to be washed and disinfected, just as a precaution. She'd have to ask Jac about using the laundry. Stepping under the shower, she turned the hot up as high as she could handle, letting the beads of water prickle her skin and beat down on her scalp. She rubbed her head as hard as she could, massaging the shampoo through her hair and letting the water stream down her back, rinsing away the residue of the day.

Once she was clean, the thought of dinner had her turning off the taps, drying and dressing in a hurry. Rustling around in her bag, she pulled out a slightly rumpled but clean pair of jeans and an even more rumpled white shirt that she really should have ironed, but it was getting late. She shoved her arms in and buttoned it up, checking herself in the mirror. Her damp hair hung in ringlets past her shoulders and her cheeks were flushed pink – either from the sun today or the shower, or both. Never mind, this wasn't a dinner party, and she was seriously starving. She slipped into a pair of ballet flats and started up towards the house.

Things seemed to have quietened down a little. She poked her head through the door.

'Hi,' she called out.

'Come on in.' Jac was seated at the table, a glass of red in hand, her husband beside her. 'Charlie, this is Brad.'

'Nice to meet you, Charlie.' He stood up and held out his hand.

Brad? Hadn't he told her his name was Joel?

'Um . . . hey,' Charlie mumbled, reaching out to shake

his hand. The smiling man in front of her seemed to have no recollection of them ever having met. Was she that forgettable or was he foxing?

'Want a drink of something?' Jac offered, gesturing towards the wine bottle.

'Yeah, that'd be nice.'

'I hear you've been having fun out at the McDowells,' Brad said, sitting himself back down at the table.

'Well, that's one way of putting it,' she replied. What was going on here? She seriously hoped she didn't look as confused as she felt. Probably best to just go with it.

'Did he give you any more trouble?' asked Jac, handing her a generous glass of wine.

'Not really. Wasn't what I'd call warm and fuzzy, but he didn't carry on too much.'

'That's good. Sit down and I'll heat up some spag bol for you. One of the few delicacies the whole family eats.'

'Thanks. Is your daughter in bed?'

'In the process. Having story time with—'

'She *was* having story time.' A voice came from around the corner, taking Charlie by surprise. 'Lasted for a whole five pages before she crashed.'

She lowered the glass she'd just raised to her lips as the body attached to the voice appeared. Her eyes flashed from the man strolling towards Jac at the kitchen bench to the man sitting across from her at the table and then back again.

Seeing her reaction, Jac laughed. 'Don't worry, you're not going crazy. This is Joel, Brad's twin brother.'

Joel's face broke into a smile. 'Charlie. I heard you were the new boarder.'

Now it was Jac's turn to look confused. 'Do you two know each other?'

Charlie hoped the flush of colour creeping up her neck wasn't obvious to everyone else, but considering she had a white V-neck on she wasn't too optimistic.

'Sort of,' she answered, putting her wine down carefully. 'We met at the pub the other night.'

'And then at Country Harvest,' Joel added. 'Charlie was demolishing a plate of pancakes when I went in for my morning smoothie.'

'Well, I didn't quite demolish them,' she shot back. 'You were right by the way, they were to die for.'

'So there were leftovers, eh? I should have stuck around.'

Jac swept past and deposited a steaming hot bowl in front of her. 'Don't take any notice of him, Charlie,' she said, giving Joel a poke on the shoulder. 'They both like messing with people and he's even worse than his brother. Here, eat. You must be famished.'

'Thanks.' The meal was a timely diversion and Charlie gladly followed instructions. Twins. So she wasn't losing her mind. And Jac's husband hadn't been flirting with her. But Joel had. He most definitely had. And now he was sitting here at the table right beside her while she tried to delicately eat spaghetti. She twirled the pasta around her fork in the smallest portions she could manage, listening as Joel filled the others in on Hannah's bedtime antics.

'Joel's a real hit with Hannah. Insisted he be the one to read her a story,' Jac said.

'This might be a dumb question,' Charlie ventured, looking from Joel to Brad, 'but does she ever get the two of you mixed up? I mean you are identical, like, really identical.'

'Well, I'm clearly better looking,' Joel answered. 'So Hannah's known who was who from day one.'

Brad pulled a face. 'You keep fantasising about yourself there, brother. Somebody has to.'

Joel lifted a beer in response.

'Do you have kids yourself, Joel?' The question dropped out of Charlie's mouth before she even knew she was speaking. She hoped she didn't sound too nosy. Or too interested.

He answered with a casual shake of his head, but Jac was more forthcoming.

'Unlike his brother, Joel hasn't found the perfect woman yet, but he's great with kids. Hannah adores him.'

'Yeah, well, she's a great kid.' There was a softness in his tone, any hint of his earlier jesting completely gone. 'So, Charlie, you didn't mention you were here for work when we met,' he said.

'I know. Sorry. I thought it was better to keep a low profile until I knew what was happening. The whole hendra thing freaks people out.'

'She's not wrong,' added Jac. 'You would not believe the phone calls and visits I've had at the station today. You still good for the meeting tomorrow night?'

Charlie nodded and took another gulp of wine. It was peppery and dry, the perfect accompaniment to the rich pasta sauce. She realised that Joel was nodding too and suddenly remembered what Jac had said about her brother-in-law.

'Wait, so you're the park ranger?'

'Yep. Does that mean we're on the same team or opposing?'

Charlie's brow furrowed. 'I'm not sure what you mean.'

'Well, you know, the hendra thing. Bats versus horses. I'm the bat man, you're the horse woman.' He quirked an eyebrow cheekily.

Charlie wiped at the corner of her mouth with a

napkin, trying hard not to laugh. 'Actually, I think you'll find we're on the same side. Not that I like the idea of sides.'

'I do if you're on mine.'

She felt the tips of her ears heat up and swallowed another mouthful of wine. 'Unfortunately not everybody looks at it that way.'

'Like Garth McDowell,' cut in Jac. 'And the dozen or so others who rang the station today asking what we were going to do about the bat problem.'

'Really?' Charlie sighed. She'd been through this before. People got scared, that was understandable, especially when human lives were at stake. Everyone looked for a scapegoat. 'Hopefully we can iron out some of that tomorrow night.' She turned to Joel. 'I'm guessing you'll be able to handle any questions about the bats?'

He ran the tip of his tongue across his bottom lip, a gesture Charlie found disturbingly mesmerising.

God, get your act together, Charlie!

She dragged her eyes back up as he answered her.

'I know about their habits,' Joel said, 'but I'm not an expert on the hendra stuff.'

'That's okay. I'm up on that,' Charlie said. 'The virus is usually spread by bats when they're giving birth or possibly urinating—'

'Oh, please, I've just eaten.' Joel rubbed a hand across his stomach.

'Get over yourself, Joel,' said Jac, throwing a scrunched-up serviette into her brother-in-law's lap. 'I don't know any of this stuff.'

Charlie knew Joel was teasing. She gave him a quick nod before continuing. 'The horses either graze on pasture that's been contaminated or drink infected water. That's why having fruit trees around horse paddocks isn't a great idea.'

'Like McDowell has,' added Jac.

'Exactly.'

'Can people get the disease from bats?' Jac leant forward in her seat, both elbows resting on the table. 'Is it like lyssavirus?'

'No, it's not.' Joel jumped in and Charlie sat back, happy to let him explain. 'Well, only in that bats are the carriers. But people can't pick up hendra from bats like they can with lyssa.'

'So what's the difference?' asked Jac.

Joel turned to Charlie. 'You'd know better than me.'

'All the cases so far have been horse-to-human transfer,' she said. 'Oh, and two dogs have been infected – via a horse, as far as we know.'

'How many people have actually died from this thing?' Joel asked, deadly serious now.

'Four,' she replied. 'Some people have been infected and survived. The more we learn about the disease, the more chance we'll have of keeping mortality rates low. The meeting tomorrow night should help people feel more comfortable about it all.'

'Don't bet on it.' Brad had been sitting quietly at the other end of the table, flicking through the local paper. He held up the editorial page. 'It's high time,' he read out loud, 'that something was done about the increased presence of the bat menace lurking in the state forest. Authorities have known for some time that these animals carry deadly viruses, diseases that cause not only illness but death. As a community, we need to band together and call on the government to cull the numbers, if not remove these pests completely from our environment.' He lowered the paper and turned the page. 'Eric Lawson, editor and big-time property owner.'

'You forgot to mention full-time dickhead,' said Jac. 'Could be a volatile meeting, guys – be prepared.'

'This is just the sort of thing that drives me nuts.' Charlie banged her glass down on the table, completely forgetting any niceties. 'People always want to blame something else instead of taking responsibility themselves. The vaccine has been out for a few years now, but how many horse owners have actually bothered to get it? Instead of taking control of the situation, they go for these knee-jerk reactions that aren't going to solve a thing. Urgh!' She crossed her arms and let out an exasperated sigh.

The others all sat speechless at the table and Charlie became conscious that they were watching her.

Joel rested a hand on one of hers and lowered his voice. 'Just so you know, we are on your side.'

Charlie saw the look of exaggerated concern on his face. 'Sorry, guys,' she laughed gently. 'I get a little carried away about all this.'

'Don't apologise,' said Jac. 'It's good to see someone who's so passionate about their job. How did you get into all this anyway?'

Charlie lifted her hands to the table, straightening the placemat she'd shifted during her outburst. 'The first hendra outbreak was in 1994, well before I started my degree. There were more cases while I was at uni and I got involved in some research and wrote my honours thesis on it. The DPI offered me a position and I've been there ever since.'

Joel nodded approvingly, his eyes finding Charlie's. The way he looked at her left her fumbling for words.

Jac came to her rescue. 'Looks like I'm not the only female around here with brains and beauty.' She laughed. 'Isn't that right, Brad?'

Brad lifted his eyes from the paper, folding it in half and placing it back on the table. 'Whatever you said, I totally agree.' He kissed Jac on the forehead. 'Well, I hate to break up the party, but some of us have to be up early in the morning. Nice meeting you, Charlie. Don't listen to too much of my brother's bullshit. Night all.' He stood, squeezing his wife's shoulders as he passed.

'Yeah, better go get your beauty sleep.' Joel chuckled as he stood up and reached for the wine. 'Goodnight.' He topped up Charlie's glass and held the bottle over Jac's, but his sister-in-law raised a hand in protest.

'Not for me, I'm on the early shift tomorrow. Can't be running the station with a hangover.'

'Guess someone has to be responsible.' Joel filled his own glass and sat back down.

'Thanks so much for dinner, Jac.' Charlie went to stand.

'Not a problem. You stay there and finish your wine. Batman here can let you out before he leaves.' She gave Joel a pat on the back and left the two of them sitting at the table, quiet music playing in the background.

This should feel uncomfortable, Charlie thought, but it doesn't. Jac had made her feel so welcome, and the brothers' banter had lightened her mood, along with the hearty food and the wine. She sat back in her chair, closed her eyes and took another sip. When she opened them again, Joel was staring at her, the corners of his mouth turned up in a grin. She fixed her gaze on him. 'What?'

'Weird we should have met twice before and then you end up here for dinner, don't you think?' he asked.

'Good weird or bad weird?' She swirled the crimson liquid, watched it lick at the sides of the glass.

'Definitely good,' he murmured. 'Since we're on the same team and all.'

Charlie ignored the quivering in her stomach. It would be so easy to join in and play the game, but she needed to keep the conversation on safer ground. 'I guess it is a little strange. Small towns, though – you're always bumping into people. Have you always lived here?'

'Nope. We lived up north when we were kids. Then my dad passed away and Mum wanted to move, so we all ended up coming south when I got this job about eight years ago.'

'Your whole family moved here?'

'Not all. My sister's in Sydney. I came first, then Brad came down and later Mum.'

'You must like it, if you're still here.'

'Yeah, it's great. The people are friendly, the town has everything you need, beach isn't far away.'

'The beach is beautiful.'

'You sound like you know it. Have you been here before?'

She chose her words carefully. 'I went out there the other day for a drive. It looks like a great spot.'

'The best. Do you surf?'

'No, but I've always wanted to learn.'

'Well, if you're up for a lesson, I'd be happy to show you the ropes.'

Charlie found herself answering before she could think better of it. 'I'd like that.'

Joel flashed her a coy look and she replied with one of her own. There was something about this guy that had her slightly breathless, feeling like a teenager again. Or at least the way she should have felt as a teenager – light and playful and free.

They sipped quietly at their drinks, Charlie suddenly aware of the musky scent of his aftershave. Had he moved closer or was that wishful thinking? Soft, sultry jazz notes hovered in the air and she found herself swaying along, deliciously relaxed.

Joel raised his glass. 'Cheers,' he whispered and she did the same, both of them finishing the remains of their wine. He pushed back his chair. 'Well, I'd better get going.'

Charlie felt a quick stab of disappointment as he stood, collecting their empty wineglasses from the table. 'Here, let me,' she said, reaching out to grab a glass.

'No, you're the guest.' His fingers brushed against hers, sending a burst of electricity sizzling through her veins. They ended up with one glass each, heading towards the kitchen, thighs bumping and arms touching as they packed the dishwasher.

'See you tomorrow night,' said Joel as he held the back door open, gesturing for her to leave first.

'Yeah, see you then.' She slipped past him, not trusting herself to meet his gaze.

'I'll be looking forward to it, Horse Woman.'

Me too.

'Goodnight . . . Batman.' She let the words float behind her as she made her way back to the granny flat, her smile firmly in place. It had been a tough day, no doubt about it, but the dinner and the company tonight had left her feeling more than a little cheerful.

Especially the company.

Fine tendrils of steam curled into the morning air from the mug of hot tea cradled between her palms. It was a ritual she loved – sitting alone in the pre-dawn stillness watching the day begin to wake. She hadn't bothered at the motel, but here in Jac's garden, surrounded by the roses and their sweet, delicate perfume, there was a sense of peace that she sorely needed after yesterday's cluttered turmoil. As tired as she'd been last night, she'd still ended up tossing and turning, trying to rid her mind of the image of the pony's thick black eyelashes fluttering for the last time as he fell to the ground beside the hole that was soon to be his grave. It had stirred up fragmented dreams of other graves. Those of the two people she loved the most, who had been her entire world.

Her parents.

Even now, she only recalled snatches from that day. Her mother's favourite songs, 'Imagine' and then 'Amazing Grace'; hands on her shoulder and cheeks brushed against her own; words, supposedly of comfort, whispered into her ear. What she remembered most was the feel of the dirt between her fingertips as she bent to grab a handful to throw onto each of their coffins. Gritty. Cold. Rough. The thunk the dirt made as it landed on the lids, first one and then the other. Two sudden heartbeats of sound and then nothing. Nothing except a smudge on her fingers that stuck even after she rubbed them against the thin black silk of her dress.

It was funny the way the mind worked, thought Charlie as she took a slow sip of her tea. How one simple thing could spark such a deeply buried memory. How the smell of something as ordinary as freshly dug soil could drag you right back to a time and place you had no desire at all to ever revisit.

An ant crawled across her bare toe and Charlie flicked her foot against the leg of the wrought-iron chair. The sun had risen a little higher, the sky now a wash of violet, and noises from inside the house reminded her it was time to quit the reverie and get on with her day. Keeping her notes up to date was crucial. As worrying as a new outbreak was, there was no doubt it provided a great opportunity for understanding more about hendra. How had it spread this far south? What more could be discovered about its transmission from bats to horses to humans? Each case was a learning curve, even now, after years of research.

On top of that was the preparation for tonight's meeting, mental as well as physical. These things had a habit of getting heated, and from what Jac had already told her about the phone calls she'd been receiving, this one was going to be a doozy. Community education was part of Charlie's job, but public speaking still made her nervous. At least she'd have a support crew there and wouldn't be alone.

Joel would be there. Joel, with his sea-blue eyes and distracting grin. And that caramel hair with the sun-streaked waves she would really love to run her fingers through. Even the thought of it sent a ripple of warmth curling low down in her belly. She slurped at her tea and shifted slightly in her chair, reprimanding herself. *What the hell are you thinking, Charlie Anderson? Keep your mind out of the gutter and on the job. Today, of all days, you have to be on your game.*

Today she would be back out at the McDowells', monitoring. Then she would test three more horses at her aunt's. So far she'd managed to avoid any one-on-one contact with Hazel, but that was about to change. She couldn't hide behind Jac – or Ross – any longer. Jim Roberts might be long gone, but being back at the farm and dealing with Hazel was still going to be difficult. This job needed her full attention. There was no time to procrastinate – or go mooning around like some horny adolescent.

She tossed the dregs of her tea onto the grass. The sooner she got over herself and did what she'd come here for, the sooner she could get back to her settled, painless existence. But right now she had work to do.

Charlie looked around the small, bare room. A functional desk with metal legs was tucked into one corner next to a battered old filing cabinet. The walls were unpainted brick, and a single sliding aluminium window covered by blue verticals looked out onto the car park at the back of the police station.

'It's not exactly spacious, but it might work,' said Jac. 'We used it as an extra interview space before the renovations were done, but we don't really need it any more.' She wiped a film of dust off the desktop. 'I'll get it cleaned up for you.'

'No, Jac, it's fine, don't go to any trouble. I can sort it out.'

'Are you sure it's big enough?' The police officer stood in the doorway, a doubtful look on her face.

'Absolutely. There's only me,' Charlie assured her. 'It's really just somewhere people can come if they want information.'

Jac smirked. 'Or to have a rant.'

'Or that.'

'Can I help you set up?'

'That'd be great.'

They headed back outside to Charlie's car. It was early in the day and a light morning breeze rattled the leaves of the grevilleas lining the outside walls of the building. A plump grey wattlebird bounced on the top branch of one of the bushes, a pinch of brilliant yellow like a tiny thumb print on its cheek. It kept a close eye on Charlie as she opened the boot, picked up a plastic crate and passed it to Jac. 'Files, information leaflets and other assorted bits of paper.' She heaved a second, heavier box out to carry herself. 'Vaccines, medications, assorted veterinary supplies.'

'Wouldn't it be easier to leave all that in the car?'

'Yeah, but I need to sort it out first. I'll keep a stash with me and a second supply here.' Charlie lifted her knee and pushed the door of the boot shut. It slammed with a loud bang, sending the wattlebird off with a frantic flap of wings.

'So if your main job is monitoring, what do you need all this stuff for?' Jac asked as they re-entered the makeshift office with their loads, Charlie dumping hers on the floor, Jac depositing her crate on the desk.

'There'll probably be a rush on vaccinations — at least I'm hoping there will be — and with no local vet on hand . . .' Charlie pulled herself up short, aware Walter Murray's death might be a sensitive subject with the locals. 'Usually I assist if needed, but this time around I'm sure it will keep me more than busy.'

Jac reached up and pulled back the blinds, sliding the window open with an ear-jarring screech. She winced. 'Oops, sorry. If hendra is so dangerous and there's a vaccine available, why don't more people use it?'

'Good question.' Charlie clicked open the lid of the crate and pulled out a handful of folders, huffing away a strand of hair that had fallen across her eyes. 'To be honest, there have been a few instances of adverse reactions to the vaccine.'

'How adverse?'

'Lethargy, muscle and joint stiffness. A few claims that it's been a direct cause of death.'

Jac pulled a grim face. 'Urgh, really?'

Charlie thought about the bitterly worded email she'd

received a few weeks back from a client on the north coast, blaming the vaccine for the demise of her stock horse mare. 'Yeah, look, it's still a relatively new thing and we don't know all the ins and outs. Unfortunately it happens in a very small number of cases, but the risks of not getting it done are much higher than the outside chance your horse might have a negative reaction.'

Jac nodded. 'A bit like human vaccinations.'

'Exactly. They're not one hundred per cent safe in all cases, but at present they're the best safeguard we have.' Charlie dragged the desk out from the wall and pushed one of the chairs in behind it. 'That's why documenting everything about a case is so important. The more we learn, the more we can refine the vaccine.'

After a bit more shuffling and organising, the pair stood back and viewed the new set-up.

'If you need anything copied or printed, just pop next door and I'll organise it for you,' Jac said.

'That'd be great, Jac, thanks so much. This is perfect.' Charlie was grateful for the help she was getting. It wasn't always easy arriving in a town and being the bearer of bad tidings – having support certainly relieved some of the stress.

'Let me know if you need anything else. Better get back to it.'

'Thanks, Jac.'

Alone in her new 'office', Charlie smiled to herself. At least she had a space to work in now, when she wasn't out in the field. But as she registered the time on her phone and thought about her next stop, the smile vanished. She yanked the door closed behind her with a resounding bang.

Chapter Ten

The fluoro orange tape strung along the fence flapped in the wind. Charlie leant against the side of the car and looked down the row of coral trees lining the drive. For the most part they were bare, the gigantic leaves that clothed them in the warmer months long since discarded, leaving the limbs naked and exposed. But right at the top of the higher branches a few scraps of scarlet flowers remained, clinging on through the harsh winds and battering rain, refusing to give in. Charlie kicked at a pine cone lying on the ground by her feet. She could do this. This was just another property like so many she'd visited before, she told herself, and Hazel Roberts was just another client. Repeating that sentence in her head, she climbed back into the car and approached the house.

On her last visit – was it really only yesterday? – Hazel had remained partially hidden behind the flyscreen door. It had suited Charlie fine, but today, as the woman stepped out of the shadows of the house and onto the small porch, the words Charlie had rehearsed died on her lips. The years had taken their toll on Hazel. A deep crevice made her brow seem permanently furrowed, and strands of lank grey hair hung either side of her jaw, ending just above her stooped shoulders. The navy woollen jumper pulled down over a pair of khaki slacks stretched tightly across her middle. As the two women looked at each other, the resemblance Hazel had to her late sister struck Charlie hard.

Would her mother look like this now if she were alive?

Not likely. Philippa had been the younger by three years, tall and slender with the same blonde curls that Charlie had inherited. And the sisters' lives had been as different as their looks, Hazel living on the land, married to a man who sucked her dry – emotionally and physically – while Pippa, as she liked to be called, had ended up in the city with a devoted husband and a full-time career. Charlie's throat thickened and her eyes closed as the image of her mother flooded her mind. Her elegant, beautiful mother, who smelt like summer and rain and peppermint.

'I didn't think I'd be seeing you again so soon.' The words were enough to snap her back to the present. Hazel's voice was small, frail even. Maybe she was ill?

'I need to test those three horses.' She spoke in a monotone, focusing on a patch of peeled paint above the doorframe to the left of Hazel's face.

The older woman nodded. Charlie took it as permission – not that she needed any – to do what she'd come here for and moved back to the car to begin unpacking her gear. She kept her eyes lowered as she climbed into her overalls, the snap of each fastener punctuating the uneasy quiet.

'Do you need any help?' Hazel asked.

'No, thank you.' She opened the boot and pulled out the

storage crate the courier had left behind, along with her own equipment bag. Three horses. It shouldn't take long.

'They're in the top paddock. Probably easier if you drive up.'

Charlie nodded, turning to put the gear back in the car. The distance from the house would make the process easier – no need to worry about being interrupted – and she could make a faster getaway once the job was done.

'And you definitely don't have any other animals on the property?' Charlie scanned the overgrown paddocks and empty cattle yards. The place had never exactly been an oasis, but any sign of the farming business her uncle had once operated here seemed to have vanished.

'Only some chooks out back. Just me here now. Garth spells some of the horses on occasion.'

Charlie ignored the implied reference to Jim's death but couldn't help biting back with a comment on McDowell's deception. 'Yes, I noticed.'

Hazel scratched at her wrist, her thumb rubbing at the same spot over and over. 'He hasn't been back here yet, but when he does he's going to work out someone told you.'

'He already knows,' Charlie said.

'But Emma said she begged you not to say anything.'

'I didn't. Mr Chalmers, the LLS man, let it slip.'

Hazel's eyes widened and Charlie recognised the same emotion swimming behind them that she'd seen yesterday in Emma's. 'He didn't say we knew where the horses were, only that we knew they'd been moved.'

'He'll see the quarantine sign and know you've been here.'

'That can't be helped. It's out of my hands.'

'You don't understand. When he finds out, he'll . . .'

Hazel wrapped one hand across the other, the skin edging her nails turning white as she squeezed hard.

'He'll what?'

'Nothing.' The word was barely audible. 'Please, isn't there any way you can bend the rules, take the sign down, remove the tape?'

Charlie stifled a humourless laugh. The whole point of isolating a property was to alert people to the risk. And that meant everyone had to know about it. Including McDowell. 'I'm sorry, but it's not up to me. It's a legal requirement. There's nothing I can do.'

'I see.'

Charlie's animosity faded as she saw the look of despair on her aunt's face. But it couldn't interfere with her doing her job. She couldn't let it. 'These horses are on your land now, so unfortunately that makes them your responsibility. If they have enough feed in the paddock, it would be best if you stay as far away from them as possible. And they'll need to be tested a few more times over the coming weeks.'

'You'll be doing that, will you?' There was no malice in Hazel's voice and once again the feeble tone had Charlie confused.

'Yes.' An alert buzzed on her phone. The courier would be here in less than an hour. 'I'd better get moving,' she said. She handed Hazel the same information sheets she'd given Emma and turned to get in the car. There'd be no need for any further conversation once the testing was done. Charlie was relieved that she'd made it through this whole exchange while avoiding anything more personal.

'It's good to see you've made something of yourself.' Hazel's words dashed that last thought to pieces, stopping Charlie in her tracks as she opened the car door. 'Your mother would be proud.'

The mention of her mother hit Charlie like an arrow to the chest. It was the last thing she needed. She raised her eyes to Hazel's, saw the way they watered even as they faintly smiled. *Do you really think so?* she wanted to ask, but the question stuck in her throat. She couldn't do this now, couldn't get into some nostalgic discussion about her parents, not when she had work to do, and not with the woman who was the last living reminder of everything she had lost. The past was the past and she'd spent years putting it behind her. Now was not the time to get tangled in it again. Now was, in fact, the time to get her arse up to that paddock, do what she had to do and get the hell out of here.

The community hall was already buzzing when Charlie arrived. People milled about the doorways in clusters, a frazzled mother yelled at a group of kids skidding along the waxed floorboards in their socks, and most of the plastic chairs laid out in neat rows were already filled. Wary of running into anyone she knew, Charlie kept her eyes focused straight ahead as she made her way through the crowd. She was still slightly shaken after her visit to Hazel's, but she had to put a lid on that to prepare herself now for addressing the audience. She definitely knew what she was talking about, but having a roomful of eyes on her – not all of them friendly – wasn't the easiest way to spend an evening.

Jac was chatting to a group of people at the foot of the stage where a row of tables had been set up for the panel. Charlie slowed her steps a little. Should she make her way straight there or hover? She turned just as Joel entered the hall, clean-shaven and dressed in a pale blue collared shirt and dark denim jeans. When he spotted her, he waved and made his way straight over. He leant towards her and the scent on his skin, something exotically spicy, had her head spinning. 'Dressed to impress I see, Ms Anderson?' he said.

Really? She was only wearing jeans with a crimson shirt and a black leather jacket. The heels were a last-minute addition, conscious as she was of being front and centre tonight.

'One can only try,' she answered, matching his playfully mocking tone, trying to decide if she preferred the five o'clock shadow he'd sported last night or the scrubbed and polished Joel who was smiling at her right now. With her added few centimetres they were almost eye to eye. Certainly not an unpleasant position to be in, but not exactly what she needed when she was trying to calm her nerves.

'Shall we?' Joel motioned to the stage steps, and the two of them walked up and took the seats on the farthest side of the row of tables. Jac joined them as Charlie plucked up the courage to cast her eye over the growing crowd. While she tried not to let her gaze settle on anyone in particular, there were a few faces she recognised. Mrs Banks, her old art teacher, plumper than she used to be but with the same wildly frizzy hair, caught her eye and gave her a wave. Charlie lifted her hand in return. Ellen Mallory, her one-time rival for those high marks in the HSC, was there too, as gorgeous as ever and with an enormous baby bump. Ellen broke off her conversation with the woman sitting next to her, stood up and called out loudly, 'Hi, Charlie, great to see you!' Charlie smiled back. So much for trying to keep a low profile.

The noise began to die down as people took their seats, shuffling along to fill up each row. By the time Ross

Chalmers and Doctor Brunton arrived and the four speakers were seated on stage ready to begin, there wasn't a vacant seat in the entire place. Jac had done well getting the word out to the community about the meeting. It was standing room only – late arrivals were forced to congregate along the back wall.

'Let's get this show on the road, shall we?' whispered Jac. She stood and tapped a pen against the jug of water in front of her, waiting for the conversation to dwindle before she began. She welcomed everyone to the meeting and outlined the agenda, which would start with a presentation from Charlie. Dr Brunton, Ross and Joel would field any questions from the floor that might fall under their respective areas of expertise.

Charlie scanned the room once more as Jac finished the introductions. Emma was seated about a third of the way back, but there was no sign of her husband. Maybe he was home with the kids.

Or maybe not.

As Charlie rose from her chair, a group of men shouldered their way through the door and positioned themselves along the side aisle. There were five of them, and the one leading the way was Garth McDowell. He was smartly dressed, his broad shoulders and the sharp, square lines of his jaw giving him a definite presence. Eyeing him from a distance, Charlie suddenly realised what Emma might have seen in him when they first met, but the thought was only fleeting.

'Watch out. He and his cronies might have come to stir things up,' Jac whispered into Charlie's ear.

Great. Just what a girl needed to calm her public-speaking nerves.

When an expectant silence fell over the hall, Charlie

knew that was her cue. She stood and began speaking in a voice she hoped sounded confident. Sometimes you just had to fake it.

Slowly and clearly, she gave a brief history of the virus, explaining where it had been found up until now and the events that had led to her arriving in Naringup. As she described the way hendra seemed to be transmitted between populations, she sensed the anxiety of her audience. When she reached the part about Walter Murray's death, the tension in the room was almost tangible. She looked down at the faces in the front row. One woman, hanging on every word she said, was writing furiously in a notebook. Another pursed her lips and shook her head vehemently as Charlie set out the steps needed to contain the virus.

So far she hadn't named the infected property, but she knew it was only a matter of time before it was common knowledge. In a small place like this, most people would already have heard the gossip. It was her place, she told them candidly, to give them the facts, but she left it at that. As she concluded her presentation, she assured everyone that the department was working hard to control the virus, using the very best science they had available, and while there were still risks, there was a very good chance that no further lives – animal or human – would be lost.

'Thanks so much for that summary, Ms Anderson,' said Jac, on her feet again. She looked out at the crowd. 'I think now would be a good time to open the floor. Please raise your hand and wait to be selected, then speak as loudly as possible so we can all hear your question.'

Before Jac had even finished speaking, a dozen hands shot into the air. Charlie reached for her glass of water.

'Here we go,' murmured Joel.

The first question, from a middle-aged woman in the second row, wasn't a question at all but a statement.

'We have a right to know whose property this disease is on,' she said bluntly. Voices mumbled in agreement as the woman looked around at the audience, seeking out allies.

Okay, so maybe the rumour mill wasn't as good as Charlie had thought.

'It's well away from the centre of town,' answered Jac carefully.

'Not good enough,' the woman said. 'We want details. Your young vet here from the department talks a good talk, but it sounds like you people really know jack shit about this thing when it comes down to it. How do you know it isn't possible for it to spread from person to person? If you ask me, the people on that place should be kept away from the rest of us.'

There was a chorus of 'yeahs' and 'too rights'.

Jac opened her mouth to reply but closed it again. She turned to the panel and hunched her shoulders.

Charlie stepped into the breach, clearing her throat before speaking.

'What you're describing is a common worry, and I understand your concern, as there are still things we don't fully know about the virus. However, based on what we do know, the disease is not transmitted from person to person – isn't that correct, Dr Brunton?'

She was thankful for the calm, no-nonsense tone in the doctor's voice when he responded. 'Absolutely correct. To date the virus has only been transmitted from horse to human and in a couple of cases from horse to dog.'

'But you've admitted there's a lot you still don't know,' called a voice from the centre of the room. The hand-raising etiquette had apparently been abandoned.

'Yes, but that is something we *do* know,' Charlie said.

'Let's cut the bullshit,' a voice boomed from the far side of the hall – McDowell. Any brief idea Charlie may have had about his inherent charm evaporated as soon as the man opened his mouth. 'This thing is at my place, but I'm not taking the blame. We need to deal with the real problem here and that's the fucking bats. They've been swarming all over town since they set up digs in the forest, crapping all over the place, causing a racket at night, destroying the fruit trees. Now this. As far as I'm concerned, they're vermin, and they need to be gotten rid of. What do you plan to do about it, Drummond?'

Heads turned from McDowell to Joel, who slowly pushed back his chair. Charlie noticed the way he straightened his shoulders and tilted his chin a little higher, rising to the challenge. If this was tough for her, it must be even harder for him, being a local.

When he spoke, his voice had a distinct air of authority. 'There are plenty of things we can do to guard against the spread of the disease, as Ms Anderson has already pointed out. Vaccination of horses for one. Netting of fruit trees for another.' Joel glared straight at McDowell. 'The flying foxes are a protected species, and there will be no culling or forced removal. I want to make that really clear. Anyone who attempts to do so will be prosecuted.'

'So you're going to personally foot the bill for the vaccinations, are you? And put up the nets? Why should we have to fork out for all this?' There were rumblings of support for McDowell now that he was talking about the hip pocket.

Charlie rose to her feet, eager to take the pressure off Joel. 'It's the horse owner's responsibility to pay for the vaccines, Mr McDowell, and to take proper precautions regarding hygiene and lockdown when required. I don't think any of us want to see further deaths as a result of this disease. We're all in this together.'

'Bullshit. Who stands to make money out of this whole vaccination lark? I'll tell you who – the government and the company that makes the vaccine.' He turned to the crowd, on a roll and loving the sense of power. 'And who loses money? We do, all of us. I say the best solution is to get rid of the source of the problem. And that's the *bats*.'

Some in the audience were nodding their heads furiously now, others calling out 'hear, hear'. A smaller group shifted in their seats, looking more than a little uncomfortable.

Jac jumped in. 'Mr McDowell, it's already been established that attempting to harm a protected species is against the law, so let's move on. Are there any other questions?'

But McDowell wasn't going to be shut down. 'You're all fucking gutless if you stand by and let them call the shots.'

He strode to the front as he spoke, poking at the air with his index finger. 'All they're interested in is lining the pockets of the pharmaceutical companies and getting information for their precious research. None of them give a shit about any of us, or our horses. If you want to stay here and listen to more propaganda, that's up to you, but I've had enough.' He glared pointedly at Emma, who looked around nervously before standing and making her way to the door. The group of men who'd arrived with McDowell followed suit now as he pushed his way out, the last of them shooting a piercing look over his shoulder at the panel, who remained seated onstage.

For a few seconds the entire hall froze in stunned silence before murmurs began to ripple through the crowd. Charlie shuddered. Even though McDowell hadn't physically threatened anyone, the venom in his tone had poisoned the room.

So much for a harmonious exchange of information, she thought ruefully.

Jac dipped her head towards Charlie. 'Could've done without that.' She took the floor again, moving to the front of the stage. Her presence did nothing to calm the audience. Looking back over her shoulder, she turned her palms towards the ceiling as the noise continued. Charlie frowned. Poor Jac had been thrown in at the deep end, and she shouldn't be the one bearing the brunt of the community's wrath.

Charlie stood and moved forward, clasping her hands in front of her as she spoke in a loud enough voice to cut through the commotion. 'Excuse me, if I could have your attention for just another few minutes.'

She looked around the room, making eye contact with as many of those present as possible while she waited. It took a minute or so, while people elbowed each other and turned to face the front of the room, but gradually the voices dimmed.

'Thank you. I understand this is difficult, but despite what Mr McDowell said, I know I speak for everyone here,' she indicated those behind her, 'when I say we have the interests of the community at heart. I have personally been involved with a number of hendra cases before, including those where, sadly, people have become terminally ill.' She knew it was better not to use the word *died* or any variation thereof. It was way too emotive, especially in light of Walter Murray's recent death. Taking another look around the audience, she continued. 'There is no way I would wish this on anyone. The precautions being taken are for everyone's benefit. Yes, there is a danger the disease could spread, but we are doing everything we can to contain it – and for that we need your cooperation and for everyone to remain calm.

If anyone has any further questions or would like to speak to me individually, there is a temporary office being set up behind the police station where I will be available when I am not working on site. Please feel free to come and see me.' There was little more she could say, and it was probably best not to prolong this volatile meeting.

Charlie sat down and Jac brought the presentation to a close. 'Thanks for coming, everyone. And thanks in advance for your cooperation.' The hall began to clear of people as the panel sat back.

'Well, that was interesting.' Ross screwed up his face and scratched his temple. 'I'm betting we're going to be hearing more from that McDowell character.'

Joel pushed his chair in and shoved his hands in his pockets. 'Probably just shooting his mouth off.'

Jac's face, though, was clouded with concern.

The crowd was starting to thin, and Ross and Dr Brunton said their farewells while Charlie and Joel helped Jac lock up before heading out to the car park.

'I think I could use a drink after that. Anyone care to join me?' Joel asked.

'Not me. I've got a killer headache and Hannah wasn't well this afternoon. Better get back and see how she's doing.' Jac flashed a look at Charlie. 'But you two go ahead.'

Charlie rolled her eyes at Jac's not-so-subtle push. She always needed to unwind after things like this and she certainly wasn't averse to spending another hour or two in Joel's company, but she could do without the matchmaking. And besides, at 7.25 on a weeknight, the only place to eat would be the pub, where a few of the audience members were likely to be holding a post-mortem of the meeting.

'I think Savannah is open tonight,' Joel broke in, as if reading her thoughts. 'It's a licensed bistro. We could grab a bite to eat and wash it down with a quick drink, compare notes on tonight's events.' He was speaking to Charlie as if Jac had already left, but she was conscious of the other woman's eyes trained on the pair of them. 'If you haven't already eaten, that is,' Joel finished.

'No, I haven't.'

'Right, well, off the two of you go and *compare notes*,' said Jac wryly. 'I'll catch you tomorrow.'

The police officer disappeared into the shadows. A car door shut, an engine hummed to life, and the glow of tail lights cast a splash of red across the asphalt at Charlie's feet.

'So . . . my car's just out on the street.'

'Oh, okay.' Her voice was a little shaky. It was a bit strange now that Jac had gone and it was just the two of them. Two colleagues debriefing, that's all this was.

She followed Joel out the gate to a battered pale blue Land Cruiser that had clearly seen better days. 'Is this yours?' she asked, choking back a laugh.

Joel waved a hand theatrically towards the cruiser. 'Sure is. Charlie, meet Bertha.'

'Bertha?'

'Yeah. After her numberplate, BER-478.'

'Do you always name your cars?'

'I do. I've had Jemima, Lulu and this one, Bertha.'

'All women? You've never had a male car?'

He opened the door for her and she climbed in, buckling up as he went around to the driver's side.

'Well, they are the fairer sex,' he said, 'and generally much more fun to be around than men.'

No doubt about it, this guy was a charmer, Charlie thought as Bertha cruised along the main street. That smile, the way it went all the way up to his eyes, that way he had of wriggling his brows. She'd come across men like him before, out for a good time, or maybe a challenge. But there was something boyish in Joel's manner that told her his ribbing was a lot more innocent. And potentially a lot more dangerous.

'Yeah, in my experience, men are a lot easier to get along with than women,' she said, picking up on his previous comment.

'Is that so? And is there any one man in particular you *get along with*?'

He'd thrown out the hook, she knew, but she was happy to bite, or at least nibble. 'Not currently. Work takes up a lot of my time and . . .' Charlie stopped mid-sentence. Who was she kidding? She hadn't been on a date since she'd broken up with Chris – that would require actually going out and socialising. 'Well, I have serious hermit tendencies.'

'You know what they say about all work and no play.' Joel parked the car and turned off the ignition.

Charlie let the comment go as she stepped out of the car. He moved in behind her to lock her door, then rested his hand against the small of her back as he directed her towards the restaurant. An involuntary thrill buzzed through her limbs. It was the same jolt she'd felt last night when his fingers grazed against hers. Nothing more than a physical response, she told herself sternly, as the waitress showed them to a corner table. After a long time without any intimate contact, it was perfectly normal for your body to have some sort of reaction when a man – a rather attractive man – touched you. There was nothing more to it. But there was no harm in enjoying it, either.

Joel passed her a menu. 'Hungry?'

Charlie suddenly realised she was starving and nodded enthusiastically.

He laughed at the expression on her face. 'So, mains are a given, but are you a dessert or entree type of girl?'

'What do you think?'

'Hmm, I'd say dessert.'

'And you'd be right. Although it's not unusual for me to go all three courses.'

'Is that so?'

Charlie let her eyes fall to the menu as the waiter arrived to take their drink order. Perfect timing.

'What did you make of the meeting?' she asked when the waiter left, taking the opportunity to change the subject.

'A bit of a debacle, thanks to Garth McDowell.'

'Hmm, he sort of threw a grenade in, didn't he? It doesn't surprise me considering what I've already seen of him.'

Their drinks arrived and Charlie turned her glass between her fingers. The way McDowell had behaved at the farm had been worrying enough, but his performance at the hall tonight, spurred on by his mates, was even more of a concern.

'How well do you know him?' she asked Joel.

Joel shook his head. 'Only by reputation. I see him at the pub occasionally, but we've really never crossed paths. He's not very well liked around here.'

'So you really think he's all bluff?'

Joel stared into the beer in his glass. 'I'd like to think so, but I have heard a few stories.'

'Such as?'

'Rumour is he's done time. Went off the rails when he was a teenager. His father bought that property when he retired – he was loaded, apparently – and the horses were his hobby. Garth and his brother fell out after the old man passed away. Died after getting kicked by a stallion he was training, but . . .' He hesitated.

'But what?' she prompted.

Joel raised a hand. 'This is just hearsay, but apparently the brother claimed Garth had something to do with it.'

Charlie's glass hit the table hard. 'What? That he killed him?'

'It seems they had a pretty volatile relationship. The coroner's report said it was an accident, but the brother wouldn't believe it. Couldn't prove anything, though. That was about twelve years ago. Garth took on the property and the breeding business. He lives off that and the investments his father left him.'

'So she was drawn to the money,' Charlie said, almost to herself.

'Who?'

'Emma.'

Joel frowned. 'You sound like you know Emma McDowell?'

Charlie hadn't told Joel about her previous connection with the town, and by the looks of it, Jac hadn't filled him in either. There was really no reason to keep it secret, but there was also no need to complicate things by revealing the entire story.

'She's my cousin,' she answered eventually, with a sigh. 'But we're not close.'

It wasn't the whole truth, but it wasn't far off.

'Really? Didn't see that coming. You two are nothing alike. Not that I know her well. Or you.' He was faltering, trying hard to put the pieces of the puzzle together.

'That's true – we are nothing alike. But from what I know of Emma, I can't understand why she would be attracted to someone like Garth McDowell.'

'Who knows? Working out the way women's minds work has never been my strong suit.'

She wasn't imagining it – there was definitely a tinge of melancholy in Joel's tone that came out of nowhere. It made her curious.

'Sounds like someone who has tried and failed.' She said it lightly, in the teasing tone they'd conversed in earlier.

'You're not wrong.' Joel pushed his beer glass towards the centre of the table and back again. He took a sudden interest in the frayed edge around a hole in the white tablecloth. Charlie couldn't see his eyes, but the stiffness in his posture told her she'd well and truly put her foot in it.

She stumbled over her next words. 'I'm sorry, that was meant to be a joke.'

Joel pressed his lips together as he tilted his glass and studied what was left. 'Not a problem,' he said finally. The light returned to his eyes and Charlie could tell that whatever demon he'd been wrestling with was now defeated. 'So, how long do you think you'll be in town?' he asked.

'As long as it takes to sort out the situation, I guess.'

'Anything you need while you're around, just ask. I'd be happy to help.'

'Thanks.'

Their meals arrived in a fog of steam and garlic and the conversation drifted to food, the best places to eat in town, bands that sometimes played at the local theatre and a summary of all the other attractions Naringup had to offer. By the time dinner was finished, Charlie knew a whole lot more about the current version of the town than she ever would have thought possible. She made sure not to mention how much it had changed or to give away any clues about her knowledge of the area.

'You're really doing a good job of selling the place,' she told Joel as the waiter collected her empty plate.

'Good. I aim to please. Dessert?' He held up the menu.

She plucked it from his fingers and scanned the listed offerings. 'I couldn't eat a whole serving. Do you feel like sharing the chocolate tart with peanut and salted caramel ice-cream?'

'Why not? That means you've only had one and a half courses, though. I wouldn't want to deprive you.'

'I'll make up for it next time.'

'I might just hold you to that.' He signalled to the waiter and placed their order.

Next time? What was she thinking? Dating was so not on her agenda. But then who had said anything about dating?

'So, nobody special in your life?' She tried to say it casually, taking a sip of wine as she asked, flicking her eyes up only as he began to answer.

'Nope. Unless you're talking the four-legged variety, in which case my dog, Tilly, would qualify.'

Charlie laughed. 'I was thinking more the two-legged type of female. No offence to Tilly.'

'None taken – on her behalf.'

Dessert arrived amazingly quickly and Charlie realised they were the only ones left in the restaurant. Joel handed her a spoon and the two of them started on the tart. The rich chocolate was delectably silky and Charlie moaned.

'Sounds like you're enjoying that.'

'Oh my god, it's sooooo good.'

Joel swallowed a scoop of ice-cream. A smear was left behind, coating his mouth. Charlie stared, fighting the urge to lean forward and savour the caramel lingering on his lips.

She watched instead as they curved upwards and knew she'd been caught out.

'Sorry,' she said, wrinkling her nose and digging her spoon back into her side of the bowl.

'Oh, don't apologise. Believe me, I'm enjoying this as much as you are.' She knew by the smoky look in his eyes and the hazy sound to his voice that he wasn't just talking about the ice-cream.

They both laughed softly then and ate the rest of the dessert in silence, until the clanking of metal against the ceramic bottom of the plate had them both downing spoons at the same time.

'That was delicious.' Charlie rested back against the wall, glad she'd chosen the bench seat and had space to spread out.

'So, big day tomorrow?'

'Not too bad. Monitoring, paperwork. How about you?'

'A bus group visit in the morning, a couple of fire trails to check and then, like you, the dreaded admin.'

'No escaping it, is there?'

'You did a pretty good job of taking my mind off it tonight, though.'

He kept his eyes on hers and it was impossible for her to look away. I'm in serious trouble here, Charlie thought. 'Glad I could be of service. Guess we'd better get the bill.' She reached for her bag and pulled out her wallet.

Joel stopped her, clasping her hand beneath his own. 'My shout.'

'Uh-uh, I always pay my own way.' The stubbornness in her voice had him backing off without an argument.

'Fair enough.'

The night air was cooler than she'd expected as they made their way to the car. She pulled on her jacket, or at least attempted to before one arm got slightly stuck. Joel untwisted the sleeve, his body tantalisingly close. It only took a small turn of her head for their mouths to meet and only a few seconds until the kiss deepened into something more than a random skimming of lips. Somewhere in the back of her mind she was conscious of her legs becoming unsteady beneath her and she reached up, wrapping her arms around Joel's neck, more for support than anything else. It wasn't until she needed to take a breath that she finally pulled away.

'Hmm, I'm liking that salted caramel more and more,' Joel said, his hands settled firmly against her hips.

'Me too.'

The trip back to Jac's place was short, but long enough for Charlie's mind to start racing. Should I ask him in? Is that even appropriate when I'm staying at his brother's place? Why am I even doing this when I'm here to work? Before she could contemplate the answers, the car stopped and Joel's fingertips were resting gently against her shoulder. 'I had a great time tonight, Charlie. We should do it again. Soon.'

She was glad the darkness of the car left his face partly obscured. If she'd been able to see his eyes, there was no way she'd have the willpower to say goodnight without going back for a second kiss. But making out in a car like some randy teenager wasn't really her style.

'That'd be nice,' she said, opening the door.

'See ya, Charlie.'

She crept up the driveway, slid the key into the lock of the granny flat, flicked on the light and flopped onto the bed. Wow, what a night. Hardly what she'd expected when she'd headed into the meeting. It had been quite a while since she'd been even remotely attracted to a guy, and the distinctive tingling she felt way down low when she closed her eyes and thought about Joel, about that kiss, reminded her just how long it had been. She knew she wasn't imagining the chemistry between them, but she couldn't let herself be side-tracked by some holiday romance. Once this job was done, she'd be heading back up north. A man in her life right now would be nothing more than an unnecessary distraction. One she really didn't need.

Really, she didn't.

Chapter Eleven

Charlie watched the sugar crystals sink into the foam of her latte, turning her head to look out the window as the last of them dissolved. The café was in the perfect position to see but not be seen – unlike the vegetarian place, where there was a strong chance she'd run into Joel. Not the best idea when she was trying to keep her mind on work.

Across the road, the whole town was turning out for Walter Murray's funeral. Cars lined the main street and guests poured into the tiny church. There were a number of people she recognised among the mourners. One woman in particular drew her attention – Hazel's black skirt and jacket were suitably sombre, the plainness broken only by the string of pearls dangling from her neck. She waited by the door, glancing at her watch and then looking up and down the footpath, her fingers fiddling with the strap of her shoulder bag. Despite the more formal clothing and the less dishevelled hairdo, her face was pale and still had the harried look Charlie had seen the day before. After one more check of the time and another glance in each direction, Hazel turned and disappeared through the arched wooden door behind her.

Charlie jumped as her phone vibrated on the table.

A message from Alex: There's a backlog at the lab. Last lot of test results won't be in until after the weekend.

Great. So no information on the horses McDowell had moved until Monday at the earliest. Right now they weren't showing any symptoms, but they could still be carrying the virus. And the longer we wait for answers, she thought, the more chance there is of the disease spreading. She drummed her fingers against the side of the glass mug. There was no way of speeding up the process, so there wasn't much point stressing.

Outside, the street was deserted now. The jagged chords of an organ coming from behind the walls of the church broke the morning hush. In the car park, a driver wearing a charcoal suit leant against the door of a hearse, dropping a cigarette to the ground and grinding it out with the ball of his foot.

Poor Walter. He'd just been doing his job and this was the price he paid, Charlie thought. Being a vet had certain hazards you knew about when you signed up – dog bites, scratches, the occasional kick if you dealt with larger animals – but death by incurable virus certainly wasn't at the top of the list of potential dangers.

A blur of movement caught her eye: a woman rushing out the door of the church and crossing the road. Her face was hidden behind dark sunglasses, her head down, eyes fixed on the ground, but her body shape and colouring made her instantly recognisable. Emma. She must have arrived when Charlie was checking her phone, but why was she leaving before the service finished? There was something troubling about the way she hugged the memorial booklet to her chest, the way her body seemed to crowd in on itself. The situation at the farm must be taking its toll. Dealing with her husband's anger, her daughter's grief and the possibility that any one of them could be infected – was it any wonder she looked so distraught?

She was almost right outside the café. Charlie angled her body back from the window, making sure she wouldn't be seen from the street. As she continued to watch her cousin, a second person appeared closely behind Emma. Hazel grabbed her daughter's arm and spun her around until they were face to face. Neither woman would be considered tall, but in heels, Emma dwarfed her mother. She pulled herself out of the older woman's grasp, waving her hands as she tried to back away. Charlie edged forward. They were only a few metres away from her, their voices muffled by the glass. She didn't need to hear anything to know this was not a warm and friendly mother–daughter moment, but she still gasped when Hazel yanked the glasses from her daughter's face. A purple bruise darkened the skin around Emma's left eye. The two women froze, staring dumbly at each other. Emma glared at her mother before snatching the glasses back and turning away. She stumbled to her car and started it up, pulling out so quickly that a passing truck had to slam on its brakes. The driver yelled something through his window, shaking a fist as Emma tore off without a sideways glance. Hazel wheeled around quickly then, wiping her hands down the front of her pleated skirt. Adjusting her pearls, she made her way back across the road to the grounds of the church just as the doors opened and six dour-faced men carried out Walter's coffin.

Charlie slumped back in her seat and signalled to the waitress for a second cup. She couldn't leave now – not with so many locals milling about and Hazel still within view. Besides, she needed some time to take in what she had just witnessed. Picturing Emma's swollen cheek, the plea her cousin had made at the motel played itself over again in her head — *Please don't tell Garth.* Did McDowell beat his wife because he'd found out she'd deceived him? Charlie gulped down what was left of her coffee, right as the waitress appeared with the next one.

'Thanks,' Charlie mumbled.

Still trying to process what she'd seen, she opened her wallet, rifling through an assortment of business cards, a few old concert tickets and a book of stamps, finally finding what she was looking for: a photo, bent and worn, colours fading, of two teenage girls. One was a little older and taller than the other, with a mass of wild blonde curls. The shorter, younger girl had long dark hair, but as different as their other features were, their eyes were almost identical — almond shaped and a deep forest green. Charlie remembered the day the photo was taken. It was stinking hot and they'd spent the afternoon cooling off at the swimming pool, mucking around doing bombs and playing Marco Polo, blowing the last of the money Hazel had given them on iceblocks that dripped stickily down their wrists. On their way home, they'd spent their leftover coins in the photo booth in town.

The image blurred as Charlie gazed at the two girls: their arms wrapped around each other's shoulders, their heads angled together, their big cheesy grins, both giggling as the flash clicked. Just look at those smiles, she thought, bringing the photo closer, her heart drumming. Gorgeous, sweet young Emma who had relied on her older cousin so very much. Tears filled Charlie's eyes and slipped silently down her cheeks. She'd left Naringup all those years ago to save herself, but to her cousin it had been a desertion. A betrayal. There was nothing Charlie could do to turn back time. But there was something she could do to try to help Emma right now.

Sliding the photo back into its pocket, she tucked a ten dollar note under the saucer of her cup and ducked out of the café. The crowd had pretty much dispersed and Hazel was nowhere to be seen, possibly gone to join the other mourners at the wake. She'd be smiling sweetly and pretending everything was fine, no doubt, as she'd always done, even after such an ugly public argument with her daughter.

Charlie left her car parked where it was and headed south. It was only three blocks and a five-minute walk to the police station.

'My hands are tied, Charlie. What you've told me in no way proves that Garth McDowell assaulted his wife. I can't just go barging in and arrest him because of that.' Jac rubbed a finger across her temple. 'As much as I'd like to.'

'But you know I'm right?' Charlie shot a challenging look across the police officer's desk.

Jac rolled a pen between her fingers. She tapped the end of it against a pile of papers as she pressed her lips together before directly meeting Charlie's gaze. 'Let's just say I've had reason to speak to the man before regarding his, how should I put it, aggressive tendencies.'

The background noises of the police station faded as Charlie's eyes fell shut. It was what she'd suspected, but hearing it out loud, even with Jac's carefully chosen words, made her head spin.

'I wouldn't have thought you'd care so much, considering your history with the Roberts family.'

Charlie raked a hand through her hair. 'What? You think I want to see her hurt? What sort of person do you think I am?'

'Calm down, calm down. I'm sorry.' Jac sighed into the long, thick silence. She stood and rolled her chair around until it was right beside Charlie's, sat down again, leant forward and lowered her voice. 'Look, I've had a couple of anonymous tip-offs about domestic violence at the McDowell place. No question in my mind the calls were from Hazel Roberts. But when I went out there to check on Emma, she told me to mind my own business. Pretty much kicked me off the place. If I go out there with all guns blazing, it will only make the situation worse for her and possibly for the kids.'

Charlie propped her elbows on the desk, dropping her head between her hands.

'Any chance you could talk to Hazel and try to find out more about what's going on?' Jac asked.

'We aren't exactly on speaking terms. I don't think she'd listen to me.'

'I see.' Jac stared at the pen she was still holding. 'I'm sorry, but there's really nothing we can do. I'd love to lock the dickhead up, but no one has actually witnessed a crime taking place.'

Charlie listed into her chair, exhaling heavily. 'I'm afraid I could be at fault.'

'Unless you socked her one yourself, then there's no way you are. McDowell might be pissed off about what's happening, but you're not to blame.'

'I know, but Emma made me promise not to let on that I knew he'd moved the horses.'

'And you told him?'

'No. Ross Chalmers did. Maybe that's what got her the black eye.'

'We don't know if that's true, but even if it is, you're still not responsible. McDowell's the one with the temper, and unfortunately Emma, for whatever reason, stays. I've seen it over and over, and it frustrates the hell out of me.' She threw her pen onto the desk. 'Sorry.'

'Never mind.' Charlie stood. 'I just . . . after what I saw, well . . . I wanted to do something to help. But I understand you have to work within the boundaries of the job.' As we all do, Charlie thought, remembering Hazel's plea to hold off on the quarantine. 'I'll let you get back to work. I've got some of my own to do.'

Jac laid a hand on Charlie's arm briefly before moving back to her side of the desk. 'Hey, I meant to ask, how was your date with Joel last night?'

Charlie was almost out the door. She stopped and turned around. 'It wasn't a date, it was just dinner.'

'At a nice restaurant, with a hot guy – I'm allowed to say that since I'm married to his twin.' There was a gleam in Jac's eye. 'Two attractive single people getting to know each other over food and wine. I'd call that a date.'

'Well, if you must know – and you obviously must,' said Charlie, 'it was nice.'

'Nice? Really? Is that all I'm going to get?'

'There's nothing else to tell. We ate, we chatted, we left.'

Jac choked out a laugh. 'Yeah, right. I've been watching the way you two look at each other, and using my excellent policing skills, all the evidence suggests there's a lot more you *could* tell.'

'I'm definitely not in the market for a man.' Charlie could hear the defensive tone in her voice and decided to brighten it a little. 'Look, he seems like a great guy, Jac, but it's purely platonic. Believe me.'

Jac angled her head, studying Charlie's face. 'Hmm, you say that with so much conviction, Ms Anderson, but I'm not sure I do believe you.' She grinned. 'And, knowing my brother-in-law as I do, I can tell he's smitten. Hey, we're having a birthday bash for the boys tomorrow, out at Joel's place. How about you come along?'

Charlie huffed. 'Is this a set-up, Jac?'

'Set-up? Would I be that devious?' She chuckled. 'You'd be coming as my guest. We'll have fun. At least say you'll think about it?'

Despite herself, something inside her was warming at the thought of seeing Joel again. 'Fine, I'll think about it.'

She ignored the glow of triumph on Jac's face as they said their goodbyes.

Even as she left the police station and made her way back along the street, Charlie knew exactly what she'd be doing tomorrow.

If the state Emma was in when she'd left the church was anything to go by there was a good chance she would head straight home. At least that's what Charlie was banking on, and she needed to make sure she was okay after what she'd seen unfolding on the street. She'd made it out to Hazel's place to do the monitoring straight after leaving the police station, while the vet's wake was still underway. While she'd made a point of avoiding any further contact with her aunt, she hoped Emma would be in and willing to talk.

As she peered through the gate, everything looked much the same as yesterday – horses grazing in the paddocks, kids' toys scattered across the front lawn, a tractor parked in front of the massive garage beside Emma's silver Pajero. The only vehicle missing was the black Land Cruiser, the one Charlie knew belonged to Garth. She pressed the buzzer and the gate slid open, allowing her to drive straight in. So far, so good.

She climbed out of the car and up the steps. The front door was closed, the house noiseless. She dug her thumbnail into the pad of her index finger as it hovered above the doorbell. Emma had made it clear she didn't want any personal contact. The relationship Charlie still mourned every time she looked at that photo in her wallet was long gone. And yet she couldn't stand there knowing Emma was in trouble and simply walk away. The bell chimed three times as Charlie stood and waited. No voices from inside the house. No approaching footsteps. Not a sound. She rang the bell again and waited. Nothing.

Maybe she could leave a note. Saying what? The things she needed to say to Emma couldn't be written on paper – paper McDowell might see.

All she could do was get on with what she was supposed to be doing.

Suiting up, she grabbed her bag and began the rounds of the paddocks, checking each horse's temperature, making sure there were no nasal secretions and that they generally seemed in good health. It took well over an hour to get around to all thirteen horses, recording her findings quickly in her notebook. She packed her gear back into the car and slowly stripped off her overalls. It was only early in the afternoon, but her body was weary. As her hand curled around the handle of the car door, a noise from behind made her turn.

Emma's daughter, Tori, was standing on the verandah.

The rosy glow Charlie had seen in her cheeks that first day was gone, replaced by the ghostly colouring of a child who had seen too much.

'Hi, Tori,' Charlie ventured, 'is everything okay?' It was a stupid question. The child's pony had just died. No, not died, been put to death.

By me.

The girl didn't speak, but her eyes swam with tears. She tried to hold them back, sucking back one quick breath after another, but as the tears started to fall she flew down the steps, a string of sobs rattling her tiny frame.

Instinctively Charlie knelt and the girl came to a stop in front of her. Charlie was glad she'd already taken the time to disinfect her hands after doing her rounds. She reached forward and placed an arm cautiously around Tori. 'Hey, what's wrong? Where's Mum?'

The child gave a quick nod towards the house.

So if Emma was here, why was Tori finding solace in the arms of a total stranger? Charlie thought about what had gone on over the last twenty-four hours and her heartbeat quickened.

'Tori, are you hurt?'

The girl stood upright, making her eyes level with Charlie's. 'No, but Mummy is,' she said. 'She said I wasn't allowed to tell anyone, but she has bruises, and when I cuddled her to make her feel better, she started crying and ran into the bedroom and now she won't open the door.'

Tori had the same eyes as her mother. The same as Charlie's own. Looking into them, Charlie saw the same pain she'd seen in Emma's, years ago, as the two of them had huddled together behind the safety of their bedroom door while screams and blows were hurled outside.

I left you there.

The girl pulled away and for a second Charlie wondered if she'd said the words aloud. But Tori was wiping the sleeve of her shirt across her eyes, a tiny shiver bringing an end to her tears.

'How about we go and see if your mum's okay? She's probably just having a rest.' Charlie kept her voice casual for the child's sake. Tori took her by the hand. 'Is your brother home?' Charlie asked as they stepped inside the house.

'He's at school. Mummy let me have the day off because I'm so sad about Star. I stayed with Larissa while she went to Mr Murray's funeral.' Charlie felt a pinch of guilt at the mention of the pony, even though she knew that wasn't Tori's intention. But right now there were more pressing issues to deal with. They stopped outside a door at the end of the hallway. 'This is Mummy's room,' Tori said.

Charlie tried the handle, but the door was locked. 'Emma,' she called, knocking lightly. 'Can I come in?'

Nothing.

She was conscious of the girl's eyes staring up at her, begging her to fix this. 'Emma, Tori's here, she's worried about you.'

Shuffling from inside the room.

A key turning.

The door opening, slowly.

'Mummy.' Tori lunged, wrapping her arms tightly around her mother's waist. Emma's hand shot to her ribs.

'God, Emma, what happened?' The bruising Charlie had glimpsed from a distance outside the church this morning was darker and uglier up close, the eye itself puffy and bloodshot.

'I had a fall down the back stairs,' Emma answered, refusing to meet Charlie's eyes. 'But I'm okay.' She looked down at her daughter, stroked a hand across the girl's hair. 'I was just having a sleep, Tori, that's why I didn't hear you.'

A fall. Did Emma really expect her to believe that? I'm way out of my depth here, thought Charlie. But I need to try. 'Let me take you to the doctor,' she said tentatively. 'And I'll come with you to the police station if you want to report anything.'

'There's nothing to report.'

'Emma, please. Isn't there something I can do for you?' She could hear the desperation in her own voice and fervently hoped Emma would respond.

'I think you've done enough.'

'Look, Emma, I had no choice about the quarantining at your mother's. I'm sorry if—'

'Forget it. You should leave. Garth will be back soon.'

The last thing Charlie wanted to do was put Emma in even more danger. 'You have my number if you change your mind. Or if you want to talk.'

Emma remained in the doorway, her hands resting on her daughter's shoulders as Charlie headed back down the hall and out to the car. Things were a whole lot worse here than she had anticipated. A sense of helplessness burrowed itself deep into the pit of her stomach. It stayed with her all the way home and left her with no appetite for dinner. It was still there after her reports were written and she finally called it a day. As she lay in bed, tossing and turning, the image of Emma's battered face kept her awake well into the early hours of the morning.

Charlie sat beside Hannah in the back of the car, the toddler singing 'Baa, Baa, Black Sheep' at the top of her lungs. She wasn't one hundred per cent sure she should be here, but Jac had been annoyingly persuasive when she'd found Charlie hunched over her laptop, fumbling to come up with an excuse not to come. Even feigning a headache hadn't worked. Anyway, maybe Alex was right about her social life – it probably wouldn't hurt her to get out more.

'So I just need to warn you about Mary.' Jac's voice interrupted her thoughts.

'Who's Mary?'

'The boys' mother. She's what you might call eccentric.'

'Or a freaking lunatic.' Charlie saw the gleeful look on Brad's face in the rear-vision mirror. She couldn't get over how much he and his brother were alike – they even sounded the same. It was a little unnerving.

Jac twisted in her seat. 'Don't listen to him. She's nothing of the sort. She's just . . . exuberant. Very well meaning, but what you see is what you get. Don't be offended if she says something a little . . . blunt.'

Brad laughed. 'Yeah, she's about as subtle as a sledgehammer.'

'Thanks for the heads up – I think.' Charlie looked back at Jac. 'Anyone else I should be warned about?'

'No, that's about it. Oh, the boys' sister, Lindsay, has come down for the bash. She's gorgeous, you'll love her.'

The car turned onto a driveway winding between lofty trees dimpled with sunlight, before coming to a stop outside a split-level timber house tucked into the slope of a hill.

Charlie couldn't believe her eyes. 'This is amazing,' she sighed as the three adults climbed out of the car. 'And this is Joel's place?'

'Pretty special, isn't it?' Jac said, unlocking the wriggling Hannah from her car seat and watching her as she raced up the path behind her father. 'Architect-designed eco home.

He and his ex-wife built it before she buggered off with one of his mates.'

So Joel had been married. 'Really?'

'Yeah, they'd been childhood sweethearts and met up again about ten years after school. They got married six months later, but she neglected to tell him she fancied the best man. Didn't even make their first anniversary before she up and left. This place was half-finished, so he bought her out and kept it.'

'How long ago was that?'

'About six years now. I tried to talk him into moving somewhere with a little more nightlife, thought he might have more chance of meeting someone, but he loves it here. He and Brad are so close.'

Charlie paled as she remembered the flippant comment she'd made the other night, about Joel's failure to understand women.

'You okay?' Jac asked her.

'Yeah, I'm fine.'

'I actually think you and Joel make a pretty cute couple. I've been forbidden to matchmake, but that doesn't stop you—'

'Now hang on a minute, Jac. We've already been through this. There is no way I'm getting involved with any of the locals and certainly not one who's carrying around a whole lot of baggage.'

'I wouldn't exactly call it baggage. He was totally heartbroken when Rachelle dumped him, but he's well over it now. Besides, don't we all have issues in one form or another?' Jac took her by the arm as they walked up the steps leading to an enormous deck bordered by willowy white gums. 'Come on, let's have some fun.'

Before they could get any further, a large woman with

dark burgundy hair styled into short spikes bounded towards them holding a giggling Hannah in her arms. 'Hello, my darling,' she boomed, planting a noisy kiss on Jac's cheek. 'And who do we have here?'

'Mary, this is Charlie. She's here supervising the hendra outbreak and staying in our granny flat for a few weeks.'

'Oh, nasty business that hendra, isn't it? Nice to meet you, though,' Mary said, leaning forward and greeting Charlie with a kiss on each cheek, dousing her in a fog of rose-scented perfume.

It was clear this woman didn't stand on ceremony, and for a moment Charlie wasn't sure how to respond.

'What did I say?' Jac whispered. 'Just go with it. She'll grow on you.'

A black and white border collie sidled up and licked Charlie's hand.

'This is Tilly,' Mary announced. 'She runs the place.'

Charlie crouched down and ruffled the fur behind the dog's ears. She had one blue eye and one brown. 'Aren't you just beautiful?' Charlie asked and she could have sworn the dog smiled in reply.

'That's enough, Tilly. Come on, girls, wait until you see what delights we have for lunch,' continued Mary, depositing the now squealing Hannah on the ground.

The two women followed Mary into the house, where Charlie was again gobsmacked by what she saw: an enormous cathedral ceiling, exposed beams, a huge open-plan living area and exquisitely simple decor. She stood inside the doorway taking it all in before joining Jac and Mary at the island bench dividing the kitchen from the dining room. The entire surface was covered in platters of food, both savoury and sweet, but the one that caught Charlie's eye was a lemon meringue pie, the topping whipped into an impossibly high, mouth-watering peak.

Charlie was practically salivating.

'That's my specialty,' Mary said. 'My mother's recipe. I've won the pie section at the local show with that one for the last five years.'

'Mary's a great cook,' Jac added. 'Does a lot of the baking for Savannah and a couple of the other cafés in town.'

'Well, I'm a great dessert lover, so I can't wait to give it a try,' Charlie said.

'Maybe we can share a slice?' said a voice from behind her.

Charlie turned and there was Joel. She felt her body respond instantly and flicked her eyes back to the pie.

'Joel Drummond, don't be so presumptuous – talking like that to someone you've never met,' scolded his mother.

'Chill, Mum, we have met. In fact we had a whole main course at dinner the other night and shared a piece of chocolate pie. Charlie is definitely a great dessert lover.' His words echoed her own and she wasn't sure if there was innuendo there or if it was her imagination.

Mary gave them both a questioning look, but Joel just laughed. Charlie didn't know what to say, but it didn't matter. The Drummond clan seemed to have the talking side of things pretty much under control.

'Charlie, this is my sister, Lindsay,' Joel said. A lithe woman somewhere in her late twenties stepped forward. She had a messy blonde bun piled on top of her head.

'Nice to meet you, Charlie. The boys have been telling me all about this hendra stuff. Sounds like a nightmare. So glad I'm a city girl and don't live out here in the sticks where I can catch mysterious animal-borne diseases.' She scrunched her nose and wiggled her fingers before dipping a cracker into some pesto dip. 'You lot are nuts.'

Charlie was still too flummoxed to speak. Mary began giving directions about lunch, and within seconds there was so much movement and chatter it was hard to keep up. Maybe she should have gone with the headache story after all.

'Can I get you a drink?' Joel asked, still standing perilously close. He pulled a bottle of already opened champagne from the fridge. 'Bubbles?'

She nodded.

'Coming right up.'

While Joel played bartender, Charlie watched the rest of the family mingle together. Jac laughed at Hannah's protests when Lindsay scooped her up and tickled her. Brad wandered out to the deck and set himself up in a striped hammock. Mary hovered in the kitchen fixing plates of food. There was a warmth and camaraderie the likes of which Charlie only vaguely remembered from her childhood. This must be what it's like to be part of a proper family, she thought, to have people you really care about, who care back.

Joel reappeared, handing her a glass of perfectly chilled champagne. 'Here you go,' he said breezily. 'Are you alright?'

Charlie realised her eyes were watering. Damn it. She sipped at the cool, clear liquid, letting it fizz against her lips as she blinked. 'Fine. Great place you have here.'

'Thanks. Come on out and have a seat.' He nodded in the direction of the deck. They chatted about what they'd been doing the last couple of days, falling back into the comfortable rapport they'd established over dinner. It didn't take long for Charlie to forget her resolve to keep her distance. The sun was shining, the drinks were flowing and the mood was more than pleasant.

Lunch was a long, jovial affair. Copious amounts of food were washed down with equally vast amounts of alcohol. After the main meal and pie were demolished, Hannah helped her father and uncle blow the candles out on the birthday cake – a chocolate mud cake so devilishly decadent that Charlie simply couldn't say no to a slice. Close to bursting, she reclined lazily in her chair, totally unwound now that she'd downed a couple of champagnes and moved on to a mellow red.

'So, I'm heading out to the beach for a surf tomorrow, if you're still up for that lesson?' Joel said, refilling her glass.

She was already over her two-glass limit and thought about protesting, but what the hell, it was Saturday. But surfing?

'When I said I wanted to learn to surf I sort of envisaged hot summer sun, not late May on the south coast.'

'Not a problem,' Joel shot back. 'We have a whole cupboard full of wetsuits.' He dipped his head at his sister. 'You two would be about the same size.'

'You surf too?' Charlie asked Lindsay.

'Used to. Didn't have much choice with these two for big brothers.'

'Brad and I spent most of our spare time surfing when we were kids. Travelled up and down the coast looking for the perfect break. That's how I found this place,' Joel explained.

'And you still get out there?'

'When I can. It's where I feel most like myself.' The raw

honesty in his voice and the way his expression softened had Charlie turning to jelly. 'But you haven't answered my question about that lesson,' he said.

From the corner of her eye she could see Lindsay watching the two of them, waiting for Charlie's answer. There was no harm going for a surf with the guy, was there? It didn't mean anything. Just a couple of people with nothing better to do on a Sunday hanging out at the beach. 'Why not? As long as it's alright with you, Lindsay? Borrowing the suit, I mean.'

'Go for your life. I'm planning on sleeping off a hangover, so I won't be needing it. Besides,' Lindsay smirked, looking first at her brother and then at Charlie, 'you two will look totally cute all suited up together.'

Charlie fought the rush of blood to her cheeks as Joel picked up a bottle top and lobbed it at his sister's head.

'Didn't you say you had somewhere to be?' he asked.

Lindsay picked up her phone. 'Oh shit, I'm supposed to be meeting Kel at the pub at six. Nice meeting you, Charlie. Have fun tomorrow.' She dashed inside, grabbed her bag and disappeared down the stairs.

'We'd better get going too,' Jac said, nodding at Hannah, who had fallen asleep in her father's lap. Brad picked her up and her head fell into the crook of his neck.

Charlie went to stand too, but Joel stopped her with a hand on her arm. 'I can drop you home a little later if you want to hang around for a while. It's still early.' She could feel the heat of his palm through the sleeve of her cotton blouse.

Jac answered while Charlie hovered, completely tongue-tied. 'Great idea. But a taxi might be better. Wouldn't want my favourite brother-in-law put in the slammer for drink-driving.'

'Good point.'

Charlie's evening was being planned out for her and she found herself quite at ease with the idea. 'I guess it wouldn't hurt to stay for another drink,' she said.

Mary had been clearing away the plates and cleaning up, having insisted the rest of them leave her to it. She reappeared now and flashed a conspiratorial grin. 'I'm heading back downstairs to catch up on some reading. Stay as long as you like, dear.'

Within minutes the goodbyes had been said and only Charlie and Joel remained on the deck. The chatter of birds had fallen away, replaced by the gentle hum of crickets and the faint murmur of the evening breeze. They sat quietly, nursing their drinks. After the noise and liveliness of the afternoon, it seemed that neither of them knew quite what to say now that they were alone.

Charlie watched Joel over the rim of her wineglass. 'So you live with your mum?'

'No,' he fired back, a trace of a smile playing on his lips, 'as a matter of fact, she lives with me.'

'Isn't that just semantics?'

'Not at all. I built this house after I took the job and moved here. She came for a visit a few years back. Been here ever since. Keeps threatening to get her own place but never does anything about it.'

Charlie noted that he'd said 'I' rather than 'we' when he mentioned building the house, but she let it pass. It wasn't any of her business. 'And you don't mind?' she asked.

'No. I pretend to, though. I give her stick about being a freeloader, but we both know I'd miss her bossing me around if she left. Not to mention her cooking.'

'So she doesn't cramp your style too much then? I mean, being a single guy in a town like this must have its advantages.' Did I really just say that? The wine must be loosening my tongue, she thought.

Joel laughed. 'Sadly not. I can't say there's too many available women around here. At least none that I'm interested in.' Their conversation had quickly progressed to flirting and Charlie felt decidedly out of her depth.

While she was still contemplating her witty response, he placed his hand on top of hers. 'I really enjoyed dinner the other night.' He spoke slowly, looking down at the table. 'More than I have with anyone since my divorce.'

Ah, so here it was. 'You never mentioned you'd been married.' She kept her tone neutral, trying not to sound too interested.

'It didn't really come up in conversation. It's been six years since it ended, so it's not recent news.' He shifted his hand slightly so that his fingers slipped between Charlie's, lifting his head as he turned towards her. 'But I meant what I said about dinner. And I would like to get to know you better.'

His face was in shadow, but she could still make out the question in his eyes. Even as the rational, distant part of her counselled against it, she found herself moving forward in her chair, answering him with the touch of her lips against his, and the surge of desire that flooded her body as they kissed again was something she hadn't felt for a very long time.

It was the rioting of what sounded like a thousand lorikeets in the trees outside that woke her. Charlie cracked open an eyelid and squinted into the morning light pouring through the floor-to-ceiling glass windows. There was a distinct thumping in her head and her mouth was dry as chalk.

Where the hell am I?

Pushing up onto one elbow, she shucked off a blanket and quilt and surveyed the room. Joel's place. His living room. She was sleeping – well, waking up – on his couch. Now it was all coming back to her.

Their conversation on the deck.

The kiss.

Oh, god, that kiss.

Even with her eyes still half-closed and her brain a ball of fuzz, the memory of it stirred a sharp yearning. It hadn't been just one brief kiss either. They'd sat there making out until night had completely fallen and the cool tingling of the air against their skin had brought them indoors.

Joel had suggested a movie and she perused his DVD collection, surprised but more than a little pleased to find some of her favourites there. She made a joke about him being a lover of chick flicks and he'd told her they belonged to his mother, then they'd curled up together on the lounge and watched *Love Actually* followed by *Notting Hill*.

The fact that she was here alone on the couch covered in a pile of blankets meant she must have fallen asleep. Good job, Charlie, she berated herself, way to win a guy's heart, fall asleep on him. But then she wasn't trying to win a guy's heart, was she?

This was all so bizarre. She was a little hazy from the wine and the champagne, but she clearly remembered sitting on the lounge with Joel's arm draped around her shoulder, feeling deliriously content. Nothing else had happened, and at some point he'd covered her up and taken himself off to bed. Wherever that was.

She looked around the room, taking in each door in

turn, and then at the stairs spiralling up to what must have been the master bedroom. Apart from the screeching of those damn parrots, the place was completely quiet. What was the protocol here? If she had her car, she could slip away and drop him a thank-you text. But that wasn't happening. She could lie back and try to drift off to sleep, but once she was awake there was no going back, so that wasn't an option either. Of course, there was the possibility of snooping around and looking for him, but that might give him the wrong idea if he woke up in bed and found her loitering in his doorway. She wondered briefly whether he slept naked but pushed the thought well and truly away.

It looked like she'd just have to wait it out. But in the meantime, she really needed to do something about her head. She pushed herself completely upright and made her way to the kitchen, a little wobbly but not too bad considering the amount she must have drunk. Her bag was on a chair and she rummaged around until she found a packet of ibuprofen, then headed for the sink and filled a very tall glass with water. Rehydrate. That's what she needed to do. She swallowed the pills and was halfway through gulping down the liquid when footsteps on the stairs made her stop mid-mouthful.

'Goooood morning,' sang Mary, 'and how are we this morning?' She was wearing a bright orange and turquoise kaftan splashed with a bold leopard-skin print that even later in the day would take some processing, hangover or not.

What am I even doing here? Charlie wondered vaguely.

'Hi, I'm, uh, well, I've been better,' she grimaced, holding the tablet pack up for the older woman's scrutiny.

'You kids were getting through those drinks when I headed downstairs,' Mary laughed. 'Still, it's worth it as long as you two had a good time. Is that handsome son of mine still in bed?'

Charlie noted the emphasis on the words *handsome* and *bed* and found herself squirming. Mary clearly presumed the two of them had spent the night together – not that it seemed to bother her. 'Ah, I'm not sure.' Charlie pointed to the blanket-strewn lounge. 'I just woke up. Must have fallen asleep watching the movie.'

'Oh, I see.' Was there a note of disappointment in Mary's voice? The women in Joel's life certainly didn't hide their opinions when it came to his love-life. The whole situation was starting to make Charlie's head ache even more. Was it suddenly hot in here? And really wasn't it about time she was getting back?

'I think I might get going. A few things to do,' she stammered. 'Would you know the local taxi number?'

'Don't be silly.' Mary marched towards her and for a few seconds Charlie thought the woman was going to physically restrain her, but she breezed right past, stopping to open the fridge, and pulled out three cardboard cake boxes. 'I have to deliver these to a café in town. I can give you a lift if you like.'

Charlie could have hugged her. 'That'd be great.' She grabbed her bag and headed towards the door behind Mary, taking a look back over her shoulder just in case Joel had appeared in the last few minutes. But no, he hadn't.

Just as well.

She kept the conversation light as Mary drove, dreading an interrogation or any further reference to last night. Not that it mattered, nothing had happened. Well, nothing much. It was only the older woman's pointed comment that she hoped she'd be seeing her again soon that was slightly embarrassing. Charlie crept down the driveway to the back of the house and into the sanctuary of the granny flat, grateful that everyone inside the main house seemed to be sleeping.

Dropping onto the bed, she rubbed her hands across her face and gave herself a good talking-to. Really, Charlie, what the hell were you thinking? Come here, get the job done and get out. Stick to the plan.

Just as she was starting to convince herself, her phone buzzed with a message: Missed you this morning, hope you slept well. What time will I pick you up for our lesson?

Oh, shit. The surfing thing.

The thought of Joel, zipped up inside a wetsuit, lifting her onto a board, his hands snug around her waist, left her slightly breathless.

You're here to work, not to get caught up in some pointless romantic fantasy when you have no intention of staying, she told herself.

And there it was in a nutshell – the reason she needed to back right away from Joel. Right now. What was the point of leading him on when she'd be packing up and leaving in a few weeks?

What was the point at all?

A memory arose in answer to her question – the memory of how his mouth felt against hers, the feelings of warmth and safety that had settled so easily inside as he curled his arm around her. Before it could take hold, she typed her response to Joel's text: Not up for a surf today – and pressed send. Short, direct, no apology, zero discussion.

Her phone buzzed again less than a minute later: Okay, let's take a raincheck. See you again soon?

Really?

Her reply had hardly been warm and friendly. Now he was asking her a direct question she was compelled to answer. Or maybe not. Better to just leave that one hanging and hope he'd get the hint.

She held her thumb over the power button, staring at Joel's message before turning off her phone and leaving it on the table beside her computer and notebook. It was Sunday but there were still reports to write up, site visits to carry out, research notes to collate – plenty to keep her busy, after she dealt with that tiny hammer tapping at the inside of her skull. She pulled her water bottle from her bag, downed a few mouthfuls and slid beneath the covers, wishing away the image of Joel's blue eyes that appeared inside her closed lids.

Chapter Twelve

Charlie jolted awake. Afternoon shadows were already falling. She picked up her phone, stabbing at the black screen in search of the time, completely forgetting she'd turned it off before crashing out. Heaving herself upright, she switched it on: 2.38 pm. Damn! She'd slept for over five hours and she still needed to do the site visits. The overalls were on and she was out the door and in the car in three minutes flat, ignoring the remnants of the headache.

She hit the window button, hoping the cool air would dust the cobwebs from her brain, switch it into work mode. Hazel's place first, then Willow Vale Park. She'd squeezed yesterday's visits in before lunch and hadn't seen anyone on either property. Would Emma be there today? Would she be okay? She pictured again the ugly bruising on her cousin's face. The same sort she'd seen Hazel try to hide, time and time again. Jim Roberts. What a tyrant. So different from Charlie's own father. The loss of him – both of them – was still a solid wedge of pain deep beneath her ribs. But at least she had a vague memory of what it was to live in a happy family. Not like her cousin. Why would Emma marry a man as callous as her father?

Sometimes there's more to a story than the words on the page. Her mother had told her that once when she'd complained about a girl at school who had stolen her lunch. Charlie had seen her take it, was outraged, wanted her mother to ring the principal and make the girl pay, but Pippa had calmly refused. Instead she'd given Charlie an extra sandwich the following day and told her to offer it to Samantha, the thief. Even though it went totally against the grain, Charlie had done as she'd been told, keen to please her mother, and had been embarrassed when fat tears had spilt down the girl's cheeks. She'd taken the offering, turned away and sat alone on a bench seat in the grey shade of the schoolroom. Charlie kept her distance and watched the girl eat the sandwich, savouring every mouthful before she stood again and gave Charlie the slightest hint of a smile. They never spoke of it afterwards and the only answer Charlie ever got was the one from her mother about everyone having their own story.

The concept that things were not always black and white, that there were definite shades of grey, had always been difficult for Charlie to comprehend. It was why she couldn't understand the choice Emma was making. But there was one person who might be able to explain it to her: Hazel Roberts. As she pulled into her aunt's drive, she decided that this visit wouldn't be all about work.

Charlie clenched her fist tighter as she lifted it to knock. Each time she'd been here she was conscious of a movement at the window, of eyes she couldn't see peering out at her from behind a shifting curtain. Her aunt had taken her at her word after Charlie had told her she didn't need any help, but now Charlie was the one crossing that line she'd so firmly drawn between them.

Silence shrouded the house, a silence that reminded Charlie of earlier times, after the fights, when she would take herself on long walks, desperate to escape. The sounds of movement in the bush — birds flitting through trees, lizards scurrying between bushes, a curious wallaby watching her from behind a rock — had helped take her mind off what was happening back at the house, somehow making her feel less alone.

'Charlie.' Hazel's voice, guarded and fragile, came from behind the wire flyscreen.

'Hello.'

'Is there a problem with the horses?' Her aunt made no move to open the door.

'No . . . well, I actually haven't checked on them yet. I was wondering if I could have a word with you.'

'Of course.' The door opened outwards and Charlie took a step back, hesitating for a moment before entering. She followed Hazel into the lounge room, a familiar smell engulfing her, not eucalyptus, but a woody scent that took her back in time as she ran her hand along the timber panelling. Hazel stopped abruptly and Charlie had to pull herself up quickly to avoid a collision as her aunt turned.

'Can I get you a cup of tea?'

There was the faintest tinge of anticipation in the question and Charlie felt a sudden urge to run as fast as her legs would carry her away from the house. The braver part of her won out. 'That would be lovely. Thank you.'

As Hazel filled the kettle and pulled mugs from the cupboard, Charlie took the time to look around. Nothing much had changed, but there was a tired feeling to the place that echoed the weary movements of its owner as she went about making the tea. The kitchen, once a bright buttercup yellow, had dulled to a dirty shade of sand. A crack in the window above the sink had been covered in silver electrical tape. Her aunt's collection of ceramic teapots still lined the shelves above the bench, all of them now coated in a thick layer of grime. Photos of Emma's kids hung at angles on the fridge, held there by magnets advertising the local real estate, electrician and Chinese restaurant. A crayon drawing of a bouquet of orange flowers inside the outline of a red love heart with the words *I love you Nan* was pinned to the wall by the back door.

'Matt did that for me last year on my birthday.' Charlie could see the light shining in Hazel's eyes as she gazed at the picture. 'He's a real sweetie, that boy.'

'He doesn't get that from his father,' Charlie remarked without thinking first. She gave Hazel an apologetic look and took the tea that was offered.

'No, he doesn't.' Hazel gestured to a chair and the two women sat down, their mugs scraping on the glass overlay of the round table, a crocheted doily flattened between it and the dark wood. Charlie traced the floral pattern with her fingertip.

'Your grandmother made that. And a pile of others I've got out there in the linen closet. Don't suppose you remember her?'

'No, I don't.' She knew it was her mother's mother Hazel was talking about. Both she and her grandfather had died when Charlie was small.

'She loved all you kids. A real family woman. Soft as marshmallow. A good thing she was gone before Pippa passed away. She wouldn't have coped.'

Charlie's stomach lurched. She let the comment go, hoping her aunt would take the hint and change the subject.

'Can I show you something?' Hazel asked. Without waiting for an answer, she disappeared down the hallway.

This was not going according to plan, Charlie thought but then again she hadn't really arrived with one. Maybe coming inside hadn't been such a good idea after all, maybe she should leave. The sound of footsteps returning from the front of the house stopped Charlie from acting on that thought.

Hazel deposited something on the table and sat back down. It was a worn old school case, locks mottled and rusty, the brown lid coated in dust. Charlie leant down to read the name on the label but it had long since faded. 'It was your mother's,' Hazel said.

Even though it had been barely a whisper, the words hit Charlie hard. 'No.' She shook her head, stood and took a step away from the table. 'I didn't come here to do this.'

'Please.' Hazel reached out and Charlie felt the coarseness of the woman's hand on her wrist. She couldn't be here. This was the reason she hadn't wanted to return. It was as if all the years of grief she'd stored away were sitting right in front of her in that case on the table. Waiting to be cracked open. She wasn't sure that she could bear it, but was there a part of her that needed to flick those locks, lift the lid and take a long, hard look?

'I don't . . . I can't,' she stammered.

'Don't be scared, Charlie. It's just some things I kept for you. Some odds and ends that I found from when your mother and I were kids, and a few other bits and pieces.'

Charlie stared at the case, her body rigid.

Hazel pushed it closer. 'Go on,' she urged gently.

You can do this, Charlie.

She looked at her aunt. Hazel inclined her head and blinked. Almost in slow motion, Charlie raised her hands and placed them on the corners of the case. She sank back down into the chair. The locks were rough beneath the pads of her thumbs but they clicked open. Her fingers froze. Her breath caught as she lifted the lid. Printed in neat black lettering across the inside was a name: Philippa Martin. Charlie had never heard anyone call her mother by her full name. She had always been Pippa, or Pip. It was hard to reconcile the bright, bubbly woman she remembered with the more formal name that she must have gone by as a child. She stared down at the collection of papers, unsure where to start. Dipping into the pile, she pulled out a handful of photos. The first was a snapshot of her mother wearing a spotted one-piece swimming costume, kneeling on the sand, squinting into the camera. Her hair fell in thick waves past her shoulders, and although the photo was black and white, Charlie could see her own green eyes smiling back at her. She flipped it over and read the inscription: *Lake Conjola, January 1961.*

'She was about twelve in that photo. You looked so much like her at that age,' Hazel said.

'The same age I was when she died,' Charlie murmured.

'Yes. Do you remember much about her?' Hazel's voice was so tender it took Charlie by surprise.

'No,' she said, shaking her head. 'I try not to think about her – about them.' She pushed her tongue against the roof of her mouth to try to hold back the welling tears. 'But at least once a day I'll be doing something ordinary –

washing up, making a cup of coffee, taking out the garbage – and an image will flash into my head. Mum curled up on the lounge engrossed in a book or Dad standing in front of the bathroom mirror, his face covered in shaving cream. And then they're gone. Every now and then I'll hear their voices inside my head. I don't know if they're things they actually said to me or things I've made up. It's almost as if they're watching me.'

She wasn't really sure where all these words were coming from. Perhaps the need to talk about her parents to someone who actually knew them had been lying dormant all these years.

'I'm sure they are,' Hazel said.

Charlie looked at the child in the photo. A child who had become her mother. A woman who no longer existed. 'I don't believe in life after death. Once you're gone, you're gone. Anything else is just a myth people have made up to make themselves feel better.'

'You're so much like her. Not just in looks. The way you think. Practical. Rational. Black and white. We were so different, she and I.'

'Is that why you weren't very close?' Now that the conversation had started, Charlie's initial trepidation was giving way to an unexpected curiosity.

A wave of anguish rolled across Hazel's face. 'We were when we were children. Inseparable. But Philippa was always smarter, did better at school, was more driven. As we got older, our interests changed. She went to boarding school and stayed on in the city for university. We both married and had children, but our lives had gone in completely different directions.' She looked away from Charlie, staring out the window. 'And by the time she died,' she added wistfully, 'we were almost strangers.'

'So why did you agree to take me in?'

'She was my sister. It's what families do. Maybe it was the wrong thing for you, though. Maybe you'd have been better off somewhere else. I've never forgiven myself for letting him get his hands on your legacy.' Hazel's voice cracked and when she continued it was in a hoarse whisper. 'How did you manage? After you left here?'

'I had the scholarship for university and I still had a little bit of money left. Jim didn't take all of it.' Charlie saw her aunt recoil. The theft of her inheritance was obviously still a painful memory for both of them. 'I got myself a few part-time jobs and worked my way through uni – bar work, waitressing, tutoring. It was tough, but I managed.'

A strained silence fell. Charlie's fingers tensed around the edges of the photograph she was holding. They hadn't even got past this one photo before getting bogged down in the past. Would she have been better off with total strangers? Fostered out with people who had no connection to her whatsoever? At least she'd had Emma for those few years. They'd had each other – but the good times they'd shared had been overshadowed by the constant tension that filled the house, and then by the discovery that her aunt had signed the papers allowing Jim to get his hands on the money she was supposed to receive when she turned eighteen. It had been the final straw for Charlie. 'Look, Hazel, I know things ended badly between us, and to be honest, I wouldn't ever have come back here if it wasn't for my job—'

'You hated us that much?'

Hate was such a strong word. It was certainly the way she'd felt about her aunt and uncle when she'd left, but now, after all these years, it had faded into something more like disappointment.

'I just never understood why you let him treat you that way. Why you didn't leave.'

Hazel bowed her head, her hands clasped together in her lap, almost as if in prayer. 'I wanted to. I even packed some things one night, but he stopped me, begged me to stay, told me he'd change. And he did for a while. But never for long. When it came down to it, I had nowhere to go, not with three kids, and there was no way I could leave you all here. I protected you from him as much as I could.'

'Like Emma protects Tori and Matt?'

The older woman flinched at Charlie's pointed question. 'How do you know?'

'I saw the bruises. And I've seen the way Emma tiptoes around him, just like you did around Jim.'

'This whole hendra thing has got Garth riled up.'

Charlie jumped to her feet, unable to believe what she was hearing. 'How can you make excuses for him? The man is abusive. He should be locked up.'

'Don't you think I know that? I've tried to get her to leave him, but she won't listen. She's frightened of what he'll do if she goes.' Hazel shuddered, folded her hands together and rested them on the table. 'Emma told me if I kept on about it, she'd cut me off, stop me from seeing the kids.' Her voice wavered. She took a shallow breath, composed herself. 'They're all I've got.'

Charlie listened to the ticking of the clock on the kitchen bench, measuring out time, marking the seconds she and her aunt sat in silence. She was beginning to understand now why Hazel had stayed then and why Emma stayed now. Fear. Fear of the unknown, of what would happen to them if they left, what would happen to their children. And possibly hope. The hope that things would change. Yes, she was starting to understand, but she still found it hard to accept that staying was the best option.

'Could you talk to her, Charlie? She'll listen to you, I know she will.'

'She doesn't want anything to do with me.'

'She missed you so much after you left. Try again. Please. Don't do it for me, do it for her.'

So much time had passed since she and Emma had lived beneath this roof. So much had changed. Charlie pictured the sweet young girl she had known back then, the cousin she had taken under her wing even when she herself was so broken. It had been that bond between the two of them that had kept her going until she felt she had no alternative but to get out. They were two completely different people now. Strangers.

'I already tried,' she said. 'She told me to mind my own business.' The look of utter despair on Hazel's face left Charlie at a loss. She'd come to try to make some sort of sense of things, but really they were just going around in circles.

There was a lot that hadn't been discussed, but Charlie was finding all the talk about her mother and about Emma overwhelming. And there was still work to be done. 'I need to go check on the horses,' she said, dragging herself out of her chair.

Hazel made no attempt to stop her. 'This is yours,' she said, closing the case and holding it up. 'Take it with you.'

Charlie had no words.

Standing slowly, Hazel gave a tentative look before stepping forward and pulling her niece into a hug. Charlie resisted at first, but her aunt's fierce grip on her shoulders made her soften, just a little. It wasn't much, but perhaps it was a start.

And that was something.

Her phone rang the minute she pulled out of Hazel's driveway. She pressed the answer button on the hands-free car phone. 'Charlie Anderson.'

'Charlie, it's Joel.'

She had to hand it to him, the guy was certainly persistent.

'We've got a problem.'

There was something urgent about his tone. She turned up the volume. 'What's wrong?'

'I just got a call from Andy Phipps, the publican at The Centennial. Garth McDowell's been in there with a few mates mouthing off about the quarantine. Andy overheard them saying they should take matters into their own hands, do something to, and I quote, "stop those dirty fuckin bats causing any more trouble". Not long after that they left. Andy heard them mention something about guns.'

'You think they're going to try to shoot the bats?'

'I wouldn't be surprised. I'm going to head out to the park now. Any chance you could come with me? Your vet skills might be needed.'

'Of course.'

'I'm already in the car, so I can swing by in a few minutes and pick you up.'

Charlie looked around and got her bearings. 'Actually I'm driving. I'm not far from your place, so I'll call past.'

'Okay.' The line went dead.

Was there no end to McDowell's lunacy? Hopefully it was just the booze talking, but there was no way of knowing until they checked. She wondered if they should tell Jac where they were going, get her to join them, but it was probably too early to involve the police. If it turned out Joel was right, then she'd call Jac. She checked the clock on the dashboard – five past five and she still hadn't been out to Willow Vale Park. Right now this was more important – she was the only vet in town until the locum arrived. If there were injured animals, she needed to deal with them first. Within a few minutes she was at Joel's place and pulled up to find him packing a stack of plastic crates filled with towels into Bertha's boot.

'What's all this?' she asked.

'In case we need to transport any injured bats.' He lifted a twenty-five litre water container and packed it in beside the crates. 'Or treat them.'

Charlie opened her own boot and grabbed her vet bag, overalls and a bag full of gloves. 'I'll bring these in case we need to handle any of them. Have you been vaccinated for lyssavirus?'

'Yep. Anything else you think we should take?'

'No. I think that's it.' She piled her things into his car and climbed into the front passenger seat. 'Let's hope we don't need any of this.'

Joel started the engine.

'Do you really think McDowell is that vindictive?' she asked. Even as the words left her mouth, she recalled the conversation she'd just had with Hazel and knew the answer.

'We'll soon find out,' Joel said.

They sighed in tandem. Charlie looked out the window. There wasn't much daylight left and she hoped it wasn't too far to where the colony roosted. Conscious of Joel's body beside her, and the clean lemony smell of his clothes, she let herself glance across at him. His hair was still damp and there was a light film of stubble shadowing his jawbone that she had an urge to reach out and brush with her fingertips. But the lightheartedness that had radiated from him yesterday was gone. This was work Joel. Serious. Focused. She found herself wanting to lift his mood, fall back into the flirty ribbing they seemed to be so good at, but the sharp set of his mouth and the intensity of his gaze at the road ahead brought her back to the reason for their trip.

'So, how many bats are we actually talking in this colony?' she asked.

'Hard to say, exactly, but probably a few hundred, maybe more.'

'Wow. And he thinks that going out there with a couple of guns is going to make a dent in it.' She almost wanted to laugh at such absurdity. 'Seriously, could a person really be that stupid?'

'You'd think not, but if he and his mates had a few drinks under their belts, they wouldn't exactly be thinking – or acting – rationally. If they've gone out there to throw pot shots, all they're going to succeed in doing is freak the bats out and scatter the colony.'

Charlie fell back into her thoughts, mulling over what she knew about bat habits. They were nocturnal, of course, so at this time of day they'd still be roosting but starting to get restless. Stationary targets. She'd seen people taking their rage or fear out on bats, trying to trap or shoot them if they came onto their properties, but she'd never encountered such malicious, premeditated cruelty. Still, maybe it was cheap talk and they'd get out there to find everything was perfectly normal. There was no point jumping to conclusions.

The autumn sunshine that had washed the sky this morning was now hidden behind a curtain of cloud, giving the bush on either side of the road a desolate feel that perfectly reflected the mood inside the car. Joel turned onto a service track, trying to dodge the potholes but finding one anyway. Charlie hit her temple against the side window and didn't quite manage to stifle a groan.

'Sorry,' he mumbled, as if the state of the road was his fault. 'This track doesn't get used much.'

She rubbed at the spot. 'That's okay. I'll live.'

He turned and looked at her. 'Hope so. You promised me a raincheck on that surfing lesson, remember?'

'And here I was thinking you had nothing on your mind but work this afternoon.' She knew the tone in her voice was suggestive, knew that this wasn't really the right time, but she just couldn't seem to help herself.

'I had a lot more on my mind before I got that call from Andy, believe me.' Joel darted his eyes to hers. 'Mainly you.' Before she could even contemplate how to reply to *that*, the track came to a dead end. 'The colony roosts a bit further along, but we'll have to walk from here,' Joel said.

They grabbed their gear from the back of the car, Joel taking the crates and water, leaving her with only her bag to manage.

'Look at this.' He pointed to a set of tyre tracks etched into the muddy ground. 'Someone's been here.' Charlie's hopes that this might be a false alarm started to dwindle. Rocks slipped beneath her feet as they made their way along the rough, overgrown path, and she was glad she'd worn her sturdy boots. The bush was strangely still, not even a murmur of air through the trees, but as they walked on Charlie became aware of a feeble mewling coming from somewhere up ahead. It wasn't like any bird call she could recognise, and she turned her head in the direction of the noise to try to decipher it more clearly. As they walked on the sound grew louder.

Joel drew to a dead halt. 'Shit.'

Charlie peered over his shoulder. 'Oh no.'

They both took a few more tentative steps towards the source of the noise. She couldn't believe what she was seeing. Strewn across the forest floor were the bodies of dozens of flying foxes. Most were already dead, the soft caramel fur of their bodies stained with blood, the black skin of their wings shredded. The sound Charlie had heard was the whimpering of those that were injured, and up close, now that she knew what it was, it made her so nauseous she dropped to her knees, retching. Joel knelt beside her, his arm around her shoulder.

'You okay?' he asked gently.

She nodded but didn't look up. The sight of injured animals shouldn't bother her this way. But the scene before her was so shocking she seemed to have lost any semblance of control. Pulling herself upright, Joel's hand supporting her elbow, she rummaged around in the bag of gloves, handing one pair to Joel and wriggling her fingers into another. They were thicker than the usual surgical gloves, in case any of the injured bats decided to scratch or bite. She handed Joel a mask. 'No point taking risks.'

Her own mask secured, she turned back to survey the scene again. It was like a war zone. In places the bats had fallen so close together that Charlie could barely take a step between them. As she and Joel moved carefully through them, the collective sound of the wounded dimmed, their heart-wrenching cries fading. One by one the injured bats were dying. They finished checking on them and only a handful of the creatures seemed well enough to rescue. There were a few more who were so badly hurt that Charlie thought it best to put them out of their misery. Joel stood beside her as she gave the injections, holding the vials, handing her the needles. The horror Charlie had felt when they first came upon the scene was sparking into anger with each press of her thumb against the plunger, but it was an anger that would have to smoulder until this job was done.

Joel waited while she packed the empty syringes back in her bag. 'I can take the injured ones to my place,' he said. 'Mum's a registered WIRES carer. And she's vaccinated. She can help out and contact her network.'

'Right. Well, let's get them wrapped up and see if we can get them into the crates.'

They made their way back to the edge of the clearing to collect the crate and towels. 'Wait,' said Joel, pulling his phone from his pocket. 'Probably should get some photos.'

'Good idea.' As ghoulish as it seemed, if they were going to try to pin this on McDowell, they'd need some evidence. Charlie waited until Joel had taken photos from a few different positions. She followed his line of vision to the tree branches above where a few bats remained, hanging upside down, some with their wings wrapped tight around their fur-covered bodies, others twitching agitatedly. 'There's not many left.'

'Most of them would have been scared by the noise and flown off.'

'Will they come back here to roost again?'

'Hard to say.' Joel bent down and picked up a small object from the ground. 'Whoever was here didn't clean up too well.' A shell casing rested in his outstretched hand. 'Jac will be more than interested in this, I think.' He shoved the casing into his pocket. 'Let's get these guys out of here.' They worked together, picking up the bats one at a time, wrapping them gently and placing them side by side in the crate, ignoring the frightened hissing and attempts to scratch. There were only five Charlie had deemed worth saving. They carried the crates back to the car in the fading daylight.

Neither of them spoke as the four-wheel drive bumped its way back along the track. The only sound was the whimpering of the bats.

'You did a good job out there. Are you okay?' Joel looked across at her as he pulled back onto the tarred road.

'Yeah, now I've stopped vomiting.' She lowered her head, embarrassed.

'Don't beat yourself up about it.'

'I am a vet, you know. A few dead animals shouldn't get to me like that.' It was true. Normally she had a lot more self-discipline, but the events of the last few days seemed to have unhinged her a little, wreaked havoc with her emotions.

'It was pretty bloody unnerving.'

'Yeah,' Charlie's voice faltered. 'It was.'

'Don't think I've ever seen such wilful violence towards animals in my time as a ranger.' Joel reached across and laid his hand over hers. She turned her palm upwards, clasping his fingers in her own as if it was the most natural thing in the world. As he ran his thumb over the heel of her hand in a gentle, soothing motion, she closed her eyes, letting the tension that had built up in her body over the last couple of hours begin to ease.

'So, what do we do now?' Of course she was talking about the situation with the bats, but the double meaning behind her own words didn't elude her. Or Joel apparently.

'There are so many ways I could answer that question.' He caught her eye. 'But I assume you're talking about McDowell.'

'Yes, I am.'

'I hope like hell we've got enough evidence to arrest the prick.'

'Me too, but there are no witnesses, so it might be hard to prove anything.'

'There's a bunch of dead bats, a clearly overheard conversation, tyre tracks and ammunition casings.'

'Should be enough?'

'It will be.' Joel's jaw was set firm.

The remainder of the trip was quiet, apart from an occasional murmuring from the injured bats. When they pulled up in Joel's driveway, it was a surprise to Charlie to find their hands still entangled and even more surprising was her reluctance to let go.

'That leaves two little darlings for me.' Mary closed the door as the last of the other WIRES carers left.

'Do you think they're all going to make it?' Joel handed his mother a coffee.

She shrugged. 'Your guess is as good as mine. Our vet here probably has more of a clue than either of us.'

'I wish I did,' Charlie sighed. 'I haven't had that much experience with native animals – and none at all with bats.' She'd treated a few wild animals during her course, and the odd one in her stints around the state, but so much of her work had been with horses that she really felt out of her depth. Tilly was curled up by Charlie's feet and she reached down and gave the dog a rub behind the ears. Tilly groaned with satisfaction.

'Well, we can only do what we can do,' said Mary. 'I'm going to go check on them again and hang around downstairs for a while. There's soup in the fridge and some leftovers if you want something to eat.'

'Thanks, Mum.' Joel wrapped his arms around his mother in an enormous bear hug that brought a brief movement to Charlie's lips. A deep melancholy had descended on her since the rescue trip. Not that it had all been bad news. They'd called Jac and she'd decided to question McDowell in the morning, along with his redneck mates, once she managed to get a statement from Andy Phipps. If they could nail him on this, it might make him pull his head in, at least for the time being.

Charlie turned to Joel, who was standing in front of the open refrigerator, staring. 'You hungry?' he asked.

'No. But you go ahead and eat.' Her stomach was still churning and her usual healthy appetite had disappeared.

'Couldn't eat a thing.' He slammed the door shut, rattling its contents, before picking up his car keys from the bench. 'I'm going to pay McDowell a visit.' An ominous resolve darkened his eyes.

Charlie sprang from the stool she'd been sitting on. 'No. You heard what Jac said. She needs to talk to a few people from the pub, get some statements, gather the information. There's no point going out there accusing him of anything right now – he's just going to deny it.'

He turned and looked at her, hands on his hips.

'You know I'm right,' she said. 'Besides, confronting him about it now is just going to tip him off.'

'Probably.' His stance relaxed a little, but she could see he still wasn't convinced.

'Joel, the guy is a lunatic. Let the police deal with him.'

His keys clattered back onto the bench. 'Okay.'

'Don't worry. I'm as angry as you are.'

He nodded and shoved his hands deep into his pockets.

'Feel like watching some TV?' He was standing so close. If she was going to leave here at all tonight, she needed to do it now. She was deathly tired, and after the day she'd had, all she really wanted was to be on her own. She stood and pushed the stool into the bench, pulling her keys from her pocket.

'I'm pretty whacked. Think I'll just head home.'

'I was hoping you'd stay.'

Charlie wasn't brave enough to meet his eyes. They were too blue, too inviting. Too much. If she crossed the line now would it really be just a casual fling? 'Sorry. I have to go.'

Joel didn't even try to disguise his sigh or the resignation in his voice. 'Okay. Well, thanks for your help today.'

She gave him a hurried smile but didn't get one back, and he made no move to see her out. The door slid closed behind her with a clunk. Stepping out into the damp, dark night, she knew it was more than the cold air making her shiver.

The chill had settled deep in Charlie's bones despite the heat of the shower. She grabbed a grey hoodie from the hook on the bathroom door and yanked it over her head. Rubbing a towel over her hair to soak up the excess water, she ruffled her hair and left it to dry. It was only just after 8 pm but she was too exhausted to bother doing any more. When she came back out into the small living room of the granny flat the first thing she saw was the school case. It sat in the middle of the bed where she'd dumped it after returning from Joel's. She opened a drawer and found a pair of tracksuit pants, pulled them on and went into the kitchenette for a drink of water, but her eyes kept returning to the case. Slowly she lowered the glass to the table, crossed the room, sat down and rested her hands on the lid.

So far she'd only looked at that one photo of her mother. What else had Hazel kept for her? The conversation with her aunt had reminded Charlie how little she knew about her mother's early life – and how much she'd chosen to forget about her own.

Open it.

There was nothing in here to be afraid of, Hazel had said.

Open it, Charlie.

They were just pieces of paper, artefacts from the past, relics of a life she'd left behind.

After one final hesitation, she pressed her thumbs against the locks and opened the case, diving straight into the pile before she had time to think and pulling out an assortment of photos. She shuffled through them, stopping for a closer look whenever one caught her eye: two young girls – Hazel and Philippa – wearing matching dresses and buckled shoes, bows in their pigtailed hair; a serious family portrait of her grandparents, standing stiffly with their daughters seated in front of them on high-backed chairs; a couple gazing down at a baby, cradled in the woman's arms, nestled inside a pale pink blanket. She dropped the other photos into the case and turned the third one over: *Charlie, 5 days, leaving hospital.* Flipping it back again, she looked at their faces, first the man's, then the woman's. Her parents. Younger than she remembered them, of course. She closed her eyes and tried to picture them as they were that last time she'd seen them, but the image wouldn't come. She'd spent so much of her life willing herself to forget that now it seemed impossible to remember. 'That's what you wanted,' she told herself. A tear made its way down her cheek and she swiped at it, depositing the photo alongside the others.

Digging deeper into the pile of mementos, her hand came to rest on something solid. A book. She pulled it out and ran her hand across the cover. The gold lettering of the title stood out against the dark red embossing of the background: *The Golden Treasury of Australian Verse*. It was a hard cover, old. Her mother had loved fossicking around in second-hand bookshops. Just like I do, Charlie thought. She peeked inside at the inscription. *As a small mark of esteem, from The Thistle, 1917.* Puzzled by the obscure message, she flipped the book open to a random page, a poem called 'Good-Bye' by someone called Ada Cambridge. She scanned the lines, pausing on the final stanza:

Your love is true, your grief is deep and sore;
But love will pass – then you will grieve no more.

Do you ever really stop grieving?

She thought she had, until she came back to Naringup, but maybe there was a difference between burying the past and truly moving on. Being back here with all the reminders of her family was making her realise that there were too many things she'd never dealt with, too many people she'd tried to block from her memory and from her life. She closed the book, fitted her thumb into the curved edge of its pages, found a softer, more slippery texture mixed between the thicker paper. Flicking it open again, she came across a leaf, trapped between two waxed sheets. One of the leaves she and her mother had collected and kept. It was perfectly preserved, the strong lines of its veins dark and vibrant against the brilliant burnished orange. After all this time, it was still here. Hidden deep within the pages of a book

Charlie had completely forgotten. A sudden burst of warmth flooded through her body and she found herself smiling. She left the leaf in its place and closed the book, placing it on the bed as carefully as if she was laying an offering on an altar.

Dipping back into the box, she reached right to the bottom and pulled out a bundle of envelopes, a blue satin ribbon tied around them and fastened on top with a neat bow. Charlie tugged at one end of the ribbon and let it fall onto her lap. The envelopes were all the same size, all addressed to the same person, all in the same handwriting. They were the letters she'd written to Emma after she'd left Naringup. The letters she'd sent without ever receiving a reply, until she'd eventually given up. She shuffled through the pile, checking the postmarked dates, turning each one to find that they had all been opened. At the bottom of the pile was the last one she had written. Sliding the pages out, she unfolded them and scanned the lines: general news about finishing her course, her plans to one day open her own vet practice, an invitation to her graduation. Charlie would have been almost twenty-five when she sent this one and it too had gone unanswered. She skimmed down to the final lines, reading the words out loud.

It's been six years now since I left and I think about you every day, Emma, and hope you're doing okay. If I don't hear back from you this time I'll take the hint (maybe I should have already but you know how stubborn I can be!) and not bother you again. If that's the way it goes, please know you're the closest thing I have to family and I'll never forget you. Take care, Emma.
Love, Charlie x

She stared at the words, waiting for her vision to clear. Every word she'd written then was true now. Emma was still the closest thing she had to family. Her cousin hadn't replied to the letters, but she had opened them. And kept them. Tied them together with a blue satin ribbon. Something fell from the bundle onto the floor and Charlie bent down to pick it up, her heart skipping a small beat as she held it between her fingers: the photo of the two of them when they were teenagers. An exact copy of the one she still kept in her wallet. The picture that had prompted her to go to Jac about McDowell, to try to get Emma to confide in her. If I still feel it, maybe you do too, Charlie thought, looking down at the image of her cousin's face. There'd been a glimmer of reconnection with Hazel. If she tried harder, perhaps she could find it with Emma. It was one thing to put the past behind you, but it was another thing entirely to pretend that it never existed.

Charlie picked up her phone and checked the time. Almost 9 pm. She could go straight out there now and see Emma, let her know – properly this time – that she was here for her. And this time she wouldn't take no for an answer.

A sharp wind rustled the leaves. The house was in darkness, shutters closed. As she made her way up the steps, Charlie had only one thing on her mind: seeing Emma and making sure she was okay. Unlike earlier that afternoon at Hazel's, this time there was no wavering. She pounded her fist against the door. Waited. Listened. Nothing.

She banged again. 'Emma, it's me, Charlie.'

The distant call of a bird.

A horse neighing in a paddock.

Her own heart pounding against her rib cage.

But nothing from behind the walls of the house.

She tried the handle of the door. 'Emma.' She banged again, this time with the flat of her palm against the solid stretch of timber.

Come on, open the damn door.

Both cars were parked outside the garage. At this time on a Sunday night the kids would no doubt be in bed, so Emma, at least, would likely be inside. Something wasn't right.

Charlie turned and hurried back down the steps and around to the back of the house. Skirting the glass panels of the pool fence she crossed the width of the deck to the back door. Again the door was closed, the windows covered. She knocked, lighter this time, conscious of the quickened pace of her breathing, her eyes glued to the handle, waiting for it to turn. Nothing. She ran her tongue across the inside of her lip, swallowed, lifted her hand to the doorknob and slowly pushed the door open.

'Emma? Hello? Are you there?' Her voice sounded thin in the cavernous silence of the kitchen. Closing the door carefully, she noticed a dim light coming from one of the front rooms. She'd only been inside once, so she wasn't sure about the layout of the place. She tiptoed through the dark until a sudden thought stopped her: What if Emma – or Garth – caught her creeping around their house for no apparent reason? What would she say?

A low growling noise sent a quiver across her scalp.

Eyes wide, she moved towards the sound.

'Huh!' The exclamation escaped before she had a chance to contain it. Lying on his side on the floor was Garth McDowell, motionless, eyes closed, blood oozing from a gash on his forehead.

Charlie took a few more cautious steps. Something crunched beneath her feet and she looked down. Shards of glass littered the rug on which she was standing. A broken bottle lay on the floor not far from McDowell and the sharp smell of whisky stained the air. On the coffee table a second bottle of scotch, empty but intact, sat beside a tumbler of amber liquid. There was another low growl and Charlie jumped. McDowell's body shifted slightly as he let out a brief snore. Well, he's not dead, Charlie thought, but what the hell happened? She looked around the room. There were no apparent clues. Where was Emma? Where were the kids?

Switching her phone to flashlight mode, Charlie moved down the hall towards the bedrooms. Before she reached what she knew was the master bedroom, she heard a faint sound from behind a closed door. She turned the handle. The room was dark. It seemed empty, but a whimpering coming from inside the built-in wardrobe had her moving fast. Sliding it open, she saw two small forms huddled beneath a rack of clothes, their arms wrapped tightly around each other. Tori's cheek was pressed against her brother's forehead. Charlie fought back the tears. Now was not the time to lose it. You can do that later, she told herself, please just not now.

She crouched down until she was at eye level with the two children. 'It's okay,' she said softly, resting her hand on Matt's arm. 'Everything's going to be okay. Tori, where's Mum?'

'In her bedroom,' the girl whispered. 'I think she's hurt.' Charlie reached out a hand but the children only shrank further into the cupboard.

'No,' Tori said. 'We'll stay here.'

'Okay.' As much as Charlie hated to leave them there

like that, she knew McDowell might be back on his feet any minute.

'Emma.' She stood and hurried out of the room and along the hallway, bursting through the door of the main bedroom. The figure lying on top of the mattress was curled into a foetal position. Charlie rushed over and flicked on the bedside lamp. She dropped to her knees. 'Oh god, what's he done to you?'

A dark blemish grazed Emma's cheekbone. The eye above was no more than a slit in her swollen face, and a dried bloodstain smudged her upper lip. Her arms were folded across her ribs. 'What are you doing here?' Her voice was raspy, barely audible.

'That doesn't matter now. You need a doctor.'

'I think I killed Garth.'

'No. He's passed out on the floor in the lounge room, but he's not dead.'

'If he wakes up and finds you here . . .' Emma winced as she tried to sit up.

Charlie ignored the surge of anguish threatening to paralyse her. She took Emma's hand. 'We need to get you and the kids out of here.'

'Charlie, you don't understand. You have to go.'

'Emma, look at me.' She waited until her cousin met her eyes. 'You're right. There's a lot I don't understand, but I just found your children cowering in the wardrobe like a pair of frightened puppies. I understand that and I remember what it felt like. I know you do too.'

A single tear slid silently down Emma's cheek.

'Is that how you want them to grow up? Like we did?'

'He'll come after us.'

Charlie pictured McDowell's inert form. 'Not tonight he won't.'

A sob broke from Emma's chest. 'I just want them to be safe.'

'I know. I know you do.' Charlie tucked a strand of hair back behind her cousin's ear. 'I'll help you – we'll get an AVO. You can do this.'

'Are you okay, Mummy?' Tori stood beside her brother in the doorway, holding his hand.

Emma dragged herself up from the bed and shuffled towards her children, so damaged Charlie could hardly bear to look. She watched as Emma knelt in front of them and placed a hand on each of their shoulders. 'Yes, I am.' The quiet strength in her cousin's voice left Charlie in awe. 'But I need you to do something for me. I need you to go to your rooms, grab enough clothes to wear for the next couple of days and put them in your backpacks. Okay?'

'Are we going on a holiday?' Matt's question was innocent and heartbreaking all at once.

'Sort of. We're going to stay with Nana for a while.'

'What about Daddy?'

'He'll be okay. He just needs a few days to calm down. Now go, do as I ask.'

'Come on, Matt.' Tori led her brother out of the room.

Emma waited until they had gone to haul herself up, using the doorframe as support.

'I think we'd better get you checked out at the hospital,' Charlie said, moving to her side.

'No. I am not going to the hospital,' Emma hissed. 'Not tonight.' She staggered to the walk-in wardrobe, blanching as she reached for a bag from the top shelf.

'Here, let me.' Charlie grabbed the bag and held it while Emma plucked underwear and a couple of tops and jumpers from the drawers, and a pair of jeans and tracksuit pants from their hangers. Emma's movements were slow, and she tried to stifle a gasp of pain as she bent down to pick up a pair of runners. Charlie took her elbow and led her back to the bed, took the shoes from her and held them as Emma eased her feet in one at a time and allowed her cousin to lace them. They rose together.

'I'm so sorry, Emma,' Charlie whispered, gently folding an arm around the younger, smaller woman. 'I'm so, so sorry.' Whether she was apologising for leaving, for not coming back or for the turmoil her cousin had had to live through, Charlie wasn't really sure. But she was sorry. For all of it.

Emma allowed herself to rock into Charlie's body for a few brief seconds before pulling back. 'I hit him back. He came at me again and somehow I managed to pick up the bottle and hit him back.'

Charlie nodded, took the bag and led Emma out into the hall. She waited, listening for any sounds from the living area, while the children finished packing and appeared beside their mother. The backpacks they carried were bursting at the seams. Matt had a shabby brown teddy stuck under his arm and Tori was clutching a toy horse that was missing one eye.

Emma looked up at Charlie, and together the group bundled themselves towards the front door.

At the end of the hallway Charlie stopped. She held her hand up, signalling to the others to stop too.

'Wait here.' She edged her way out into the room, letting out a loud sigh of relief when she saw McDowell was still in the same position, sprawled on his back beside the black leather lounge, his mouth open wide like some grotesque carnival clown.

Emma stepped up beside Charlie and looked across at her husband. Something almost like a laugh broke from her lips. 'I don't know who's more pathetic, me or him.' She took the children's hands in hers and walked from the house.

Charlie followed, giving McDowell one final scathing look before she switched off the light, leaving the house buried in darkness.

Chapter Thirteen

Rain pattered against the corrugated roof of the cottage, waking Charlie from a restless sleep. She sat upright, memories of the previous night cutting through the fog in her brain. How will Emma be feeling this morning? she wondered. At least she was out of McDowell's clutches – for now. Charlie shuddered as she thought of what could have happened, how it could have been so much worse. But then it still could be – what if he came after them as Emma feared?

A gentle tapping roused her from her thoughts. Someone at the door. She scrubbed a hand across her face. 'Just a sec.' She stumbled to the door and pulled it open.

'Thought you might still be here.' Joel stood on the porch, two takeaway coffees in his hands. He held one out to her. 'Dark and sweet, if I remember rightly from the café?'

'Oh, hi . . . thanks.' Charlie was immediately conscious of the skimpy PJs she was wearing and wished she'd thought to throw on more clothes before opening the door. Too late now. 'Come in.' She placed the cup on the table. 'I'll just grab some clothes.'

'Don't bother on my account.'

She answered his teasing comment with a quirk of her lips and turned towards the bedroom.

'Did I wake you up?' he called through the divider.

'No, no, I was already awake, just taking things a bit slowly this morning.' She picked up the clothes she'd dumped on the floor last night and stabbed an arm into the sleeve of her sweatshirt, pulling it over her head before climbing into the pants.

As she rounded the corner, she couldn't help but notice the look of disappointment on his face when he saw her now-covered body. 'So, what brings you here at this almost sensible hour?' She peeled the lid off her coffee, eyes closing as she inhaled, before letting a mouthful of the hot liquid slide down her throat. 'This is ridiculously good, by the way.'

'Almost as good as mine,' Joel countered, watching as she took another sip. The annoyance Charlie had sensed as she'd left his place last night seemed to have vanished, replaced by his usual cheekiness. 'Anyway,' he continued, 'I thought we should go see Jac about the bats together.'

So much had happened in the last twenty-four hours and Charlie's brain was totally scrambled.

'Sorry, I should have asked sooner. How are the bats?'

'The ones Mum's looking after are doing okay. They don't seem to have succumbed to the shock. She was going to call and check on the others this morning.'

Charlie nodded.

'So, we probably should go see Jac,' Joel said.

'Right. Yeah.' She glanced down at what she was wearing – not exactly professional attire.

'She hasn't left for work yet, so we could have a chat to her here if you like.'

'Lead the way.' Charlie drained her coffee, leaving the cup on the table, and the two of them headed up the path to the main house.

'Knock, knock. Where's my favourite girl?' Joel called out as he stepped inside.

'Right here.' Jac appeared from the next room, laughing. 'Sorry to disappoint you, but Brad dropped the little princess at day care this morning, so you've missed her.'

'Lucky I'm actually here to see you then.'

Jac's eyes shifted to Charlie, then back to her brother-in-law. 'And what are you two doing here – together – so early in the day?'

Charlie gave an exaggerated frown. 'We're here about the bats.'

'Ah, yes, of course. You really are taking the whole Batman thing seriously, aren't you?' Jac smirked at Joel but saw her attempt at a joke had fallen flat. 'Sorry. It's pretty awful, I know. I'm going to need an official statement from you both, but going on what you told me, I may be able to charge McDowell with harming a protected species. Certainly seems like we'll have enough to pin it on him, although he is an expert at dodging the law.'

'Maybe not this time.' Charlie looked at Jac, then flicked her eyes to Joel, weighing her options. Emma had promised she'd call the police station first thing this morning, but what if her resolve faded?

'Am I missing something?' Joel quizzed her.

She lifted a hand to her mouth, pressing her fingers against her lips, her eyes drifting closed for a few seconds. Emma's safety was at stake here, and her children's.

'Last night, after we sorted out the injured bats,' she

nodded to Joel before continuing, 'I started worrying about Emma. I wanted to make sure she was alright.' She swallowed. 'So I went out there.'

'After you'd told me not to?' Joel's voice had a prickly edge.

Charlie looked him straight in the eye. 'Yes. I wasn't going there to tackle McDowell – I was going to talk to my cousin.'

'And you thought that was a smart thing to do, to go out there on your own when you pretty much knew McDowell was the one who shot the bats?'

'Yes . . . no . . . Look, I was hoping he wouldn't even be there.' She could feel their eyes on her, Joel's accusatory, Jac's curious. 'But he was there. He was passed out.'

'What happened?' Jac asked.

Charlie ignored Joel's scowl. 'He smashed Emma up pretty badly. She retaliated this time, hit him over the head with a bottle and knocked him out.'

'Good for her.'

'Yeah. I persuaded her to leave with the kids. She was in a bad way but wouldn't let me take her to hospital. She promised she'd call you this morning, but—'

'She may not.'

'It might be different this time.'

'Let's hope so.' Jac picked up her bag and keys. 'Charlie, I know you weren't actually there when he hit her, but you were there in the immediate aftermath and that makes you a witness of sorts. I can serve an interim order on him. But I have to do it in person. What state was he in when you left?'

'Comatose. Totally out to it. The cut on his head was still bleeding a bit.'

'So he would have woken up to an empty house and a sore head.'

Charlie nodded.

'Let's hope he hasn't already made a visit out to Hazel's.' Jac pulled her jacket from the back of a chair. 'I need to get to the station. Leave this with me. I can go out there and question McDowell about the bat incident, but this business with Emma is my main concern at the moment.' She moved towards the back door. 'Charlie, I suggest you don't go out to the McDowell place on your own for any more monitoring. Maybe take Joel out with you, even if he stays in the car.'

'You don't think McDowell would try anything with me, do you?'

'Think about it. From where he stands, his life was pretty peachy until you arrived. Now he has another dead horse, a property in lockdown, and to top it off his wife has finally walked. I don't think he's going to be too happy to see you.' She headed for the door, brushing a hand against Joel's arm. 'As for the bat situation, I'll get a statement from Andy this morning. Can you both come down to the station a bit later and do yours? Just lock up when you leave.'

Charlie listened as the clicking of Jac's boots on the concrete path faded. Joel was leaning against the kitchen bench, arms folded, staring out into the backyard.

'You shouldn't have gone out there.' His face was expressionless, but she could tell he was trying to keep his voice steady.

'Maybe not. But it's done now. And Emma might still be there if I hadn't.'

'I'm confused,' he said. 'I thought you said you two weren't close.'

Charlie didn't have the energy or the inclination to get into it with Joel right now. Her family issues were her own business. 'We're not, but I needed to talk to her. On my own.'

'Seems you like doing a lot of things on your own.' He echoed her words sourly.

'What's that supposed to mean?' This whole conversation had taken a strange turn and Joel's attitude was really starting to piss her off.

'Charlie, every time I've tried to get to know you a little more, you've backed away. You give off this vibe like you're interested and then you shut down.'

The truth in his words was a little too close to home. Charlie folded her arms tightly. 'I may have indulged in a little harmless flirting with you, but that's as far as it's gone. As far as it will go. I'm doing what I came here to do and leaving.'

Joel pulled his keys from his pocket. 'Right. Well, thanks for letting me know where I stand.' He opened the back door and waited for Charlie to leave without even bothering to meet her eyes. She lowered her head and marched past him, her heart racing.

Back in the granny flat, she stripped off her clothes and stepped into the shower, turning on the water as hard and hot as it would go, reminding herself again why she was single and needed to stay that way. Okay, so the connection between them was stronger than the word *flirting* implied, but that wasn't a thought she really wanted to entertain right now. She didn't have time to waste worrying about her love-life – or Joel's bruised ego. There was something – and someone – more important who needed her attention.

'Hi, Emma, it's me.' Charlie arranged some loose sheets of paper into a pile on her office desk as she spoke into the phone.

There was a long pause on the other end of the line.

'Emma?'

'Yeah, I'm here.'

'I just wanted to call and see how you're feeling.'

'I'm okay.'

Charlie frowned. Emma sounded aloof, like she didn't want to talk, but that was probably to be expected after last night's ordeal. 'And the kids?'

'They're good.'

Charlie wasn't sure she should ask the next question, but she had to know. 'Has he been out there?'

Again it was a while before the answer came. 'No. He called a few times, but I didn't answer.'

'Did you want me to come out and pick you up? I could come with you to the police station.'

'No.' Emma's response was lightning quick this time. 'You don't need to do that.'

A sickening suspicion swirled in Charlie's stomach. 'You are going to make a report, aren't you? Like we talked about last night?'

There was another, longer silence before Emma spoke. 'I am going to, just not today.' Charlie rose from the chair in her makeshift office and started to pace. She pinched the bridge of her nose between her fingertips, shaking her head. Her cousin's *not today* might mean *never*.

'He's not going to change, Emma. You of all people should know that.'

A quiet weeping began on the other end of the line. Charlie waited while her cousin composed herself.

'I know. I know you're right,' Emma said. 'You and Mum. I just—'

'Look, I know you're scared, but I spoke to Jac Pearce and she's going to have an interim AVO issued. It'll take a couple of weeks for a proper application to be processed, but this will make sure he stays away from you and the kids in the meantime.'

'You really think he's going to take notice of a piece of paper?' Emma was sounding frantic.

'If he doesn't, the police can step in.' Charlie paused, choosing her next words carefully. 'But you need to commit to it, Emma, and not let him talk you into going back.'

Charlie waited patiently for Emma's response, willing her to agree. This was her cousin's chance to make a stand, a chance for Emma and her kids to be safe.

'Okay. I'll call Jac.' Emma sounded resigned rather than decisive, but at least it was a step in the right direction.

'Good. If you need anything, give me a call. I'll be out there later to check on the horses.'

'Okay . . . and Charlie, thanks . . . for last night.'

'I wish I could have helped you sooner.'

'Bye.'

The conversation over, Charlie looked out the window at the sullen, wet day. Puddles of water had formed in the parking lot at the back of the station. Raindrops clung stubbornly to the windowpane. They looked like tears someone had collected and arranged, just so, against the glass. She wanted to feel elated that her cousin was doing something to protect herself and her family, but Emma's reticence had her worried.

'Please follow through with this,' she whispered.

The sky had cleared when Charlie pulled up once more outside the gates of Willow Vale Park. Or at least the rain had stopped falling. What was left of the day was now grey and misty, the wind that had whipped through the trees last night having returned to blow away much of the cloud. Her visit to Hazel's earlier in the afternoon had put her mind at rest about Emma – the phone call to Jac had been made, the application for the AVO lodged. Now it was up to the police to serve McDowell with the order. But that was proving more difficult than they'd anticipated. The man was nowhere to be found.

According to Emma, McDowell had a visit to Sydney scheduled for the first half of the week so, presuming his head hadn't been too sore to get behind the wheel this morning, that was where he'd most likely gone. It meant the place would be deserted, so Charlie didn't have to worry about bringing Joel with her for the site visit. A good thing, after their altercation this morning. But now that she was here at the gate, her heart was all but jumping out of her chest. She peered through the windscreen, trying to see which cars were parked in front of the house. Emma's was there, and the horse truck was still parked in front of the shed. The tightness in her diaphragm loosened a little when she saw that McDowell's car was missing. She hopped out, punched in the code, waited for the gates to retract as she jumped back in the car and drove on in.

It was okay, he wasn't around. She could do this quickly and then leave.

Grabbing her bag from the back seat, she slipped into her overalls and made her way around to the back of the house. McDowell had agreed to keep all the horses close to make the monitoring process quicker. And that was just fine by her.

She pulled a handful of liquorice pieces from her bag, the black stumps sticky in her hand, and made her way to the first paddock. A few of the horses whinnied as she approached – they were getting to know her now, and a bribe always helped. Working quickly, she moved from one to the next, recording each horse's appearance, temperature and heart rate in the shorthand she'd developed on a previous job. Only a few of them were a little difficult, prancing on the spot when she inserted the thermometer or pulling their heads away as she prised open their mouths to inspect the colour of their gums. She gave each one a thorough scratch behind the ears and finished off with a second treat, and before too long the process was finished. Her last stop was the stable, where Emma's grey mare was being kept, since she'd been in closest contact with Star.

'Hello, beautiful.'

Jewel gave a low whinny and moved to the front of her stall.

Charlie rubbed her muzzle and held out the last piece of liquorice. 'You like that, don't you. Hopefully it won't be too long and you'll be allowed out of here.' Emma had been letting her out into a smaller, separate paddock each day. Charlie knew it would be killing her not to be here to look after the horse.

She went through the usual procedure and dropped her notebook into her bag.

'See you tomorrow, girl.'

The mare nudged at her shoulder, almost as if saying goodbye.

Blinking in the almost-dark, Charlie rounded the corner of the house. She had her head down as she checked her phone for messages, so engrossed in what she was doing that she didn't notice the scratch of tyres on the driveway or the closing of a car door.

'Didn't think you'd be paying us a visit today.'

Charlie jumped at the deep growl of the voice, staggering back a few steps before coming to a halt. McDowell was leaning against the bonnet of her car, hands shoved into the front pockets of his jeans. Charlie took in his expression – the razor-sharp line of his mouth, the jut of his chin, the cold flint of his eyes. She stiffened. Her instincts were telling her to get the hell out of there as fast as she could, but he had positioned himself between her and the only escape route.

Keep cool, Charlie. You can do this.

'The horses needed to be checked.' She heard the nervousness in her voice and knew he would have detected it too.

McDowell stood and took a step closer. Charlie's eyes flew to his forehead. A wad of cottonwool was wedged beneath some plaster masking the wound from last night. 'You want to know where I got this?' He pointed and went on without waiting for Charlie's response. 'Your bitch of a cousin attacked me with a bottle. Lucky I didn't lose an eye.' His laugh sent a tremor through Charlie, deep down into her bones. 'Lucky for her I'm a forgiving man.'

She curled one hand tightly around the handle of her bag, grasping her phone in the other.

'Some man you are, beating a woman who's half your size with your children there to witness it.' You probably shouldn't antagonise him, Charlie, she told herself. But the anger the man stirred inside her wouldn't be restrained.

'Is that what she told you?' McDowell stepped forward again.

She could see the tiny beads of spit dotting his lower lip,

the veins rising in his rigid forearms. The rage exploding from his face.

'You listen to me . . .' he said.

Charlie's eyes fell to the phone in her hand and she saw him track her gaze. 'Oh, I'm listening,' she said, swiping her phone on, her thumb resting on the zero of the keypad. 'I'm all ears to hear how you justify it to yourself.'

'I don't need to explain myself to you – or anybody else, including that fucking policewoman.'

So Jac must have paid him that visit. 'You keep telling yourself that,' Charlie said. 'Good practice for when you get to court.'

He was so close to her now. She wanted to take a step back, get away from the acrid odour of his body, but that would be retreating and she was loath to let him think he had the upper hand.

'There won't be any court. They've got nothing on me, nothing they can prove.' The laugh he gave was quick but brutal. 'Don't go betting on Emma to follow through with any of this AVO crap. There's no way she's going to give up all of this.' He nodded towards the house. 'She'll be back.'

'I wouldn't be too sure about that. There's only so much a person can take.' She knew it was true, knew from her own experience. 'She'll do what she has to do to protect her children.'

'My children. They're mine.' He was shouting now, losing control. 'And no one – not you, not her, not any stinking copper or judge – is going to take them away from me.'

'They don't have to,' Charlie said before she could think better of it, 'they're already gone.'

McDowell dived at her and dug his fingers into her bicep, sending a searing bolt of pain through her arm. But she wasn't going to give him the satisfaction of knowing how much it hurt. She choked back a scream and braced her body as she tried to drag a quick mouthful of air into her lungs.

'Listen, bitch, you mind your fucking business and get off my property or you'll be sorry.' His breath was hot and reeked of whisky. He still had her by the arm, twisting it, making her shoulder burn.

'With pleasure.' Charlie wrenched her arm from his grip and sidestepped around him, throwing her bag into the back of the car before climbing into the driver's seat. She reached up and pressed the auto-lock. McDowell took a step forward as all four doors clicked shut. As she stared at him through the protection of the windscreen, his lips twisted into a sneer. It was all Charlie could do to stop herself pressing her foot to the accelerator and mowing him down. Scowling back at him, she rammed the gearstick into reverse, turned the car around and sped away.

It wasn't until she was a good way down the road that she felt safe enough to pull over. Hunching forward, she dropped her head, surrendering at last to the fright. When the tears finally subsided and her body calmed, she was struck by a sudden realisation: for the first time in as long as she could remember, she didn't want to be alone.

Charlie stood shivering on the deck. As she looked at her reflection in the huge panel of glass, it was McDowell she saw glaring back at her. Hard and soulless. Filled with hatred. She closed her eyes to shut out the image, her upper arm aching where he'd seized it, and tried not to think about what *could* have happened. Desperate to chase away the thought, she lifted her hand to knock but the door slid open before her knuckle connected with the glass.

'Charlie.' Joel stood in front of her, the look in his eyes hard to discern. 'What are you doing here?'

'I . . .'

'You're freezing.' His hand cupped her elbow. 'Come inside.'

She let him lead her to the middle of the room, where he picked up a throw rug from the back of the lounge and draped it across her shoulders. The soft fur was instantly snug.

Joel rested his hand against the column of her spine, guiding her to sit. 'Can I get you a drink? Tea?'

She nodded, not sure yet that she could speak without falling apart. Joel disappeared into the kitchen and she closed her eyes, resting her head against the plump cushions. The reassuring sounds of domesticity filled the room. The clatter of metal against metal, water running from the tap, cups clinking together, a kettle humming as it came to the boil . . .

'Here you go.'

'Oh, thanks.' She sat up with a start, taking the mug from Joel, the china hot and solid in her hands. They settled beside each other, sipping tea. She knew he was watching her, waiting. What *was* she doing here? All of the bravery she'd been able to muster against McDowell seemed to have vanished. It took another two good gulps of scalding tea before she could say a word.

'I've just come from Willow Vale.'

Joel frowned.

'I know, I was advised not to go out there on my own, but I thought McDowell was in Sydney.' She bit hard on her bottom lip. 'He wasn't.'

'What happened?'

'He bailed me up as I was about to get in my car to leave and started carrying on about Emma, blaming her for last night, saying she'll be back.'

'Did he know you'd been there the night before?'

'I don't think so.' She swivelled around to face him. 'Has Jac filled you in on any of my past?' It was a strange turn to the conversation, but she needed — wanted — to tell him the whole story.

Joel gave a slight shake of his head. Jac had been as good as her word.

'You know that Emma is my cousin . . .'

He nodded but looked confused.

'What you don't know is that I lived with her and her family for six years when I was a teenager.' She paused. Somehow she'd managed to get that whole sentence out in one go, even if her voice was shaky and raw.

'Here? In Naringup?'

Charlie nodded back. 'My parents were killed in a light plane crash when I was twelve. It was their sixteenth wedding anniversary.'

Joel sat straighter, staring at her more intently.

'My father flew as a hobby. I was on a school camp and he was taking my mother away to celebrate. I can't even remember the weeks after their deaths — shock, I guess. Hazel is my mother's sister. My closest living relative. She took me in. She and her husband, Jim.' Charlie took another mouthful of tea as the memories came rushing back. She had no idea why she was telling Joel this, couldn't look directly at him, but now that she'd started, the story seemed determined to tell itself. 'Emma was two years younger than I was. She looked up to me. Her brother, Nathan, was a few years older and did his own thing. Jim must have been on his best behaviour for a while after I arrived, but it didn't last. Pretty soon he showed his true colours. He'd go out drinking and gambling. If he won, everything was good, but if he lost he'd take it out on Hazel.'

She watched Joel's forehead wrinkle and knew what he was thinking. 'Not on us,' she explained, wryly, 'just on the woman he'd promised to love and cherish for all eternity.'

'But she stuck it out with him?'

'Yes. I never understood why, but I finally asked her the other day. She said she had nowhere to go, that she had to keep a roof over our heads.' Charlie paused as a thought formed. 'Ironic, really – she stayed for us, but we left anyway. At least two of us did. Nathan. Then me. I had to.' She stared down into the empty mug.

Joel moved closer and rested a hand on the blanket covering her knee.

She lifted her head, made herself look at him. 'I think I tried to kill myself.' The words she had never uttered to a soul spilt out so easily. She laid her hand over Joel's, the blanket slipping from her shoulder but the warm touch of his skin grounding her. 'That sounds weird, but drowning wasn't what I actually intended when I went to the beach that day, not consciously, anyway. I just . . . I waded into the water and sank beneath the surface. It was so peaceful, so calm, it seemed like it would be better.'

Joel sat patiently beside her, waiting for her to continue.

'But something dragged me up, some instinct willing me to survive. I walked out of the water and back onto the beach, and that was when I decided I was going to leave. That I *had* to leave. I didn't tell anyone, just threw myself into my schoolwork, and the day I finished my HSC I packed everything up. Emma begged me not to go.' Charlie's voice broke at the mention of her cousin's name. 'I loved her. We were like sisters. She was the only one who made my life worth living.' Lifting her hand from Joel's, she wiped at her cheek. 'But I knew I had to get out. I would have taken her with me, but she wouldn't leave her mother, and I knew it would be hard enough looking after myself. I promised I'd come back for her one day, but I got caught up in my studies and my work and I never did.' She choked on a sob. 'I don't think I ever really meant to.'

'That's why you went out there last night,' Joel said softly.

'Yes.'

'Charlie.' He said her name so earnestly, like a promise. He opened his arms and she fell into them. For the first time in her adult life she'd truly confided in someone, told him things about her past and herself she'd never shared with a single soul. She inhaled deeply, her ribs expanding against the arms that held her. Joel slackened his hold, allowing her to move back a little, and brushed at the wet patch her tears had left on his sweatshirt.

'Sorry,' she whispered.

'I'll live,' he smiled.

Charlie sat up and looked into his eyes, saw that they were filled with genuine concern.

She drifted closer, and when their lips touched the sensation was totally different from the almost adolescent lust she'd felt the last time they'd kissed. That yearning was still there, but there was something more, something stronger that the sweep of his mouth pulled her towards, something she'd long denied needing.

There were no words when they moved up the stairs and into his bed, just the heat of his skin against hers, the rush of fire in her belly as he barely kissed her throat, the burning need that consumed her as his lips glided over her breasts. She relished the weight of him pressing her to the mattress, holding her firmly in place, the sure, solid reassurance of him. She cradled his face between her hands as he slid inside her, watched the momentary flicker of his eyes. And then they were moving together, slowly, effortlessly, falling into a steady rhythm, the friction building between them until she arched against him, her whole body trembling in a white-hot wave of release. She held him close as his own release followed, her breath echoing into the curve of his cheek, her skin tingling, her blood pumping, wild and intoxicating through her veins.

Later, as she lay in the dark beside him, falling to sleep in his arms, she realised what that elusive something was, the thing she had felt but been unable to name.

It was the feeling of swimming safely to shore.

Chapter Fourteen

Charlie woke to an insistent buzzing. peering around the unfamiliar room, she tried to get her brain to zero in on the source of the noise. She forced her eyes to open wider and rolled onto her side, flinching as a hot spear of pain shot through her right shoulder. Her left hand instinctively moved across to her upper arm and she grimaced as she saw the bruising that looked uncannily like the skin of an overripe eggplant. Turning her attention back to the noise she zoomed in on the offending object, but as she grabbed her phone from the chair by the door and dived back beneath the covers the ringing stopped.

It chimed a few seconds later. Missed call from Alex.

'Who is it?' Joel stirred beside her, groggy with sleep.

She turned and looked at him – the thick brown waves of hair her fingers had combed through last night, the barely there dimple above his chin, the broad, bare chest she'd fallen asleep against as she listened to the thumping of his heart, solid and sure beneath a luscious pillow of flesh. And as her eyes dropped, memories of another part of his body sent a ripple of heat through her own. 'I can think of better things to wake up to than a phone call from my boss,' she laughed softly.

Joel trailed the back of his hand over her cheekbone and down the arc of her neck, letting it come to rest on the patch of skin just above where the sheet covered her breasts. 'Me too.'

'Well, hold that thought, Batman, because I have to ring him back.'

He gave her a frown and Charlie couldn't stifle her laugh as she dialled.

'Charlie, is that you?'

Alex had picked up straight away. She cleared her throat. 'Yeah, yeah, it is.'

'Are you okay? You sound a little—'

'Fine, I'm fine. Just had a late night and slept in.' A hand shimmied across her waist and she placed her own firmly on top of it to still the roaming fingers. She was on the phone to her boss and this was no time to be starting anything. As much as she'd like to. There'd been plenty of *that* last night, as the tightness in her thighs so loudly reminded her.

'What's up?' she asked.

'The test results are back on the second property.' Alex paused. Her stomach dropped. 'Not good news, I'm afraid. The black mare tested positive.'

Charlie sat upright, forcing Joel out of the way as she pulled the sheet tight around her, suddenly conscious of being naked. The ramifications of what Alex was telling her spun through her brain – McDowell's prize mare was going to have to be put down. How would he take it? What would he do? How was she even going to tell him about this, after everything that had happened?

'Charlie?' Alex said.

'I'm here.'

Joel was watching her intently.

'Is the horse showing any symptoms?' Alex asked.

'Not as of yesterday.'

Her boss sighed. 'Can you get out there asap and check on it this morning? If it's still asymptomatic, we'll have to wait for the follow-up results to come back from the lab in Geelong. But if there are obvious signs, you'll need to go ahead and euthanase. Are you okay with that?'

'Of course.'

'Let me know how things go.'

'Will do.'

The line went dead and she let the phone slip from her hand onto the bed. Wrapping an arm across her middle, she closed her eyes, forgetting for a moment that she wasn't alone.

'Charlie?'

Joel's face was full of concern.

'I need to head out to Hazel's and take a look at McDowell's mare.'

'Hendra?'

She nodded.

'Shit. He's going to go off his nut.'

'Like he hasn't already.' She pictured McDowell towering over her, swollen with anger. Joel was right, there was a good chance this latest event could push him completely over the edge.

Joel sat up beside her. 'Will you have to put the horse down?'

'If it's showing any symptoms. Otherwise we have to wait for more tests to confirm the initial findings.'

'So you'll have to tell him what's happening?'

Charlie knew what he was getting at – at some point she'd have to contact McDowell. Not a thought either of them wanted to entertain. 'I don't need his permission to euthanase, but obviously it would be better if he cooperated.'

They gave each other a knowing look. Garth McDowell cooperate? That wasn't going to happen.

'I'm sorry, but I have to get out there straight away.'

'I'll come with you.' Joel rolled away from her and picked up his watch from the bedside table.

Charlie laid a hand on his back. 'No, you don't have to. McDowell's not going to be out at Hazel's. If it looks like I need to do anything with the horse – if I need to contact him – I'll call you.'

'Are you sure?'

She nodded. 'Positive.'

While Charlie was still trying to work out how to get out of bed and dress discreetly, Joel got up, collecting her clothes from where they lay in various locations around the room. He seemed totally oblivious to the fact that he wasn't wearing a stitch, as if they'd done this a hundred times before. 'You might be needing these,' he said, handing her the bundle and leaning down to give her a gentle kiss. 'Want a shower?'

She did, she really needed a shower, but she also really needed to get out of here and get her head sorted about the next step with McDowell. 'I might just throw these on and get going.'

'I do a mean scrambled egg,' Joel's forehead creased hopefully, 'and you still haven't experienced my breakfast coffee brew.'

Hmm, caffeine. Made and served by the man standing right in front of her, currently stark naked. She was tempted, but decided against it. 'I think I'd better get going,' she said.

Joel's face fell as he began to turn away. She reached out and caught him by the wrist before he moved off. 'Hey, I just need to get my head around this work stuff. Can I take a raincheck on breakfast?'

'I'll hold you to that. You're building up quite a list of rainchecks, you know?'

'Good. I plan on cashing them in very soon.'

She dressed quickly while he headed into the bathroom. When he returned to kiss her goodbye, she remembered exactly why she'd turned up on his doorstep last night and how she'd ended up in his bed. There was something about him – about *them* – that had her wishing she could stay. Not just now, here, but later, when this was over. But at the moment that time seemed a long way off.

It was slightly after 9.30 and Hazel's house was deserted. Probably taking the kids to school, Charlie thought. Just as well. The fewer people here to distract her, the better. She drove as close as she could to the paddocks where the horses were being kept, suited up and started the walk up the hill.

A small patch of blue peeked from between the low grey clouds that had been a permanent fixture for days now. She had a sudden urge to reach up and grab at the clouds with her fingers, break them apart, let the light burst out from the invisible wall it kept hiding behind – the same way she wanted to break herself open and pull herself apart and put herself back together again. Make the pieces fit.

Starting something with Joel had been stupid, completely against her better judgement, but it had also been the first time she'd followed her instincts in a long, long time, and even though she knew it could never develop into anything serious, in her heart she wished it could be more. But that was impossible. Her time here would end in a few more weeks and she'd return to Lismore. This was just a holiday romance – without the holiday. No, it wasn't even a romance, she told herself, it was just sex, two consenting adults doing what people who are attracted to each other sometimes do.

You keep telling yourself that, Charlie.

She could hear the grin underlining the words. If that was her mother's voice speaking to her, it was kind of creepy. They'd never had that whole mother–daughter birds and bees talk – there'd never been time for it, and Charlie had never really had anyone to talk to about sex or men or love. She'd never been one to confide in friends or share secrets, so she'd learnt purely from experience. Mostly good experiences. A few bad. Some utterly forgettable. But she'd never felt as safe with anyone as she did with Joel. So, yes, whoever it was speaking in her head was probably right, she was delusional, but there was no time to be anything else.

Cresting the top of the hill, she lifted a hand to shield her eyes from the glare as she scanned the paddocks. The bay wasn't hard to spot, standing at the far end, neck twisted as she stretched under the wire fence to pull at some grass that obviously looked greener. The stallion was grazing in a separate area a little further along. But there was no sign of the black mare. Had McDowell moved her again? Charlie continued on, and after a few more steps something to her left caught her eye – a dark form beneath a clump of trees. A horse. Lying down. Panic vibrated beneath her skin. Even though the tests had come back positive, Charlie had hoped they were false, that the second round of results would prove them wrong. As she approached the prone mare, those hopes were dashed: the rapid rise and fall of the horse's flank, the layer of sweat soaking her jet black coat and the frothy, bloodstained secretion spilling from her nostrils all pointed to one thing. There was no need for any other confirmation.

Charlie fell to the ground a short distance away from the horse. 'This is so unfair,' she whispered.

The mare blinked at the sound of her voice. Charlie wanted to reach out and stroke the horse, but even though she was wearing all the right clothing there was protocol to follow. Standing, she took a few steps back, peeled off her rubber gloves and called Alex.

'And?' Typical Alex. No small talk.

'We won't have to wait for the test results. The mare's in a bad way.'

'You said she was fine when you checked her yesterday.'

Charlie baulked at the implied accusation. 'She was. All her vital signs were good and her temp was normal. I've recorded it all if you want to see for yourself.'

'Of course not. Don't be silly.' He groaned. 'Well, you know what you have to do. Is the owner there with you?'

'No.'

'Get a hold of him and let him know the situation. As usual, the sooner this is done, the better.'

'This horse is worth a lot of money to him, Alex. He's not going to be happy.' The mere thought of having anything else to do with McDowell made her want to heave.

'I don't care whether he's happy or not, Charlie. He doesn't have any choice and neither do we. You sound a little uncertain about this.'

She looked over at the horse. She hadn't filled Alex in on any of the family details that had complicated this job, preferring to keep her private life private. The poor mare was suffering and that was the most important issue.

'No, I'm not,' she said. 'I'll try to contact him, but if I can't, I'm going to go ahead, put her out of her misery.'

'Stay in touch.'

'I will.'

She looked towards the house, but there was no car. Emma and Hazel still hadn't returned. Probably better that way. No point involving them. It was McDowell she needed to inform. She'd promised to call Joel first. She found his number in her directory and pressed it. One ring, two, three . . .

'Come on, Joel, pick up,' she said, impatient.

'You've reached the voicemail of—' Charlie ended the call. Damn. Where was he?

The mare jerked, her body surrendering to a series of spasms. She gave a low moan.

'Shit, I have to do something.' Charlie found McDowell's number and dialled. As she so vividly recalled from their encounter last night, he hadn't left for Sydney yesterday as planned. Maybe he was still around. After six rings, it too went to voicemail.

Fuck, can't anyone answer their bloody phone?

This time she left a matter-of-fact message: 'Mr McDowell, it's Charlie Anderson. Your pregnant mare has tested positive for hendra. She's in a very bad way. I need to put her down immediately. Please call me back.'

Should she wait for him to ring? Wait for Emma?

Charlie pulled another set of gloves from her bag, slipped on a mask and moved back to the mare, crouching down beside her. A fly hovered around the horse's face and landed on her cheek, but she didn't twitch or shake it off as a horse normally would. Such big, beautiful creatures and yet so sensitive. Charlie reached out and brushed the fly away, stroked the mare's face. 'I don't even know your name,' she said.

Had Alex been right? Had she missed something yesterday? Had all this mess with Emma and McDowell – not to mention Joel – distracted her from doing her job properly?

No. Charlie thought back to what she'd learnt about the virus. It could lie dormant, as it had with Star, and then make a sudden appearance, taking its host downhill very fast, which was what must have happened here. She'd never had to euthanase a pregnant mare before. It wasn't one life she'd be ending but two. It seemed even crueler. And yet she had no choice, especially when the mare was so clearly distressed. Charlie waited out the next onslaught of seizures, talking quietly to the horse, but when the mare's body calmed and she looked up, her dark, liquid eyes almost pleading, Charlie knew what she had to do. She whisked the needle and vial from her bag, keeping her eyes on the fluid as it filled the syringe.

Don't think about it.

Just do it.

Her thumb pushed against the plunger.

Charlie folded her legs beneath her and sat next to the mare, resting her hand on the horse's neck, as a final string of small convulsions shook the animal's body and she slipped away. Only then did Charlie stand and think about what needed to happen next. Now firmly back in vet mode, she snapped the second set of blue rubber gloves from her hands, making a mental list of what needed to be done. The body had to be covered – there was a tarp in her car. Arrangements would have to be made for burial or cremation as soon as possible – no point doing an autopsy when the tests and the symptoms all pointed to the same thing. Containment of the virus was more important.

When her phone rang, she stopped and whipped it from her bag, staring blankly at the screen when she saw the caller's name.

Garth McDowell

'Put that horse down and it'll be the last thing you ever do.' His voice was gruff, abrasive.

'It's too late. She's gone.'

'What the fuck do you mean, she's gone?'

As terrified as she'd been of McDowell after yesterday's encounter, Charlie had no patience for bullies and his aggression only served to fuel her own. 'I *mean*, the horse was in pain and I did what had to be done.'

'Without my permission.'

'I didn't need your permission. Euthanasia is mandatory for horses afflicted with hendra.'

The line went dead.

Charlie almost dropped her phone. She had no idea if McDowell was in Sydney or out at Willow Vale Park. Or what he would do next.

She looked down at the mare. Flies were swarming around her face, crawling into her ears, wading through the mucus filming her nostrils. This had to be dealt with quickly.

The question of McDowell's whereabouts burnt in the back of her mind, but she tried to ignore it as she made her way towards the car. A small white sedan appeared in the driveway when she was halfway across the paddock. Hazel. Perfect timing.

Charlie picked up her pace, not the easiest thing to do with her Blundstones snagging at tussocks on the uneven ground, but she pushed her legs harder and harder, her gaze fixed on the parked car as two women stepped out.

'Emma,' she called out. 'Hazel.' They turned simultaneously.

She hurried towards them. Her hand found the metal chain on the gate, but it caught on the top of the latch and she struggled, eventually yanking it free. It was only a few more metres to where her aunt and cousin stood, their faces clouded in bewilderment.

Hazel spoke first. 'Charlie, is something wrong?'

'The mare,' Charlie gasped, 'the black one, I've had to put her down.'

The colour leached completely from Emma's face, the dark purple stain of her bruises stark on her skin. 'Does Garth know?'

Charlie nodded. 'He hung up on me when I told him.'

'At least he's in Sydney.' A tinge of relief softened Emma's face.

'Have you spoken to him?' Charlie asked.

'No.'

Charlie dragged her hands through her hair and looked back towards the paddock. 'I'm not sure he is in Sydney,' she said. 'He was out at your place when I went there last night. But I know Jac issued the order, so he's not allowed on this property anyway.'

'You think that's going to stop him?' Emma asked shrilly, her eyes glazed.

As if in answer, the sound of a motor hummed from the far end of the driveway. They watched silently as McDowell's Land Cruiser came into view. He must have been close by when he'd called.

'Oh, god.' A bag of groceries fell from Emma's hand. Glass cracked against the cement. Charlie heard something like a whimper and turned to see Hazel's eyes fill with panic. The four-wheel drive jerked to a halt and within seconds McDowell was standing in front of them, an angry storm raging in his eyes.

Slowly Charlie lowered her gaze to the object he held in his right hand. Her stomach lurched.

A rifle.

'Hazel, Emma, go inside. Garth's come to see me, isn't that right?' She stared straight at him, hoping he'd see that she was giving him time to think about what he was doing.

'Stay where you are,' he ordered, lifting the gun vaguely towards them. 'You think you're so smart, don't you?' he hissed at Charlie. 'Coming down here and throwing your weight around, barking orders, telling people what to do with their own animals, their own property.' His eyes darted to Emma as he emphasised the last word.

'Garth,' Emma began.

'Shut up!' he screamed at his wife, lunging forward, startling them into huddling closer. 'Shut your fuckin mouth.'

From the corner of her eye, Charlie could see McDowell's thumb resting on the barrel of the gun. It was a standard farmer's rifle, one he no doubt had a licence for, the same one he had probably used to shoot the bats. *A lifetime ago.*

'I can see you're upset, but how about we discuss this calmly?' she said, trying to get him to see reason.

He threw his head back with a hollow laugh. 'Calm? You want me to be calm? You quarantine my property, ruin my business, convince my wife to leave me and take my kids away, put down my most valuable horse and you want me to be calm.' The rifle swung to and fro as he paced back and forth.

Charlie could feel Hazel's hands resting on her back. Emma, beside her, had fallen mute. It was up to her to try to defuse the situation. 'I was just doing my job.'

McDowell wheeled around. 'Destroying my family, is that doing your job?' He was shrieking, totally irrational, and Charlie wished she'd just shut her mouth and not said a thing. She was a vet, not a cop or a psychologist, and she had no idea how to deal with a gun-wielding lunatic.

'Charlie didn't destroy your family. You did that yourself.' Emma's voice was only a whisper, but it was loaded with conviction. While Charlie admired her courage in finally standing up to the man, this probably wasn't the best timing.

'Is that right?' he snarled. 'You seemed happy to put up with a bit of rough stuff as long as someone paid the bills for your fancy house and your clothes and your manicures. From what I could tell, you even liked it. Kept coming back for more.'

'I stayed for the kids. But it was a mistake,' Emma said.

Charlie swallowed back the bile that rose in her throat as she wondered what other sorts of humiliation her cousin had tolerated.

'A mistake? Let me tell you what the mistake was.' He was getting more and more riled up, poking a finger at the air in front of Emma's face. 'Letting your high and mighty cousin here onto my property so you two could cook up a scheme to ruin me. I bet it was you who tipped off the DPI – you knew she was working there. You planned this whole thing together.'

'What the hell are you talking about?' Emma was incredulous. 'You're completely insane.'

Charlie watched McDowell's expression darken. 'Did you want to see the horse?' she interrupted, desperate for a diversion.

He looked at her, confused. 'What?'

'The mare. She's in the top paddock. I can take you up there. Prove to you how sick she was.'

He tipped his head slightly to one side, considering her. Fine red lines dissected the whites of his eyes. A thick shadow of stubble darkened his jaw, and Charlie was pretty sure he was in the same shirt he'd been wearing last night. He hadn't made it to Sydney and, going on the putrid smell of him, apparently hadn't showered, so he'd probably spent the last twelve hours drinking and brooding.

'Alright, alright. Show me.' He seemed less flustered and Charlie felt the knot in her gut loosen a little. This could be their chance. 'We'll all go and take a look.' He waved the gun, directing them away from the house. 'Go.'

Damn. 'Maybe it would be better if just you and I go.' It was futile, but she was running out of options.

'How stupid do you think I am? Walk.'

Making her way slowly towards the paddock gate, Charlie kept Emma and Hazel in her peripheral vision. She noticed the careful way they moved their bodies, kept their eyes down, both well trained in compliance. Lives lived in fear. She was feeling the paralysing effect of it herself now as she moved one foot in front of the other, the way it clutched at her insides and numbed her mind as she tried to come up with a plan. It was the will to survive that had them all submitting to him, and although that will had almost left her once, it pumped through her body now as sure as the blood that carried it.

They were approaching the gate, keeping their eyes forward, McDowell walking behind. A noise sounded in the distance and Charlie turned, straining to hear. A car engine. Close. Coming closer. She turned to McDowell, and in the split second their eyes met she knew he had made a decision.

'Get in the house,' he screamed. 'Now. Do it. Get the fuck inside.' He yanked Hazel by the arm and spun her around, shoving the gun first into Emma's side and then Charlie's. 'Move.'

'Don't hurt her, please,' Emma sobbed, clutching at her husband, who had Hazel's arm twisted behind her back, pushing her ahead of him.

Charlie clasped Emma's hand, the pair of them stumbling forward. 'It's okay, it'll be okay,' she said softly, wishing she could hold her cousin like she used to when the violence outside their door was the worst she thought it could ever get. Until now.

They were almost at the porch. The whine of the approaching car grew louder and louder. McDowell released his grip on Hazel long enough to fling back the flyscreen door and push open the heavier timber one before shoving the older woman inside. He shoved Emma in after her, yanking the door closed. What was McDowell playing at? Charlie wondered briefly as he grabbed her by the wrist and spun her around. The car stopped. A door opened. Jac stood behind it. A thinner, taller figure stepped out from the opposite side and positioned himself behind the passenger door. Charlie recognised him – the young officer from the police station.

'Stop right there, McDowell,' Jac ordered. How had she known? Someone must have contacted her. Joel?

McDowell growled. In one swift motion, he let go of Charlie's wrist and wrapped his large, meaty hand around her throat. She gagged, unable to move. He pushed her backwards, holding her at arm's length.

'Put the gun down, Garth.' Jac's words were measured.

Charlie felt McDowell raise his arm. A deafening sound cracked the sky like a whip. The jolt reverberated down his arm into her body, forcing her eyes closed, but she opened them in time to see him point the rifle at the window on the far side of Hazel's front door and fire again. Splinters of glass showered the ground around their feet. 'I'm not playing fuckin games.'

A cry rang out from behind the walls of the house.

'Neither are we,' Jac replied, not missing a beat, 'so put the gun down and we can talk.'

McDowell lowered the rifle, and for one fleeting second Charlie thought he was going to do as Jac said. Until she felt his fingers tighten at her throat, his nails piercing the soft pouch of her larynx. Until everything started to move in slow motion. Until she wasn't Charlie Anderson any more but an extra on one of those TV crime shows, in the wrong place at the wrong time, snatched at random by some crazed gunman who any moment now would be kneecapped by the handsome detective.

A voice. She heard a voice.

The detective?

She tried to force herself to concentrate, but her head was about to explode. Her lungs were burning, the space under her ribs getting smaller and smaller.

Try harder.

Was it her own voice?

Listen.

No.

But it was a woman's.

Jac. It was Jac's voice.

Something snapped.

Her legs?

She could feel herself falling, her body a sagging, intangible thing as it hit the concrete path, a stone biting into her cheek.

Listen, Charlie, stay with it.

She worked on filling her lungs, willing her body to suck in a little more air.

'Just put the gun down . . . we can work this out.' Words, ebbing away, then surging forward again.

Her eyelids flickered.

Were they opening or closing?

Was it seconds or minutes or hours since she arrived at Hazel's?

'Shut up and let me think.' Definitely McDowell's voice this time. From somewhere above her. Fractured.

Bit by bit she was coming back to consciousness. The round muzzle of the gun was pointed at the ground, in her direct line of vision. She looked across to where Jac was still standing behind the car door.

Now that her head had stopped spinning, she realised her television fantasy was in fact a reality. This was a siege. There was a possibility that she could die. The logic of her thoughts amazed her – death, or near death, seemed to be accompanied by a certain clarity. Had it been that way for her parents? Had they known they were going to die or did it happen so fast they hadn't seen it coming?

McDowell's shoulders hunched. Beads of sweat dripped from his brow. Charlie was in between him and the police car, but with the gun now pointed straight at her there was no chance of making an escape.

'Garth.' Charlie registered another voice coming from

somewhere to her right. Emma? She must have sneaked out the back door and circled the house.

'Get back inside,' McDowell yelled.

'No,' Emma said sharply. 'This has gone far enough.' Charlie watched her cousin moving towards McDowell, her heart swelling with equal amounts of pride and alarm.

Emma stopped in almost the exact same spot she had been in when Charlie had hugged her goodbye sixteen years ago. That day her eyes had been filled with tears. Today they were filled with a dry, prickling terror.

'Mrs McDowell, you need to back away, you're not safe.' Jac was trying desperately to salvage the situation, but Emma simply lifted her hand and kept walking. She was coming closer. Charlie could see McDowell's chest heaving, rising and falling faster and faster with each step his wife took, and in an instant he pounced, knocking his body into Emma's and forcing her to the ground. He pinned her there with a foot on her hip, the rifle pointed at her temple.

'You think it's gone far enough, do you? How about I show you just how much further it can go?'

McDowell's challenge was met with grim silence.

Charlie could hear the beating of her own heart, ticking away the seconds. Someone had to do something. Maybe that someone was her. Maybe the something was a distraction. She pushed herself up onto her side and waited. She watched McDowell. He was facing away from her, side on to the police car, his attention on Emma. Slowly, using her elbow as a lever, she angled herself into a kneeling position.

'Move another inch and I blow her head off.'

Charlie froze. Her eyes hadn't left the back of McDowell's head and he hadn't turned around. How had he even seen her moving? She glanced across to where the constable had changed his position and realised McDowell's warning had been for him.

'Garth. Stop and think,' Charlie implored. 'How are Tori and Matt going to feel if you pull that trigger?'

Emma moaned.

McDowell fidgeted, his foot pivoting against Emma.

'Think about your kids,' Charlie said.

He swivelled towards her. Emma thrust herself upward, unbalancing McDowell. The constable stepped out from behind the door of the car.

The sounds that followed turned Charlie's blood to ice.

A short, sharp shot.

A thin, ear-piercing scream.

A heartbreaking, earth-shattering silence.

Chapter Fifteen

She wasn't sure how long she'd been sitting in the back of the ambulance. There was a dark splotch on the wall opposite her and she wondered vaguely if it was blood. Not hers. Or . . . no . . . no, it's an old stain, she thought, one that someone had tried to scrub off, but it had been too stubborn to budge. She was glad. It was something to focus on. That one single mark might keep her from falling if she could concentrate on it hard enough.

She heard noises outside: car doors banging shut, voices calling, the blunt edges of conversations. It was almost enough to drag her eyes away from the spot. Almost.

Someone climbed into the ambulance and sat right in front of her, right in front of her line of vision, so she couldn't see the spot any more. He gave her a gentle smile. His hair was greying at the temples and the lines round his eyes crinkled. He's someone's father, she thought.

Not mine.

'Hi, I'm Michael,' he said. 'Sorry it's taken a while to see you.'

Charlie nodded, not sure that words would come out even if she tried.

He held her chin and tipped her head a little. 'You're going to have some bruises coming out in the next few days, but I think that's all the damage. Does it hurt to swallow?'

'A little.' The two small words clawed at her throat.

'Try not to talk too much for a while and maybe stick to liquids until you're feeling better.' Taking her wrist, he placed two fingers on top of the vein beneath the heel of her hand and pursed his lips together for a few seconds. He held a stethoscope to the skin just above the neckline of her T-shirt. The coldness of the metal made her jump.

Michael wrapped a black rubber cuff around the top of her arm, pumped air into it and checked the gauge. 'Your pulse is a bit weak. Low blood pressure,' he murmured. 'To be expected. Do you feel dizzy or faint?'

'Bit dizzy.'

'You need to take it easy for the next few days. Shock is your body's way of telling you to rest.'

Charlie nodded, staring at the spot again as he shifted to the side, packing up the equipment.

'Is there someone at home when you get there? You probably shouldn't be alone for a while.'

'She won't be alone.' The voice was kind, familiar.

She turned her head to the door of the ambulance, to the man standing there, his hands in his pockets. It took her a few seconds to register the khaki work pants, the Parks and Wildlife logo on his shirt pocket, the soft blue light in his eyes.

'Good. You can go as soon as you're ready then.' The ambulance officer scooted away.

Joel stepped up to the back of the van and Charlie

inched along the seat towards him until she reached the door. 'Emma?' she whispered.

'She's okay, Charlie.'

'And Hazel?'

'Both of them. They're pretty shaken up. It must have been . . .' Joel struggled to continue. 'Horrible. But it's finished. You're all safe now.' His hand covered one of hers where it gripped tight to her thigh, and she relaxed just enough to let their fingers slip together.

A perfect fit.

The thought pushed at the corners of her lips, but she couldn't make them go any further. She let him guide her out the door, their hands still entwined. All the air had left her body. It made it hard to stand, like her feet had nothing to moor them to the ground. She felt weightless, like she didn't really exist.

But the circle of Joel's arms around her, holding her close, and the sweet warmth of his breath against her cheek let her know that she most definitely did.

She woke the next morning to the feeling of fingers around her throat. Her hand flew to the bare strip of skin she knew must be black and blue by now. Ghost fingers. The pressure of them still lingering. All of it nothing but history.

Everything had happened so fast after the gunshot – shouting, sirens, lights – that Charlie had a hard time comprehending most of it. But there were things she remembered clearly now: Emma helping her up, the pair of them staggering away from McDowell's lifeless body where it lay in a crumpled mess on the ground, the wan face of the young constable who had fired the shot. She had a vague memory of Hazel's arms around her, the older woman's body vibrating against her shoulder, but then she had disappeared and Charlie was led away.

There'd been no discussion of her spending the night when Joel had brought her back here after she'd given her statement. He'd wrapped her in a blanket and sat with her while his mother made them eat soup. He hadn't pushed her when she'd hardly touched a mouthful, her stomach still cartwheeling as her mind replayed images of the day over and over, like montages from some B-grade horror film. His hand had held hers as she sat numbly on his lounge and, as they'd stood together and moved upstairs to his bedroom, she let her thoughts be drowned out by the awareness of his arms enveloping her, so new and yet so easy, until everything else fell away. That was when she'd finally cried, curled into Joel, their bodies tangled together under his cool cotton sheets. The tears fell heavily, a deluge of shock and grief, until she eventually lost herself to the oblivion of sleep.

Now, with morning light peeking beneath the shuttered window, Charlie had the urge to move. She needed to see Emma. When McDowell had tried to blame this whole scenario on Charlie, she'd denied the accusation, but a small, silent part of her acknowledged he was right. If she hadn't quarantined his place, put down his horses, disrupted his life, the man would never have acted the way he did. Logic, of course, told her it was foolish to think that way, but there was no denying that she was at least partly responsible for yesterday's nightmare.

Sitting up, her eyes roamed to the man not yet awake beside her. There was a gentleness about him, even as he slept, but there was a strength too, a hidden strength that had comforted her and held her through the darkness. She traced a finger over the faint lines of his forehead, reached down and pressed her mouth to his, pulling back just in time to see his eyes blink open.

'Hey there.' The raspy sound of her voice was a surprise.

'Morning.' He blinked and sat up. 'Been awake long?'

Charlie shook her head.

'Sleep okay?' She could see the worry in his eyes, knew he was asking more.

'Strangely enough, yes.'

'Good.'

'Thank you.' It was a strain to speak, but there were things she needed to say. 'For looking after me yesterday.'

'You don't have to thank me, Charlie.' He reached a finger to the side of her neck. 'How's it feeling?'

'Like I've swallowed a carton of razor blades.'

'I'm sorry you had to go through all that. As badly as it ended, though, it could have been a lot worse.'

Charlie sighed. 'I guess so. I just wish it hadn't happened at all. For Emma's sake.'

'I know what you mean. I knew the guy was an arsehole, but I never would have expected him to pull a stunt like that.'

'Me neither. Why would someone do that?'

Joel gave her a wry smile and shrugged. Charlie remembered the look on McDowell's face as he'd turned towards her before that single fatal shot. It was the fierce, dogged look of a predator about to devour its prey. 'Emma has to live with that memory imprinted on her brain for the rest of her life.' They both knew what memory she was referring to – she didn't need to spell it out. 'And that poor young police officer . . .'

'How about some breakfast?'

'Yoghurt?' Charlie asked, pointing to her throat, happy to change the subject.

'Of course. How about I make you a Drummond special smoothie? Want a shower first?'

'Both sound divine.'

Joel headed into the ensuite. She knew if she lay back and closed her eyes the images would be there, waiting. But she also knew that they would fade, with time. She hoped they would eventually fade for Emma too, and she would be able to begin her life again.

'Shower's on,' Joel called, his voice muffled through the bathroom door.

'On my way.'

And she felt the truth of it in more ways than one.

The thick, full flavour of the drink was a balm to her aching throat.

'You can make my breakfast any time you like.' Charlie ran her tongue over her bottom lip, licking off the bubbles of froth.

'How about tomorrow?' Joel closed the door of the dishwasher and moved towards her. He leant across the bench, eyes on her mouth, and she felt her body respond instantly. Placing the silver milkshake cup to one side, she moved forward, not even trying to disguise her delight. His hand reached up and cradled the back of her neck, drawing her closer. She could smell the scent of the banana . . .

A loud bang startled her back onto the stool. She turned towards the sound.

'Alex!'

Her boss was standing on the deck, his sunglasses dangling from one hand as he curved the other over his eyes and peered in through the glass.

'Your boss?' Joel looked totally perplexed.

She nodded, jumped up and raced over to open the door. When Alex greeted her, it was with a frown. 'Morning, Charlie.'

'Hi.' She held one arm awkwardly across her body.

'Sergeant Pearce told me where to find you. Mind if I come in?'

'Of course not.' She slid the door open, motioning towards the kitchen. 'Alex, this is Joel. Joel, Alex.'

The two men met in the middle of the room with a handshake. 'I'll leave you to it.' Joel gave her a quick wink and jogged upstairs. A few tricky moments of silence followed before Charlie decided this conversation might be easier if they were both seated. She made her way to the lounge.

'You look like hell,' Alex said, sitting heavily beside her. He'd never been one for censoring his thoughts and it didn't look like he was going to make today an exception.

'Could say the same for you,' Charlie shot back. His strawberry blonde hair was poking out at all sorts of angles. Puffy bags hung beneath his eyes and he definitely hadn't shaved.

'Yeah, well, that happens when you get zero sleep because one of your best workers was part of a hostage drama. And then doesn't answer her phone.'

Her phone. *Shit*. She didn't even know where it was. 'Oh, god, Alex, I'm so sorry, it must be dead.'

'Well, thankfully, you're not.' He narrowed his eyes at her. 'At least someone was keeping me in the loop.'

'I really am sorry, Alex.'

'Hmm, I suppose it wasn't the first thing on your mind. Are you okay?'

It had taken him a while to get around to asking, but Charlie could tell by the strained look on his face that he was more anxious than annoyed. 'I'm fine, really,' she said.

'You don't sound fine. In fact I can barely hear you.'

'It sounds worse than it is.'

She saw his eyes drop to her neck. 'Honestly?'

'Yes, honestly.' She reached out and rested a hand on his shoulder. 'You didn't need to come all the way down here.'

'I was worried. And I thought you could use some help.' He sighed. 'You should take some time to get over this. I can't believe you didn't tell me this case was on your cousin's property.'

A surge of guilt washed over her. While she hadn't lied to Alex, she had failed to tell him certain facts – facts he'd apparently been told by Jac. 'The family connection didn't get in the way of me doing my job.'

'I have no doubt about that, Charlie, but—'

'But it's exactly why I want to *keep* doing it,' she interrupted. 'Emma – my cousin – has been through enough the last couple of weeks. She and the kids still aren't out of the woods with the virus, and I don't want her having to deal with strangers coming and going from her house after what's happened.'

She watched Alex's face for some sort of sign he was at least considering her argument. Despite everything – or possibly because of it – Charlie wanted to be the one to get this job finished, to make sure all the loose ends were well and truly tied up before she left Naringup.

'If you really think you're up to it, then okay. But if it gets too much, you make sure you call and I'll have someone else down here straight away.'

'I will, Alex, I promise. There's a locum vet in town now who can help out if needed. Don't worry. I have a pretty good support team.'

'So I see.' He tipped his head towards the staircase. 'There's one condition, though. Two, actually. I do the site visits today and you take some time off when the monitoring period ends.'

As much as Charlie wanted to get straight back out there, Alex was probably right. And Joel. She wasn't really up to it today. 'You're on.'

'Good. I'll book it in. And Charlie, don't let me see any more stories about you on the six o'clock news.' Alex had reverted to a casual tone, but she knew that was his way of telling her to stay safe.

'I promise.'

He clapped his hands against the knees of his jeans. 'Right. Well, I'd better get moving. Ross Chalmers arranged for the mare to be buried yesterday, but I said I'd meet him out there this morning to check on things. Then I'll head out to the McDowell place.'

They walked to the door together. A rainbow lorikeet fluttered from a tree beside the deck and settled on the rim of the bird feeder, nibbling on sunflower seeds while it eyed them warily.

'Nice place.' Alex looked around, amused.

Charlie knew exactly what he was thinking. She rolled her eyes. 'Yeah, it is.'

'I'll call you later. You might want to look for that phone and charge it. Take care, Charlie.' He pulled her in for a hug and she blinked away the moisture in her eyes at the gesture, which was totally out of character.

'I will. Thanks, Alex. Talk soon.'

She watched him disappear downstairs and drive off through the garden of eucalypts.

'Tell me you're not going back to work today?' Joel was at her back, his arms draped around her middle.

'No. Tomorrow.'

She couldn't see his face, but the tensing of his body told her what he was thinking.

'I have to see this through,' she said.

'Even after all that's happened?'

Charlie eased his hands away from her hips.

'Emma and Hazel are my family.' She fixed her eyes on his. 'My only family. I can't just walk away from them, or from my job.'

'I get that, I do. But ...' She watched his face as he struggled to find the words. 'You could have been killed out there yesterday,' he said. The brittleness of his voice had her reaching for him again.

'McDowell can't hurt any of us any more, but the virus potentially can.'

His shoulders drooped. He ran his fingers through the strands of hair that had fallen across her face. 'You're amazing. Do you know that?'

Charlie's fingers found the wispy curls at the back of his neck.

'You're not going to change your mind, are you?' he said.

'Nope. Stubborn as the day is long, or so my mother used to tell me.'

'Seems to be a trait with the women in my life. Isn't that right, Tilly?'

The dog was lazing on the deck, lapping up some morning sunshine. She thumped her tail against the timber at the mention of her name.

Charlie blushed a little at Joel's reference to her as 'one of the women in his life', but there was also a thrill of excitement at the idea. She ran her hand over the logo on his shirt. 'You have to go to work?'

He nodded. 'Unfortunately, I do. We have a school visit organised and guess who's the tour guide?'

'Lucky you.' She looked down at her clothes – she was wearing one of his sweatshirts and a pair of rolled-up trackpants. 'Can you drop me at my place on your way?'

'Only if you promise to let me cook you dinner tonight. No rainchecks.'

She pressed a gentle kiss to his lips. 'Deal.'

Charlie pulled up at the open gate and looked towards the house. On the outside, nothing looked any different from the last time she'd been here – apart from the small white car parked out front beside the two four-wheel drives. But she knew that inside the doors of Willow Vale Park everything had changed. Her hand floated to the collar of her polo shirt, and she pulled it back, stretching up so she could see her reflection in the rear-view mirror. A mottled collection of bruises covered her neck – she swore she could see the imprint of his fingers in the midst of them all, but she was probably imagining it. There was a scratch on her left cheek where she'd hit the ground, too, but all things considered, the damage wasn't too bad. Emma was the one she was worried about, and it was the damage beneath the surface that had her most concerned.

Hazel opened the door before Charlie was even at the top of the stairs and the two women stood for a few seconds taking each other in. Her aunt's eyes were bloodshot and ringed with grey. Was it possible for someone to age ten years in the space of twenty-four hours? You're not looking so crash hot either, Charlie reminded herself. Neither of them spoke, and it wasn't exactly clear who moved first, but their arms were quickly around each other, Hazel collapsing into her niece.

'Nanny, don't cry,' said a small voice. Charlie looked down to see Matt standing beside them, his hand on his grandmother's hip. Hazel moved back slightly, wiping at her damp cheeks with the cuff of her sleeve. 'Mummy said we need to be brave,' the boy continued, looking up at them both.

Hazel stroked his head. 'That's right, darling, we do. Do you remember Charlie?'

Matt nodded. 'She comes to check on the horses. And she took us to your house the other night, when Daddy was mad.' He turned to Charlie. 'My daddy died,' he said matter-of-factly.

'I know.' She crouched down in front of the boy. No matter how much of a bastard McDowell was, he had still been the child's father. 'I'm very sorry about that.'

'What happened to your neck?' he asked. Charlie was uncertain how to respond. She didn't know what the kids had been told about the situation. 'I got kicked by a horse,' she lied.

'One of our horses?'

'No, on another farm, but it's not as bad as it looks.' She stood, her eyes flicking to Hazel, who thanked her with a slight nod of her head.

'Come in.'

Charlie followed her aunt through to the kitchen. Emma was seated at the table, a mug of tea in front of her, Tori nestled into her side.

'How about we go and feed the bunnies?' Hazel held a hand out to each of the children. While Matt instantly complied, Tori shifted closer to her mother.

'It's okay, go and help Nana,' Emma urged, leaning down to kiss her daughter's forehead. 'I just want to talk to Charlie for a bit.' It took a few more seconds before Tori rose from her seat and followed her grandmother and brother out the back door to the yard.

'How are they doing?' Charlie asked, sitting in the chair beside her cousin.

'Matt doesn't really understand what's going on. That's the first time Tori's left my side. I told them the gun went off accidentally, but I'm sure Tori has her suspicions. I'll keep it from them for as long as I can. The truth is hard enough for an adult to stomach, let alone for a child to hear.'

'I'm so sorry.' Charlie silently cursed the tears welling in her eyes. She wanted so badly to be the strong one, but as she looked across at her battered, broken cousin, her resolve faltered.

'So am I.' Emma pointed to the bruises on Charlie's neck. 'He did a good job on you too.'

'He had me seeing stars for a minute there, but then you appeared and . . .'

Emma shivered. 'I think he would have killed me if you hadn't talked to him about the kids.'

'It was a long shot.' Charlie cringed at the bad word choice. 'When I heard the gun go off, I thought it was you.' She took her cousin's hand. 'You were so brave, the way you tried to talk him down.'

Emma huffed. 'Yeah, instead of my usual cowardice.'

'What do you mean?'

'All these years I stayed with him when I should have

had the guts to leave. I justified it by saying I was doing it for the kids, but really I was too afraid.'

'Afraid of what?'

'Of what people would think, of Mum saying *I told you so*, of being on my own. But there are worse things than being on your own.'

'You did what you could at the time, Emma. That's all any of us can do.'

'I understand why you left.' Emma lifted her eyes. 'I hated you for going, and I missed you, but most of all I was jealous. Jealous that you were getting out and I wasn't. That I was stuck. I stayed for Mum, but when I met Garth it was a way out. And I took it. I didn't even see that I was stepping out of one bad situation into something so much worse. I'm sorry I didn't reply to your letters.'

Charlie moved closer and gave Emma's hand a gentle squeeze. They were both crying now, years of sorrow and resentment and regret bubbling to the surface. 'I should have tried harder,' she said. 'I should have come back.'

'No, you shouldn't have – you did the right thing. You did what *you* had to do.' Emma forced a smile and Charlie tried to return it, but both were feeble attempts and fell away almost instantly.

'What will you do now?' Charlie asked.

'After the funeral I want to take the kids away for a while, maybe up to Nathan's in Queensland, with Mum. We'll wait until the monitoring's finished and our tests are all done. Hopefully we'll all have a clean slate.'

'You're going to the funeral?'

Emma looked out the window, to where the kids were lying on the grass, playing with their rabbits. 'He wasn't always such a monster. I loved him once, and whatever he did I know he loved me once too, in his own way. And he loved the children. They need to say goodbye. We all do.'

'Fair enough. If you need anything at all I'm here – today, tomorrow, next week.' Charlie's voice cracked. 'Next year.'

As they consoled each other in a silent hug, Charlie felt the small piece of herself that had been missing all these years fit gently back into place.

Chapter Sixteen

Charlie tugged as hard as she could, stretching the girth, guiding the prong of the buckle into the second hole on the leather strap. She let out a puff of air, patting Jewel's round belly. 'That was hard work, girl. You've got a bit fat with all this pampering in the stable.'

'The exercise will do her good.' Emma was saddling up a chestnut gelding in the pen next door.

'Are you sure you're okay with me taking her out? It's been a while since I've been on a horse.'

'You know as well as I do it's like riding a bike. Besides, she likes you, I can tell.'

Charlie thought back to her first meeting with the grey mare. She laughed. 'How? Because she doesn't pin her ears back flat at me any more?'

'Right. Even if you have spent the last month poking and prodding her.' Emma opened the gate and led the chestnut out into the centre of the stable block. 'Ready?'

'I guess so. We're only walking, though, aren't we?'

'Your pace, Charlie.'

'Okay.'

They walked the horses outside. The sun was shining, but the cool winter breeze had Charlie reaching for the zipper on her fleece jacket. Placing her foot into the stirrup, she hoisted herself up onto Jewel's back. 'Urgh, that was an effort.'

'You look good on a horse.' Emma grinned. 'Always did. Let's go.'

She turned and headed across the front paddock to the start of a trail. True to her word, Emma went at a slow gait and, after her initial bout of nerves, Charlie found herself settling in more than comfortably on Jewel's back. They rode in silence, taking in the sounds of the bush – finches flitting through the scrub, the rustle of hidden creatures among the leaf litter, a creek gurgling somewhere up ahead.

Today was her last official visit to Willow Vale Park, the monitoring period that had been extended after the death of the black mare now at an end. No more horses had tested positive, and six weeks after her arrival Charlie was finally able to declare both properties virus free.

When Emma, Hazel and the kids received their last results and were also given the all clear, Emma had suggested a celebratory ride and Charlie jumped at the idea. It was good to be out in the fresh air, good to be riding a horse instead of treating one. And even better to be spending time with her cousin again. Charlie took the opportunity to study Emma. The bruises had completely faded, but her face still looked drawn and gaunt, and her eyes had a look that Charlie could only describe as haunted. At least she'd started venturing out – a short trip into town, a visit to the hairdressers at her mother's insistence, and now a ride. It was healing for both of them, Charlie decided.

'So how are things with you and Joel?' Emma asked, breaking into her thoughts.

She hadn't talked much with Emma – or anyone for that matter – about her love-life, but Joel had come out to the property with her a few times. 'Not bad.'

Emma twisted around in her saddle, one hand on the chestnut's rump, the other holding the reins. 'Charlie Anderson, spill the beans.'

Charlie smiled. 'I'm not one to kiss and tell, Emma. But let's just say I haven't been spending too many nights on my own lately.'

'Good for you. I expect regular updates. What's going to happen when you head back up north?'

Charlie fell quiet, focusing on Jewel's movements as she found her way around a puddle. 'I'm not sure,' she said finally. 'We'll have to wait and see. I'm not keen on the idea of a long-distance relationship.' It was a revelation to Charlie that she was keen on any sort of relationship at all, but the thought of packing up and leaving Joel behind left her insides curdling.

The track opened out into a wide clearing and Charlie pushed Jewel forward until the horses were level. They rode along for a few strides side by side. 'How about you?' she asked, tentatively. 'How are you feeling about . . . everything?'

While the two of them had spent the odd hour together over the last few weeks, there hadn't been any direct conversation about McDowell since the day after his death.

'I feel like I'm just starting to wake up from some sort of terrible nightmare.' Emma's voice was only a murmur above the regular footfalls of the horses. 'I've made a decision. I'm going to sell up and move up north permanently. There's a place for sale not far from Nathan's, twenty-five acres. It looks nice in the photos. I can set up a riding school. Start again.'

Charlie wasn't exactly surprised. She knew more than anyone about the importance of fresh starts. 'That's a great idea. I can come and visit you when I'm back in Lismore.'

'I'd like that. So would the kids. And Mum.'

'So Hazel's going with you?'

'Yes. I couldn't go and leave her here.' Emma gave her a wistful look. 'Just like I couldn't back then.'

Charlie nodded. 'I know. It's going to take a while, Emma, but things will get better. I know they will.'

'I hope so.' Emma pointed up the grassy slope. 'You up for a trot? Maybe even a canter?'

'Oh, I don't think so.' Charlie frowned nervously.

'You'll be fine. Jewel knows what she's doing. Come on, Charlie, let loose.'

Charlie looked across at her cousin, saw the challenge on her face and gave her one back. Just like old times. 'Alright. Lead the way.'

Emma made a clicking noise with her tongue and the chestnut sped up. Charlie did the same, her legs gripping the horse's side firmly until Jewel settled into a slow rocking movement. She sat back in the saddle and let the motion of the horse carry her along, the soft brush of the wind on her cheeks like a quiet whisper of contentment.

Tilly flipped onto her back and rolled in a mound of seaweed, jumped upright, gave herself a shake and took off along the beach, chasing a seagull. Charlie watched her disappear behind a dune.

'You need to concentrate.' She could tell by the sound of his voice that Joel was getting testy.

Keeping her mind on what she was doing was pretty damned hard when she was standing right over him, his arse fitted snugly inside a wetsuit.

She swallowed a giggle. 'Okay. Right. What were you saying?'

He lay back down on the board. 'You'll probably feel a bit ridiculous when you try it, but—'

'Ridiculous? Why would I feel ridiculous lying on top of a board on the sand pretending to paddle? Can't we just do this in the water?'

'This is the best way to learn,' he said. His tone was schoolteacher serious. 'Now. The thing you need to get your head around is hopping up as quickly as possible. You need to get the feel of the wave beneath the board, then jump up and try to balance.'

He pushed himself onto his elbows and then his feet in one fluid motion, taking up a semi-crouching position in the middle of the board, facing her, with his arms outstretched.

'So you don't kneel down first or anything?'

'That'll just throw you more off balance.' He stepped off the long board and directed her towards it, his hand on her back.

Charlie lay flat on her stomach.

'Pretend you're in the water and paddle.'

She looked up at him, unable to hold back a smirk. 'Just do it.'

She moved her arms in a sweeping motion, her fingers trailing through the sand. Joel was right, she did feel ridiculous.

'Good, now, jump onto your feet and imagine you're on a wave.'

Mimicking the actions he'd just shown her, Charlie followed his instructions. She wanted to make a joke about the squatting position she was currently holding, but he was so earnest she thought better of it.

There was a gentle breeze blowing and a few strands of hair had slipped from her ponytail. She tucked them back and resumed her stance. When Joel didn't follow up with any more advice, she spun her head towards him. He was standing there with his arms folded, a devilish smile on his face.

'What?'

'Do you know how hot you look in that wetsuit?'

Charlie followed his eyes down to where they were trained on her cleavage, the suit not yet fully zipped.

'Really? You leave me standing here looking like a total idiot just so you can perve.' She straightened up and hopped off the board, brushing her hands together to remove the grains of sticking sand.

'Tell me you weren't doing the same when I was down there.' He lowered his arms and she stepped into them, folding hers around his waist.

'I have to say, I do kind of like you in black rubber – sort of fits with the whole Batman thing.' She dropped a hand and pinched his backside, laughing loudly when he jumped. 'So can we get into the water now?'

'Patience, Charlie.'

'What's the worst that can happen? The surf's not exactly pumping.'

They turned together and looked out at the water. It wasn't flat – there were a few decent-sized waves forming every now and then – but the surface was smooth and even. Joel had waited until the conditions were just right for a beginner before bringing her out.

'Okay,' Joel said, 'but we'll start in the white water until you get the hang of it.'

He picked up the board and stuck it under one arm, taking her hand with the other. Charlie used her free hand to zip up her suit. The sand squelched beneath their feet, and when they hit the water she let out a high-pitched squeal.

'Uh, it's freezing.'

'That's why you're in a wetsuit.'

Charlie rolled her eyes at him. 'Right, let's do this.'

He dropped the board into the water and pushed it out, explaining everything he'd already said all over again as they waded into the foam. She spent the next hour trying to do what she'd practised on the shore. It was a lot harder than Charlie had anticipated and she found herself getting frustrated.

After her zillionth attempt at standing and then toppling straight off the side of the board into yet another bubbling wave, she grunted, lay on the board and refused to move.

'Is this Charlie Anderson having a tantrum?' The smart alec tone in Joel's voice wasn't helping. She ignored him, letting the water rock her forward but making no effort to try again.

'How about we go out a little further,' he coaxed. 'You're getting to your feet really well. Once you're out in the green water you'll get a better sense of what comes next.'

Charlie peered over her shoulder. The last time she'd been in the ocean at Curlew Point she almost hadn't come out. Joel was saying something about posture and balance, but the quiet lapping of the waves drew her mind back to that day . . .

Lowering herself beneath the water, the gentle fingers of the ocean had caressed her skin. She could see her parents, both of them smiling, waiting for her, their soft voices beckoning.

Soon, I'll be with you soon, she replied, but even as the words floated out of her head another voice called, softly at first, the faintest whisper you could imagine. Ignoring it, she chose instead to listen to the rumble of blood beating in her ears, but the longer she lay there, the louder the words became. The whisper became a murmur and then finally a chant, echoing in her head until she was forced to listen.

Live, it repeated.

Live.

Live.

Live.

Until finally, just as she felt the strain in her muscles start to ease, as her body gave up fighting and the grey specks dancing behind her lids joined together, she opened her eyes and forced herself up and out of the salty coffin, breaking the surface and emerging into a hazy twilight.

Cold air screamed into her lungs. She gagged on it, her chest heaving as she let the swell of the waves carry her back towards the shore, that same voice whispering in her ear.

Live . . .

'Charlie, do you want to keep going, or have you had enough?'

She looked up at Joel, suddenly remembering where she

was and what she was supposed to be doing. 'Yes, yes, let's go.'

He swam beside her as she paddled out. The water was cold between her fingers and toes, but the suit was keeping her surprisingly cosy. They made it out to where the waves were forming, lifting the board up and down, her stomach rising and falling with the movement of the water.

Joel grabbed the board and spun it around, holding on to the front, his face just centimetres from hers. 'You okay?'

'Yeah.' She looked deep into his eyes. 'I'm great.'

'Now remember what I told you about getting up fast, and going across the wave, not straight ahead, once you start to move.' He looked behind him. 'There's one coming now. Ready?'

She nodded.

'Okay . . . and . . . go.' He pushed her off and she listened to his voice in her head. *Hands, feet, crouch, balance.* She let the momentum of the water pull her along as the board sliced across the surface of the wave. There was a whooping sound from somewhere behind her and a smile stretched wide across her face. It was like being a kid again for the few seconds she managed to stay upright.

Unexpectedly exciting.

And joyful.

The board wobbled and she tumbled off the edge. Pushing back up to the surface, she spluttered out a mouthful of water, wiped her hands across her face, opened her eyes and laughed.

Joel was swimming towards her, and within a few seconds he had his arms around her, the pair of them treading water, smirking like a pair of naughty children. 'You did it.' He smacked a wet kiss straight on her lips. 'You actually did it. How do you feel?'

'Alive!'

Despite the arrival of winter, the days were pleasant – warm enough to have Charlie sliding into her wetsuit a few more times and working on her surfing technique.

Alex had been shocked when she'd actually agreed to take the vacation time he'd suggested. 'You must be getting a little soft around the edges, Charlie,' he'd scoffed. 'Not that that's a bad thing. About time you started looking after yourself. I'm surprised you're staying on down there, though. I thought you couldn't wait to get out?'

She'd smiled to herself, remembering her desperation to leave the place as soon as possible when she'd first arrived. 'Yeah well, it's grown on me,' she'd replied.

It was true. All the things she loved about the country were here – rolling green hills, the easygoing vibe, people who said hello as you walked down the street. She'd found the same friendliness in many of the towns she'd lived in, of course, but once she'd relaxed about being back, the familiarity of Naringup made it all so easy. Or maybe it was the people.

Or one person in particular.

There was an openness between the two of them that she'd never felt with anyone else, and when he wasn't around she found herself counting the minutes until she would see him again. And then there were the nights. So steamily blissful that she never wanted them to end.

Just thinking about *last* night now as she sat in Jac's backyard made her blood simmer. Joel was standing beside Brad at the barbecue, his hands wrapped around a beer, and Charlie's mind filled with memories of what those hands had done to her not that many hours earlier.

'Why the red face?' Jac said, reaching across the table to scoop a cracker in the French onion dip.

'Sorry?'

'Your cheeks, they're blooming,' Jac laughed. 'Although based on where your eyes have been roaming, I'm pretty sure I know why.'

Charlie shoved her shoulder into Jac's. 'I can't help it if you have a dirty mind.'

'And you don't?'

Charlie arched an eyebrow.

'What are you girls gossiping about?' Mary's voice boomed from behind them as she stepped up to the table and took a seat.

'Nothing important,' Charlie mumbled, flashing Jac a warning look.

'Hmm, not sure I believe you, but whatever you say,' Mary shot back. 'So how much longer are we going to have the pleasure of your company, my lovely?'

Charlie had grown used to Mary's terms of endearment, but it still gave her a warm, fuzzy feeling each time the older woman addressed her so affectionately. 'Well, I have another three weeks' leave up my sleeve.'

'Is that right? And I hear the vet who's been filling in since Wally passed on is leaving at the end of the month.'

'Yeah, I heard that too.' Charlie had more than heard about the opening. The locum had actually paid her a visit and suggested she might want to consider taking over the practice. Her stomach had backflipped at the thought. That would mean putting down roots, making a commitment not just professionally but financially, and she wasn't sure she was up for either. 'I already have a job, though,' she said, keen to deflect Mary's probing, 'with the DPI.'

'You know what they say about change – as good as a holiday.'

Joel's mother was great, she really was, but her lack of tact was a little confronting.

Charlie knew Jac was watching, waiting for her response. 'So they say,' Charlie replied, giving away as little as possible. 'Anyone want a refill?' She picked up her glass and made a beeline for the back door without waiting for an answer. The kitchen was empty and she leant against the bench, relishing the opportunity to take a break. But the interlude didn't last long.

'Hope my mother isn't bugging you too much.' Joel stepped inside and moved close.

A shiver ran through her body at his touch. No point fighting it, she thought. She lifted her hands, interlocking her fingers at the nape of his neck. 'She thinks I should become the new town vet.' She hadn't broached the subject with Joel as yet – hadn't seriously considered the possibility herself.

'She's a smart woman, my mother. And what do you think?'

Before she could reply, the doorbell rang. 'Ah, saved by the bell.' Joel skipped a kiss across her lips. 'Guess I'd better get that.'

Charlie retreated to the fridge – now she really did need that second drink. She watched the bubbles fizz around the rim of her champagne glass as Joel returned to the kitchen with Hazel, Emma and the kids in tow. 'You have visitors, Charlie.' He turned to the guests. 'Can I get anyone a drink?'

'No, thank you,' Hazel said. 'We can't stay. We just wanted to speak to Charlie for a few minutes.'

He winked at her and headed out the back door.

'Take a seat.' Charlie gestured towards the table, feeling weird since this wasn't even her place.

Emma seated herself beside Charlie, Matt climbing onto her lap and Tori, as always, standing at her mother's side. Hazel took the seat at the end of the table. Charlie studied her cousin. She was looking so much better – her cheeks fuller, her eyes a little more alight, her smile quicker.

'I won't beat around the bush, Charlie,' Emma said. 'We've decided to leave town earlier than we'd planned. We're heading out today and we wanted to see you before we left.'

'Today?'

Emma nodded.

'We're going to see my uncle,' Tori said, beaming. 'And Mummy said if things work out I can get a new pony.' It was the most animated Charlie had seen the child since she'd first met her at Willow Vale Park.

'Me too,' Matt added, bouncing on his mother's lap.

'Why the sudden decision to leave?'

'It's Nathan's fortieth birthday in a couple of days.' Hazel's voice wavered. 'We haven't seen him in a long time and he's asked us to come up for it.'

'And you're not coming back? What about your places here?' She looked over at Emma. 'The horses?'

'One of our business associates has agreed to manage the place and sell off the horses for me. He's buying some of them himself. The others are quality thoroughbreds, so we won't have any trouble. I've had an agent in and he's putting the property on the market in the next couple of weeks.'

Charlie turned to her aunt. 'And yours?'

'My neighbour's been after it for years,' Hazel said. 'I've already signed it over.'

'Wow. That's great.' She was a little shell-shocked at the idea of such a sudden departure.

Hazel reached into her purse and pulled out an envelope. 'I didn't want to say anything earlier, in case the deal fell through, but this is for you.'

Charlie stared at her name on the envelope, scrawled across the front in black biro. She looked back to her aunt.

'Open it,' Hazel urged.

She wriggled her finger under the seal and pulled out a rectangular slip of paper. A cheque. A cheque made out to Charlie Anderson for $250,000. She held it firmly, trying to stop her hands from shaking.

'It's nowhere near the full amount Jim took from your account, but I hope it makes up for some of the hurt. I never should have let him touch that money – it was yours.'

And then it clicked. The one thing she'd avoided really addressing with Hazel, the blow that had added insult to injury.

'No, no, Hazel, I can't. That was your house.' She dropped the cheque and slid it back across the table.

'A house I would have lost long ago if your money hadn't been used to pay my no-good husband's gambling debts. I finished off what was left of the mortgage and have enough to keep me going. Everything else I need is right here.' She waved a hand towards Emma and the kids. 'Please, I want you to have it. For you and for Philippa.' Hazel pushed the cheque back.

Charlie picked it up. 'I don't know what to say.'

'You don't have to say anything.'

'We'll have more than enough to buy a new place once

my house is sold,' Emma said. 'Garth was a lousy husband, but he was a good businessman.'

Charlie nodded. 'We were just getting to know each other again and now you're leaving.'

'We'll keep in touch, I promise.'

'And you can come and visit us and our new ponies,' Matt added.

'When you get back to Lismore, you won't be that far away,' Hazel said, patting Charlie's hand.

'*If* she goes back.' Emma flashed a knowing look out into the backyard at Joel.

'We'll see.' Charlie bent across and held her cousin close. 'But you can definitely expect a visit.'

'Good.' Emma sighed and stood. 'We'd better get going.' The kids skipped ahead down the hallway, the three women moving more reluctantly behind. 'This is like deja vu, only this time it's me going and you staying,' Emma said.

Tears stabbed at the back of Charlie's eyes as they lingered in the doorway. 'Be happy, Emma.'

'You too.'

They hugged each other tightly, neither wanting to let go.

'Come on, Mum,' Matt called from the gate.

Charlie released her hold and turned to her aunt.

'I'm glad you came back,' Hazel whispered.

'Me too.'

Charlie stood on the verandah and waved goodbye. They were doing the right thing by leaving the past behind, but there was a huge hole inside her now that the family she had found again, albeit under the strangest of circumstances, had gone. That feeling of loneliness she'd learnt to live with had finally started to fade, despite the horrible events of the last few weeks, but now it came seeping through her again.

Back in the kitchen she stared down at the cheque. An errant tear dripped onto the date. She wiped it away, smudging the ink, and slipped it into her bag. It wasn't the cheque itself that was important, or the numbers written on it – it was that her aunt had wanted to make amends, the fact that she really had cared. Charlie picked up her glass. The bubbles had disappeared, but she took a good long sip before heading back outside.

Pausing on the verandah, she stopped for a moment to take in the scene: Brad handing the tongs to Joel and chasing a giggling Hannah around the yard; Jac and Mary deep in conversation, the older woman's story earning a belly laugh from her daughter-in-law; a bright yellow butterfly dancing over Tilly's head as she stretched out on the lawn in the winter sunshine. There were worse ways to spend an afternoon.

Or perhaps a life.

Joel looked up and saw her standing on the step. 'Everything okay?'

'Everything is perfectly fine.' She didn't even try to hide her smile.

Also in The Homecoming Collection

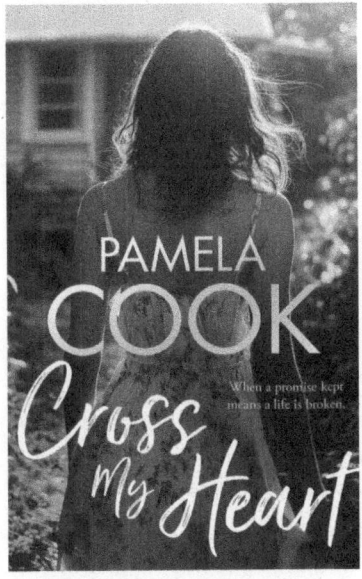

vinci-books.com/crossmyheart

Secrets, sacrifice, and the power of redemption.

Tessa's orderly life in Sydney is shattered when her childhood friend Skye passes away, leaving her as the foster mother to ten-year-old Grace. But a secret from her earlier life with Skye refuses to remain hidden, and Tessa is forced into a decision that will either right the wrongs of the past, or completely destroy her future.

Turn the page for a free preview…

Cross My Heart: Prologue

Do you remember the time we found that baby bird?

We were sitting on a rock by the creek. Cicadas were singing and the bush mint was making my nose itch. There was a shrieking noise from over near the scribbly gum. I jumped up and ran over, and there he was all puffed up in a ball. You reached down and picked him up. A magpie, you said, or maybe a butcher bird. It was hard to tell because he was so young. His body was grey, but his tail feathers were black and white. You held him so gently, and he stopped squawking and watched us, with eyes like rusty pebbles. There was a cut in his chest and he'd been bleeding. We looked around, but his parents were gone. He was an orphan, you said. I held out the bottom of my T-shirt like it was a hammock and you rested him in there, and he just sat like that all the way home.

Remember we dug up worms from the garden and tried to feed him? Except he wouldn't eat. We put him in a shoebox with some straw and I tried to stay awake to look after him, but I fell asleep. When I woke up he was still and cold.

Like you.

Cross My Heart: Chapter One

Even now, the click of a closing door could make her flinch. One long, deep breath, and the familiar citrusy scent of furniture polish was enough to pull her back.

Home.

Safe.

A faint glow softened the darkness beyond the hallway. The proverbial light at the end of the tunnel. She hurried towards it, the heels of her boots beating a staccato rhythm on the polished timber, the wheels of her suitcase drumming along behind. She stuffed her keys into the handbag dragging on her shoulder, dumped it on the living-room floor and heaved a sigh of relief. Her hands found the nape of her neck, rubbing out the kinks—the usual long-haul gremlins. Something cracked beneath her fingertips—sinews, bones, muscle, maybe all three—and she groaned. A massage would be perfect right about now.

Finally, a movement from the far corner of the room. Josh spun around in his chair, pulling the headphones from his ears, the screen of his laptop shining brighter as he turned.

'Shit, Tess, you scared the hell out of me. I didn't even hear you come in.'

The knot between her shoulder blades tightened. 'Yeah, I noticed.' She dropped her hands to rest by her sides. The last thing she wanted right now was an argument. 'What are you doing working so late?'

'Trying to make some headway on this project. Not getting very far.' He swivelled his chair back to the desk in front of him. 'How was the conference?'

Same old question, but at least he bothered to ask. 'Fine.' Same old answer, but it was too late to bother with details. She walked over and stood beside him. Once upon a time, she would have laid an arm across his shoulder, leaned down and brushed a kiss to his lips. Once upon a time, Josh would have greeted her at the airport—or at least the door—with a dozen red roses. She'd never had the heart to tell him the scent of them made her gag. It was crazy how some things never changed even when so much time had passed. She swallowed down the burn in the back of her throat.

'Did you dazzle them all with your brilliance?' A smile in his voice. His eyes glued to the screen.

She coughed. 'Naturally.'

'Have you eaten?'

'I picked at a few things on the plane.' To be honest, she could do with something decent in her stomach, something that didn't come from a foil container and smell like it belonged in a soup kitchen. Something they could share over a chilled glass of wine while they sat side by side on the couch, catching up on their respective weeks. Laughing. The fridge, no doubt, would be empty, and in all probability she'd be eating alone.

She gave her neck another twist, closed her eyes and waited for the pop. Blinked her way out of her daydream. It was late and they were both tired. 'Might just have a shower and collapse into bed.'

Josh half turned, one of his hands hovering on the touch pad, the other cradling his chin. Had he sensed the note of disappointment in her voice? Was he about to shut up shop and suggest a nightcap?

'What?' His head angled slightly in her direction.

'Nothing.'

'I won't be long.' He was already back to work, fingers tapping against the shiny surface of the desk.

How many times had she asked him not to do that? And it was a lie, of course, about not being too long. He'd be up all night. As always when a deadline was looming. Then again, when wasn't one?

She lifted her suitcase, a cramp stabbing at the arch of her foot, and grabbed the bundle of unopened mail from the island bench. A veritable mountain.

Was it that damned hard to open a few envelopes?

She glanced back to where he sat, completely absorbed with the numbers on his spreadsheet. She could strip off and dance naked around the room and he probably wouldn't even notice. The suitcase thumped against each step as she dragged it upstairs. She didn't bother lifting it to dampen the noise. Josh was totally in 'the zone', with any extraneous distractions, including his wife, completely blocked out. It wasn't like she could complain. They were as bad as each other when it came to work. Focused. Determined. Driven. It was what had drawn them together in the first place. Five years of marriage and they were both still the same in that sphere of their lives.

Even if other things had changed.

There was no point thinking about it all now. Not when the spray of hot water on her skin was beckoning, closely followed by the cool weight of high-thread-count sheets against her arms. She tossed the mail onto the bed, the dozen or more envelopes falling like a hand of cards across the crisp white doona. Probably bills or bank statements; nothing that couldn't wait. She undressed and headed for the ensuite, her bra and knickers hitting the tiled floor as she stepped into the shower. Hot water, almost scalding, streamed onto her scalp and she moaned. She sounded positively R-rated. Luckily there was no one around to hear.

Certainly not Josh.

Oh, the irony. Over a week, she'd been away. They'd shared plenty of phone messages, some of which could only be described as sexting, and now here they were under the same roof barely able to utter two words to each other. Not that she was up for anything anyway, it's just that the option would have been nice. Having *some* sort of conversation would have been even nicer. How long had it been since they'd talked about anything meaningful? She tipped her head back and let the heat pummel her face, to wash away her question. A few more minutes of mindless soaking and she turned off the taps and reached for a towel.

White, thick, fluffy and perfectly arranged on the rail. She gave her body a quick once-over before rubbing it across her head. As a kid she'd been scolded for going to bed with wet hair, told she would catch 'her death of cold', whatever the hell that meant. It had stayed with her, though. That grandmotherly warning still niggled behind her closed lids whenever she defiantly pressed her freshly washed head against the pillow. Now that it was cut short it hardly mattered. A quick shimmy and just like that, it was almost dry. The bathroom was surprisingly clean considering Josh had been home alone. Everything gleaming and in its place—no smears on the mirror, floor without a mark, the lid down on the toilet seat. Of course. It was Thursday, so the cleaner had been. Yes, it was an extravagance she'd justified to her mother on more than one occasion; the office hours they both kept didn't leave much time for household chores. Hard work might be its own reward, but a floor you could eat off and clothes pressed by an ironing service weren't too shabby, either.

She tossed the towel in the laundry basket and pulled on her pyjama top. The usual remnants of airsickness lingered from the flight; she knew they'd be gone by morning. Once she'd had a good night's sleep and sorted out her body clock.

Lamp on, light off.

There was something so comforting about your own bed. Even if you were in it alone. She sank into it, pulling the covers up to her chin as she curled into a ball on her side and closed her eyes. Serious bliss. A rustling noise had her eyelids flickering: the unopened envelopes scattering to the floor. No problem, they could be dealt with in the morning. Everything was easier to deal with in the bright light of day.

'Missed you.'

Josh's breath was damp on her cheek and the evidence supporting his words firm against the small of her back. Tess shifted forward, struggling against the heaviness of an arm draped across her middle. She cracked open one eyelid. Then another. Watery pre-dawn light leaked through the blinds. How could it be tomorrow already? Hadn't she just gone to sleep?

She reached over and switched off her bedside lamp. 'God, what time is it?' Her voice had the groggy, slurred sound of someone who'd stayed at the bar long after closing time. Jet lag was a bitch.

'Time we said a proper hello.' A hand rubbed at the underside of her breast and his mouth against the curve of her neck made her rouse. She could argue it was his fault their reunion last night had been more like colleagues passing in the coffee room than a married couple who were actually pleased to see each other. But at least they were connecting now.

She closed her eyes and drifted as his fingers floated across her skin, a warm, familiar thrum between her legs. Blood heated her cheeks, and the other parts of her body with which Josh was quickly becoming reacquainted. She dropped her hand to join with his. Her habit of wearing no underwear to bed and his of sleeping naked, often led to early-morning sessions. Not that she minded. Not at all. She pulled the singlet over her head, tossed it onto the floor and rolled over to where he lay, propped up on one elbow.

'Hello there.' She looked up at him, a smile forming.

He replied with a wicked curl of his mouth and a raised brow. His eyes, normally a sweet shade of caramel, had darkened into something more like treacle. Something in which she could happily drown. 'Is that the best you can do?'

She ran a hand greedily through the silky strands of hair at the back of his neck and followed up her earlier perfunctory greeting with a longer, deeper kiss.

'Hmm ... that's more like it.'

His body engulfed hers and she arched into him. Gripping his shoulders, she hooked one calf around his and gave him a quick shove, flipping them both over so she was the one looking down. She reached between his legs, positioning him in just the right spot, and with one single, sharp upward thrust he was inside her. Her chest billowed. She flattened her hands against the hollows below his shoulders and he rocked beneath her until they became a sweaty, ragged tangle of limbs, and she was completely overwhelmed by the glorious bone-shattering ache she'd been chasing. Josh followed quickly after, his palms searing her hips, his limbs rippling. She collapsed on top of him, her forehead nestled against the dark stubble of his jaw. Even after hours at the computer, minimal sleep and a sweaty round of wake-up sex, he had that just-washed, deliciously minty smell.

She rolled over and lay on top of the sheets, her hands tracking the rise and fall of her ribcage as she waited for her heart rate to return to somewhere this side of normal. The room heaved with their tandem panting. A horn bleated from the street outside, and another echoed back. The world was out there, ready and waiting, demanding attention, but she remained still, eyes closed, willing it away.

'Now *that's* a good morning.' Josh sat upright, reached for his phone from the bedside table and switched off the beeping alarm. He looked like a Cheshire cat. 'Best I've had all week.'

She stretched her arms above her head with a languid yawn. 'Certainly beats *Good morning, ma'am, this is your five am wake-up call.*'

'You've got the accent aced.' He laughed. 'I'd better get moving. I've got an eight o'clock meeting.' He threw her a wink before sauntering off for a shower, wiggling his bare backside more than was strictly necessary.

Tess snuggled back under the covers, any sign of the tension her body had stored up during the flight—and afterwards—now vanished. Sex had always brought them closer, stitched them back together even when their relationship had frayed. Her mind leap-frogged to those looser threads—the days, nights and weeks that sometimes rolled by when they barely saw each other. Hours spent working or doing their own thing: Josh with his cycling crew while she procrastinated about the gym by watching mindless reality-TV shows. More and more it felt like the seam holding them together was splitting, yet they were always able to patch it up with a workout between the sheets. It was how they found their way back to each other.

But was it enough?

She stared at the vacant space beside her, placed her hand on his empty pillow, the cotton cold beneath her palm. A weight heavier than the doona settled on her. She shook it away. There was nothing to worry about. Life had its ups and downs. They were all good.

Something crinkled under the sole of her foot as she swung her legs over the edge of the bed: the mail she'd been too tired to deal with last night. She gathered it up and shuffled through the envelopes. As predicted most were bank statements addressed to them both, one was an electricity bill—overdue—and a few were for TDS. A thrill tripped through her veins. It was the same whenever she saw the acronym, especially in logo-form, the letters entwined with a rough sketch of a heart: *Team-Driven Solutions*. A play on her own initials joined by the *heart* of her own human resources consultancy, which just happened to be going gangbusters. Not bad for a thirty-five-year-old. Even if it was Plan B. One last envelope fell from her lap as she stood. This one addressed to Ms T. De Santis, her full name, and while it looked official, it didn't seem to be a bill. She slid her finger under the seal and ripped, unfolding the single-page document.

FACS, Department of Family and Community Services.

Why would they be writing to her? Her stomach hollowed as she skimmed over the first few lines, and she dropped back onto the bed. She needed to read from the beginning, but each word sucked her a little further out of her own skin, so by the time she reached the end of the letter she was watching herself from somewhere outside her body.

She stared down at the signature and the department-speak at the bottom of the page, the muscles in her chest tightening as if a too-small elastic band had been wrapped too many times around her heart.

This could not be happening.

No.

It was *not* happening.

She folded the paper back into the torn envelope and placed it deliberately on the bedside table, pinching the points of her elbows tightly as she crossed her arms, holding herself together.

'Tess?' Josh's voice came to her through a cotton-wool fog. 'What's wrong?'

Somehow he was right there, standing by her side, already showered, the brown waves of his hair wet and towel-ruffled.

'It's …' She tried to pick up the letter, but it fell from her grasp like a hot coal. Her hand flew to her mouth. If she didn't say the words then they wouldn't be true, would they?

'Tess … what is it?'

As much as she didn't want it to be real it was right there at her feet, black print blurring into a haze of grey.

She pressed her fingers against her palms, scoring the soft pads of flesh with her nails.

'It's Skye.' The name was foreign on her tongue after all these years, like a rare fruit she'd tasted long ago, in another lifetime, and then forgotten. But it wasn't as strange as the answer to Josh's question. It came out quickly in a strangled cough, a bitter seed she couldn't stand to swallow. 'She's dead.'

Cross My Heart: Chapter Two

A crescent moon of white arced at the base of her thumbnail, below the navy gloss. Regular manicures might draw attention away from her ravaged cuticles, but they didn't change her disgusting habit. One day she might stop chewing the skin until it was raw and red. One day. Not today.

Josh leaned over, picked up the letter and sat beside her, the paper taut between his hands. 'Jesus.'

Somewhere outside a garbage truck rumbled, the bang and clatter of bins reverberating like a set of cymbals. Tess coiled back in on herself as the noise ebbed away.

'What happened?' Josh's voice was muffled, as if he was speaking from a distance. 'Tess, when did you last talk to her?'

She shook her head and let out a long, slow breath. 'I'm not sure. Six months ... longer maybe.' It was July now. Had it been this year or last when she and Skye had spoken? 'She wrote to me, a while ago.' But was that letter before or after the Christmas card? The one she'd replied to with a promise to visit soon. The same promise she'd been making for the last eight years. Her stomach plummeted.

Josh moved closer and tried to draw her into his embrace. She pulled herself upright, and he settled for resting his arm across her shoulders. 'I'm really sorry. I know how much you cared about her.'

Did he know? Really know? How could he when Josh had only met her friend once, when she had barely mentioned Skye in the entire time they'd been together. Not talking about her didn't mean she didn't think about Skye, though. Her memory hurdled over the intervening years back to earlier days, a series of disconnected images flickering like an old home-movie reel to a soundtrack of childhood laughter. Those dark spiral curls, the pale, freckled face, eyes that shifted like the sea on a hot summer afternoon—clear and blue one minute, grey and stormy the next.

'Guess you'll have to call them first thing. The letter's dated almost a week ago.'

The letter. She clenched her teeth until her jaw ached. If he'd bothered to tell her about it on the phone, she might have asked him to open it then and there. She jerked at her shoulder, forcing his arm to fall away.

'So what will you say?'

'I'm sure you have some suggestions.' The words came out in a hiss and Josh sprang from the bed, the towel around his waist slipping to his knees. He secured it back into place, hooking one thumb into the fold below his hip. 'Well, I mean you'll have to tell them we can't do it.' He was floundering now, flapping the letter around in the air, but a sharper, more defiant edge had crept into his voice. 'You either do that over the phone or go in and see this person. End of story.'

He'd already made up his mind. Presumed she agreed. That piece of paper in his hand was asking about *her* intentions in regard to Grace, asking if she would be honouring the agreement *she* had made to be the child's legal guardian. Skye was dead; her daughter was now Tess's responsibility. This was her decision.

She pushed herself up from the bed. They were almost exactly the same height when she wasn't in heels, making it easy to stare him down. 'So we're not even going to discuss it?'

'Tess, come on.' He dipped his head, raked a hand through his hair and snorted—actually snorted—as if this was some kind of joke. 'There's no way we can take on someone else's kid.'

'It's not just *someone*. It's Skye.'

'No, it's not Skye. It's her daughter. Shit, the kid is ten years old. When was the last time you even saw her?'

She couldn't look at him anymore. Couldn't stand that I-know-better-than-you jut of his chin and the tell-me-I'm-wrong tone in his voice. She covered her bare breasts with one arm and bit down hard on the inside of her mouth. The last time she'd seen Grace the little girl had been a preschooler, but so what? It didn't change the facts. 'That's not the point. I signed the papers when she was born.'

'Well, that was your first mistake.' And right on cue, there it was, the pointing finger. 'You should have thought it through more carefully in the first place. That was a legal document.'

'Skye didn't have anyone else.'

'A simple no would have worked.'

His same old attitude, everything black and white. She was the one who'd signed the papers, made the promise, not Josh. This was not his call to make. She wanted to grab a handful of that dripping hair and yank it out of his stupid fucking head. Not that it would change anything. Josh had total tunnel vision when it came to his life plan, and right now he was on track to corporate stardom. Nothing—and no one—would be getting in his way. She whipped her top off the bed and pulled it on, shoving past him as she stalked to the window.

The padding of feet on carpet signalled his retreat to the ensuite. Tess folded her arms and peered down at the street. People were out there as if nothing had changed. Women in coats and scarves braced against the winter wind. Men in smart suits striding along the pavement, mobiles to their ears, brows furrowed as if the future of the world depended on their every word. All of them going about their lives, oblivious to what had happened. Skye was dead and yet everything outside was completely normal.

Across the road Rocco, her favourite barista, popped up an umbrella out the front of his cafe. A young woman in a short denim skirt, black top, fishnet tights and Docs pulled up a chair. Rocco tossed his head and laughed at whatever joke passed between them, before he gave an exaggerated bow and ambled back inside, leaving the girl to her phone. A peacock tattoo covered the bare skin of her upper chest. Her short-cropped hair was dyed the darkest shade of black. Boots and tats. Almost a replica of Tess's own teenage self. Light years ago, well before Skye had asked her to be Grace's guardian. The request had seemed so lovely at the time, but she'd never considered it legally binding. Could she actually turn around now, a decade later and change her mind? Apparently, Josh thought that was perfectly fine. From the sounds of the opening and closing of drawers in the room behind her, he'd already moved on with his day. She turned to watch him do up his tie in the full-length mirror inside the wardrobe door.

Almost fully dressed now, he stuffed his wallet into the back pocket of his perfectly pressed pants and shrugged on his suit jacket. 'Tess. I get that you're upset, but you need to be practical. We both work crazy hours, live in an apartment, don't have any children of our own. There's no way we're equipped to look after a kid we don't know, who doesn't know us. I've never even laid eyes on her.'

She edged back towards the window, let his words percolate through the layers of emotion the letter had exposed. *Was* it stupid to even be entertaining the idea? She'd really only seen Grace a few times herself: when Skye came down to the city to buy her first lot of school supplies, briefly as a toddler at Skye's grandmother's funeral service, and before that in those early weeks of her life as a newborn. A tiny baby with fresh pink skin and that puzzled where-am-I expression. Totally helpless and completely dependent on her mother. Who could she depend on now if Tess didn't step up? 'She's going to be fostered out to total strangers.'

'Babe, to her, we are total strangers.' The cloying scent of his Armani aftershave was suddenly too strong, too close, but at least he was smart enough not to attempt to touch her. 'Don't you think she'd be better off with a real family? People who actually know what they're doing.'

Tess closed her eyes as the shrapnel from his 'real family' grenade cut deep. Kids had never been on his agenda. He'd made that perfectly clear the minute they'd become engaged. He didn't want to risk creating another broken home, he'd said, like the one he'd come from, and it had suited her at the time, when the concept of bringing innocent children into the world had made her insides quiver. They hadn't discussed it since, had rolled their eyes and changed the subject when others had brought up the b-word, but never seriously talked about it again. So when she'd married him, hadn't she implicitly agreed to the no-kids deal? Anyway, they were a pair of workaholics who had hardly any free time and lived in the inner city with designer furniture and white walls. None of it was conducive to raising a child, and if it didn't work out it wouldn't be fair to dump Grace back into foster care, would it?

Across the street the peacock girl's perfectly gelled hair gleamed in the winter sunlight. In ten years' time she might regret that tattoo, or other choices she'd made. People's lives can take such different directions to what they'd imagined. The Tess who'd signed the guardianship papers had been living out some kind of Disney godmother fantasy, but now that bubble had well and truly burst, leaving behind the cold, hard stain of reality.

'I'll call the woman …' She cleared her throat. 'Tell her to make other arrangements.'

'I am sorry about Skye.' He squeezed her shoulder, as if that was supposed to make her feel better. 'Maybe they can tell you more about what happened with her when you call. It would be good for you to have some closure.'

Closure. Psycho-babble for 'The End'. Everything all neatly packed up in a box, stored away and forgotten, exactly how Josh liked it. The bedside clock clicked over. Seven-thirty. Time was slipping away. Josh needed to get moving, and she needed space. 'You'd better go.'

He pressed a kiss to her cheek and was gone, no further urging required. In an instant the room, the whole apartment, was quiet, the kind of quiet she imagined that followed the felling of an ancient tree in a forest or the deafening seconds of silence that come after a raging, calamitous storm.

Or perhaps before.

She made her way to the bathroom. Only ten hours ago, she'd stepped into the same shower and scrubbed away the exhaustion of the flight. Now it was something much deeper she needed to remove, something no amount of body wash or exfoliant could cleanse. How was it possible that someone was here on the earth one moment and gone the next? *Skye.* The letter didn't even give the cause of death. A razor-sharp pain pierced her chest, swelling into a lump stuck deep in the base of her throat. She opened her mouth, tried to sluice it away, but it refused to budge. She'd always meant to get in touch, meant to check in on her friend and see if she was doing okay. Plan an actual visit. Now it was too late.

Hunched over, naked and dripping, she watched the water swirl around the drain and disappear. A sob broke from her mouth, echoing against the tiles. There was only one thing she could do: rip off the Band-Aid, the faster the better. The FACS office from where the letter was sent was in Redfern, which wasn't far away. She would call in before her scheduled meeting and see the caseworker. Explain the situation.

And find out what happened to Skye.

Jabbing away at the traffic button wouldn't make the lights change any quicker, but it was vaguely satisfying. Cleveland Street, as usual, was a virtual car park. A bus lurched past, spewing out a stream of black vapour, making Tess's stomach roll. Most days she could handle the noise and fumes—it was part of the fabric of the suburb. Chaotic. Loud. Colourful. One big noisy carnival. Surry Hills was so far removed from her childhood in southern Sydney, it was like another planet. As far away from suburbia as you could get. That word, 'suburbia', was as bland as the notion, and thankfully she and Josh had been on the same page about where they'd wanted to live. Granted, the craziness wasn't for everyone. Certainly not Skye. Her idea of heaven was the total opposite: sustainable living on an isolated country property, homeschooling her daughter, sculpting and painting, making just enough money from her artwork to survive.

Two completely different worlds. Was it any wonder she and Skye had drifted apart?

Tess pressed a hand against the ache in her chest. 'Drifted apart' was such a handy euphemism. Made it all sound so gentle, so inevitable. So okay.

The beep of the walk signal jolted her forward and across the intersection through the throng of pedestrians. On the corner, a wolfish-looking dog lay sprawled on the footpath beside his owner, who was scraping a squeegee across the windscreen of a car. People rushed past, heads down, absorbed in whatever was flashing on the screens of their phones. Worker bees, all part of the Sydney hive.

She stopped outside a nondescript building, number 219. It was already after nine am, so the FACS office should be open. She pulled the letter from her bag, ignoring the contents as she searched for the name of the person she needed to see. Regina Martin. A woman—a stranger—who had been appointed by a government department to supervise custody arrangements for Skye's only child, who was now an orphan. Like her mother. History repeating itself in some sick, cruel joke. Skye's grandmother had loved her like she was her own, but it couldn't possibly be the same. Tess's thumb throbbed. She pulled it away from her mouth, wincing at the blistered skin, and wriggled it to get the blood circulating. Where would Grace be right now? Probably stuck in some awful orphanage, or had she already been placed in foster care? All those stories you heard on the news about kids being shoved from one home to the next, at the mercy of people who only wanted to collect a payout ... or worse.

Under the cool silk of her long-sleeved shirt, the fine hairs on her forearms stood on end. Surely there were good, honest people out there who did want to do the right thing? People who genuinely wanted to provide a stable, loving family; care for a homeless child. People who were better equipped for parenting than she and Josh were. Of course those people existed. Procrastinating wouldn't help anyone, certainly not Grace.

Slipping through the automatic doors, Tess checked the directory and made her way up in the elevator, the folded document pulsing like a heartbeat against her palm.

The woman at the reception desk gave a tight-lipped smile. 'Can I help you?'

'I need to speak to Regina Martin.'

'Do you have an appointment?'

'No ... no, I don't.'

'I can make one for you if you like.' Her fingers skipped over the keys as she scanned the screen. 'I can get you in to see her next Tuesday at three forty-five pm.'

Tuesday was four days away. Far too much time to consider her options. Reconsider.

'I need to see her urgently. It's in regard to a guardianship case.' She handed the document across to the receptionist.

A few flyaway hairs sprang from the woman's centre

part as she bowed her head to read, frowning behind her thick-lensed glasses. 'And you are the guardian named here? Tessa De Santis?'

'Yes.'

'Take a seat.' She rose from her chair and disappeared, the letter still in her hand.

Tess settled back against the hard plastic seat. The waiting room was too warm and reeked of disinfectant. Photos of children of various ages lined the walls, some holding hands with an adult, all of them looking happy and contented. Were they real kids who had been placed in homes, or idealised versions the department wanted the public to see? A door opened and closed along the hall and the receptionist returned, resuming her seat without a word.

'Ms De Santis?' A second woman appeared in the waiting room. 'I'm Regina Martin. Please come in.' She had a faint accent, maybe Spanish, a lusciously thick set of dark brows, and an air of absolute authority. A bright-orange scarf was wound around her neck and her ripped jeans, definitely not traditional work wear, were a sharp contrast to the tailored charcoal of Tess's business suit.

The caseworker led the way to her office and waved Tess into a chair. 'I thought we might have heard from you sooner.'

Snippy, but probably best not to fight fire with fire. Tess put her bag on the floor, took a breath and pasted on her best conciliatory smile. 'I'm so sorry, but I've been overseas for work.' Considering the gravity of the situation, it was hardly surprising the woman would be questioning her tardiness. 'I only got back late last night.'

'We did try to contact you on the phone number found at Ms Whittaker's house, multiple times.'

Those few missed calls while she'd been in LA, the voicemail she hadn't bothered listening to. Tess cringed inwardly. No wonder the woman was snaky. Regina Martin leaned forward and shuffled through a pile of manila folders, slid one out and flicked it open. A computer and a wooden carving of an elephant were the only decorations on the desk. Tess plucked away a piece of white fluff caught in the weave of her skirt while the woman read through paperwork, probably re-familiarising herself with the case. She looked drawn, slightly harried. It couldn't be easy dealing with such fraught situations day after day. Eventually she looked up, rested her elbows on the desk and balanced her chin on the arch of her clasped hands. 'So, you are Grace Whittaker's legal guardian.'

Was she asking a question or stating a fact? Either way the answer was yes. 'That's right.'

'There's no father involved?'

'No. Skye fell pregnant when she was travelling. It was an accident, but she wanted to have the baby.'

'And when is the last time you saw Grace?'

Tess shrank back into the chair, shifting again as it creaked. The heat in her cheeks was a dead giveaway. She'd read somewhere that if you acknowledged the blush it would subside. And yet her face remained on fire.

'Ms De Santis?'

'About five years ago, I think.'

'You think?'

The incredulity was well warranted. 'No, it was. I mean … I know it was. In Sydney.'

Regina Martin sat back in her chair. 'And you haven't seen her since? Haven't visited? They didn't visit you?'

'No.'

The caseworker tipped her head to the side and

frowned. 'So, I'm curious as to why Grace's mother would leave her in your care.'

'We were friends, close friends.' Tess sucked in a breath. The explanation sounded totally lame, considering the length of time since they'd actually seen each other. 'Skye had an aversion to the city and I've ... well ... I have a very busy job.'

'I see.' Regina Martin pursed her lips as she considered the documents in front of her. 'It's my job to make sure that the child is placed with the right people.' She glanced at Tess's hand. 'You're married?'

'Yes.'

'Do you have any children?'

'No.'

She was noting down every word. 'And what is it you do for a living?'

'I'm a human resources manager. I have my own consultancy.'

'So you would be financially able to care for Grace?'

'Yes. Absolutely.'

Another scribble in the file. Surely financial stability had to count for something? 'Have you discussed this with your husband?'

'We've ... talked about it.' Finally, they'd come to the point of the meeting. She'd started off on the wrong foot, given the wrong impression about why she was here. 'To be perfectly honest ...'

'Let *me* be totally honest with *you*, Mrs De Santis.'

The sudden, incorrect change in title niggled, but there were more important issues at stake. If the woman wanted the floor, she could go for her life. In the end, the outcome would be the same. Tess crossed her legs and gave a slight nod.

'If there was any extended family in this case, we would prefer Grace be placed with them. Are you aware of any relatives who might be able to take her in?'

'No.' The short, single syllable came out far too loud and Regina Martin widened her brown eyes. Tess's stomach hollowed. She made a conscious effort to lower her volume, soften her tone. 'I was the closest thing to family after the death of Skye's grandmother.' It was the absolute truth. Family wasn't just about blood. She was right there in the room when Grace was born, watching on as the midwife laid the tiny bundle on her friend's chest, those smoky eyes looking up into her mother's. Days later, as they had sat together on the lounge of Skye's rented flat watching the baby sleep, Skye had taken her hand.

Promise me you'll take care of her if anything happens to me.

Those had been her exact words.

'And you are one hundred percent sure you can provide a safe, loving, long-term home for the child, as her mother wished?'

'Yes.' The word sprang from Tess's lips, the same answer she'd given her friend. Wherever it had come from, there was no taking it back. Not then. Not now.

Grab your copy…
vinci-books.com/crossmyheart

A Note on Hendra Virus

The initial idea for this story came from my involvement with horses and discussions about the pros and cons of the hendra vaccine. While the novel evolved into something much bigger, I have spent many hours researching the virus and tried to make the details of the detection, monitoring and reactions to it as accurate as possible. That being said, there may still be errors and this is a work of fiction, not fact. Although there have been no outbreaks of hendra as far south as the fictional town of Naringup, my sources assure me that this is not beyond the realms of possibility. Charlie's views on vaccination – or any other opinions expressed in the book – are not necessarily my own.

About the Author

Pamela Cook is an author, podcaster, writing teacher and mentor. Her debut novel *Blackwattle Lake* (2012) was published by Hachette Australia in 2012 followed by three rural fiction titles. She subsequently published two independent titles (*Cross My Heart* and *All We Dream*) and is now publishing with Bolinda Audio and Vinci Books.

Pamela writes stories of longing and belonging, delving deep into the psychology of her characters and the complexity of relationships in all their forms. She explores the impact of trauma, grief and generational conflict, drawing on the resilience and courage she finds in inspirational women. Her writing is imbued with a deep love of the natural world and its power to heal.

Producing and hosting *Writes4Women*, a weekly podcast that supports women writers and celebrates women's writing, is one of Pamela's not-so-guilty pleasures. She is also a Writer Ambassador for Room to Read, a not-for-profit organisation promoting literacy and gender equality in developing countries.

An experienced teacher, Pamela loves to mentor emerging authors. When she's not writing or reading, she wastes as much time as possible riding her handsome quarter horse Baloo, hanging out with her family and menagerie of animals on her dream-come-true rural property in the beautiful Illawarra region of NSW, and dreaming of a road trip in Virginia, her vintage caravan.

Acknowledgments

Thanks so much to everyone who has helped me with this book...

Michael Higgins, for your veterinary expertise. Your knowledge of hendra was invaluable.

My buddies in The Writers' Dozen – Terri, Jen, Yvonne, Angella, Annabel and especially Monique – for your wisdom, feedback and continual support. Krystina Pecorari-McBride, your editing tips were spot-on – thank you for 'getting' the characters and the story. To Wanda Wiltshire, thanks for your speed reading and honest appraisals. Kerry Rogerson, thanks so much for sharing your knowledge of the law and police practices – your input made the story so much stronger.

The amazing and awe-inspiring Cate Kennedy, for your time and editing skills. I learnt so much about writing from you.

Denise Fisher, my cherished friend, for sharing your memories of how you learnt to surf. Your descriptions almost made me want to give it a try, but I think I'll stick to horses.

Trusted friend and reader Carrie Green, for your beautiful comments and delicately worded suggestions.

My friends and family, for your interest in and support of my writing.

Amelia, Georgia and Freya, for indulging my hours at the computer and for your faith in me. John, this book wouldn't exist without your pep talks. Thank you so much for listening and keeping me sane through this whole process.

. . . and to everyone who read *Blackwattle Lake* and *Essie's Way*, thank you for the gift of your time and for the privilege of being able to publish this book.